LIVING LEGEND

"Make yourself comfortable, Jack," said the man, casually waving to a chair in front of his desk. "We have a lot to discuss. . . . I think you're the man we need."

Jack grinned. Today was his lucky day.

He sobered almost instantly. There had been no mention of salary. Or exactly what position he was being offered.

"How does a thousand dollars a week sound?" said the bearded man, as if reading Jack's mind.

"A thousand a week?" repeated Jack, stunned. "For doing what, Mr. Ambrose?"

"The forces of darkness and everlasting night are rising in our city. Civilization is terribly threatened. Humanity needs a champion to battle them. You're that man, Jack. And there's no reason for you to use the Ambrose alias. I prefer my real name. Call me Merlin."

"Merlin?" asked Jack. "Like the famous magician of King Arthur's court?"

The bearded man laughed. "*Like* him? You misunderstand, Jack. *I am him.* I am the legendary Merlin the Magician."

A LOGICAL MAGICIAN

ROBERT WEINBERG

ACE BOOKS, NEW YORK

This book is an Ace original edition,
and has never been previously published.

A LOGICAL MAGICIAN

An Ace Book / published by arrangement with
the author

PRINTING HISTORY
Ace edition / April 1994

ISBN 0-441-00059-2

ACE®
Ace Books are published by The Berkley Publishing Group,
200 Madison Avenue, New York, NY 10016.
ACE and the "A" design
are trademarks belonging to Charter Communications, Inc.

PRINTED IN THE UNITED STATES OF AMERICA

10 9 8 7 6 5 4 3 2 1

To my son

Matthew Phillip Weinberg

Who has taught me a great deal
in fourteen years

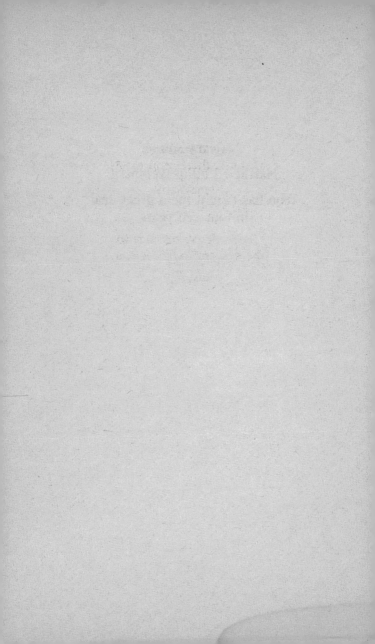

cogito ergo sum
(I think, therefore I exist)

—DESCARTES

facilis descensus Averno
(the descent to hell is easy)

—VIRGIL

∞

Prologue

Roger Quinn considered himself a very careful man. Each morning, while still lying in bed, he planned out his day's activities in excruciatingly fine detail. Afterward, he followed that outline in strict order, refusing to deviate one whit from the proper routine. Twenty years of computer programming had instilled in Roger an appreciation for exactness. He thought his actions perfectly normal and extremely logical.

Such a rigid adherence to schedule caused numerous problems for those who had to deal with him on a regular basis. They had to play the game his way or not at all. No one dared drop in unexpectedly on Roger. If they weren't listed in his appointment book, he completely ignored them. It didn't matter who they were or what company they represented. Roger refused to make exceptions. His rules were never bent, much less broken.

Business lunches began exactly on the hour, not a minute late. Presentations ran by the clock. Thirty minutes for a report meant that one second afterward Roger refused to listen to another word. His world ran like clockwork, and everyone on his payroll worked by the same schedule. Or they didn't work for Quinn Enterprises.

Behind his back, most of Roger's several dozen employees agreed that their boss belonged in a lunatic asylum. However, one

and all they kept their doubts strictly to themselves. They jumped
to obey their boss's slightest whim. In a period of retrenchment
and recession, working for a lunatic was a lot better than not
working at all. For, where most other scientific consulting and
marketing companies had fallen on hard times, Quinn Enterprises
continued to expand.

Without exception, all of the major financial experts agreed that
the phenomenal growth of the company related directly to the
unique genius of its founder and CEO, Roger Quinn. Virtually
unknown only a few years before, he entered an already crowded
field and beat the biggest companies at their own game. Started as
a small sideline operation in Roger's apartment, Quinn Enterprises
had become a major West Coast corporation, poised on the brink
of global expansion. In the last six months, QE had opened offices
in New York, Chicago, and several other major metropolitan areas.
Rumor had it that foreign offices were soon to follow.

What baffled his rivals and many of his own employees was
Roger's amazing skill at exploiting the problems and failures of
his rivals. Whenever another company experienced difficulty in
fulfilling a contract, Roger and his team were there with the
necessary answers just in the nick of time. If a material shortage
caused a backup in manufacturing a new product, Roger knew
where to find the necessary ingredient. Moreover, he oftentimes
controlled the only available supply of the goods and priced it
accordingly.

It was almost as if Roger knew when and where problems were
going to occur before they happened. His rivals suspected sabotage, but there was absolutely no evidence to support such claims.
No one could find a thing to link Roger or his employees with any
of the problems or failures experienced by the other firms. The
only explanation consistent with all the facts, incredible as it
seemed, was that Roger possessed a hidden talent for sensing
trouble. No one accepted the theory gracefully, but they had little
choice in the matter. Roger wisely kept his mouth shut. He didn't
really care what his rivals thought. As long as they never guessed
the truth.

Humming softly to himself, Roger made his way down the lone
staircase leading to the subbasement of his mansion. A tall, thin
man with a scraggly beard and bright blue eyes, he wore a pair of
battered jeans and a faded black sweatshirt embossed with his
company's logo—a five-pointed star with a large R in the center.

Surprisingly, no one drew a connection between the symbol and a pentagram. A fact that pleased Roger no end.

Always the maverick, he delighted in thumbing his nose at the establishment. Corporate executives considered Roger eccentric. But plenty of other CEO's of major corporations were equally odd. All each of the money men cared about was that his firm delivered on tough assignments when other businesses failed. Quinn Enterprises had saved dozens of important contracts that otherwise would have collapsed. It provided a necessary service and charged premium prices for that work. "We help you out when you need us most" was the company motto, one that had become famous throughout the manufacturing industry.

Roger chuckled softly. He shook his head, imagining the shocked looks of those same corporate executives if they ever learned the truth behind his success. They might not be so pleased if they knew the whole story. Which was why he kept his revelation locked in the subbasement in a room that only he could enter.

The stairs ended abruptly at the base of a huge steel door that took up the entire rear wall. There was no keyhole or lock visible. A solitary metal plate some six inches square was the only break in the cold, unyielding surface. Roger flattened his right hand against it. It required the built-in sensors a few seconds to recognize his palm print. Silently, the huge door swung open.

Technically, criminals intent on discovering his secret could kidnap Roger, force him down to the subbasement and press his hand against the entry plate to open the vault door. He strongly doubted that corporate raiders would be so bold. And even if they were, the payoff inside the inner room would prove to be something outside their usual line of business.

With a confident smile, Roger entered the nerve center of his secret headquarters. Shaped like a square twenty feet long by twenty feet wide, with a seven-foot ceiling, the chamber was entirely devoid of furniture. The walls were stone, the ceiling and floor both concrete. A pair of naked hundred-watt light bulbs provided the only illumination. More than anything else, the Spartan room resembled an army pillbox.

In the exact center of the room was a vermilion circle some nine feet in diameter. Roger had carefully painted it there a few days after moving into this mansion two years ago. Before that, a similar pattern, drawn in chalk, had decorated the living room carpet of his apartment. Vermilion was used because its color came from mercury and sulfur, key ingredients of the fabled Philosopher's Stone.

Inside the first circle was a second, eight feet in diameter. Together, the two drawings resembled a round plate with a narrow rim. Names of great power were written on that rim, transforming it into a barrier that nothing evil could cross.

Inscribed inside the two circles were the Pentagram of Solomon, as specified in *The Key of Solomon*, the most famous of all magical texts. It was constructed with two points upward, symbolizing the twin horns of the infamous Goat of the Witches' Sabbath. The sign of a black magician.

Nowhere was Roger's exactness more evident than in the construction of the mystic design. Here his computer background served him well. One wrong MS-DOS statement and your program refused to run. One misdrawn line or incorrect symbol in your pentagram and all hell broke loose.

Roger knew quite well the dangers he faced practicing the black arts. The literature of demonology specified in gruesome detail the grisly penalties paid by those not extremely careful in their dealings with the inhabitants of the nether regions. Death was the least of the fates suffered by the unwary.

The pentagram served as more than a doorway for the inhabitants of the outer darkness to enter our world. It also acted as a trap, holding those monstrous beings prisoner inside the design. Only by performing a specific task demanded by the summoning wizard was the demonic presence allowed to depart. Once banished, the being was never again subject to the whims of the sorcerer. One wish per demon was the rule. But, as Roger discovered early in his experiments, there were many thousands of demons.

Four years ago, he had been a second-rate computer hacker stuck in a go-nowhere job in Silicon Valley. His obsession with exactness had earned him a reputation as a difficult employee. None of the major firms in the area were willing to hire him. So he slaved in obscurity, designing computer games at a salary that barely covered his living expenses.

Supremely egotistical, Roger never once considered changing his behavior. There was no question in his mind that the world was wrong, not him. Thus, he was resigned to earning half of what he should and being routinely passed over when it came time for promotions. Life seemed to have passed him by.

That all changed in the course of one evening. A group of programmers at work, the closest to what might be loosely defined as his friends, invited Roger along to a party where a well-known Channeler was guest of honor. Imbued with the typical disdain felt by all scientists towards New Age mysticism, Roger treated the entire experience as one big joke. Until the Channeler, a short, stocky woman with piercing black eyes that stared directly into your soul, sank into the deep trance necessary for her to call upon her Spirit Guide.

"Who seeks the hidden knowledge?" The voice that emerged from the woman's throat was deep and harsh, a man's voice. A vague thrill of fear swept through Roger as he listened to those guttural tones. In one astonishing instant of epiphany, he transformed from a harsh skeptic to an ardent believer. "Who seeks the hidden knowledge?" the voice repeated, and Roger felt it spoke directly to him.

The rest of the evening passed in a blur. Whatever revelations the Spirit Guide offered, they made no impression upon Roger. His mind was already buzzing off on tangents far beyond his initial revelation. For once Roger accepted the fact that the occult existed and could be contacted, it opened an entire Pandora's box of possibilities to be explored. A man with unlimited ambition and ambiguous morality could achieve great things if he dared. And Roger dared.

Within a few days, he assembled an occult library consisting of some of the greatest and most frightening volumes of black magic lore ever written. Many of the books were readily available in cheap paperback format, thus leading to Roger's second great revelation. Over the centuries, many thousands of people had access to these same works and the spells they contained. But little evidence existed to show that any of those other seekers successfully mastered the powers described.

It was obvious that the spells as written were not enough to summon the forces of darkness. Ever the computer hacker, Roger guessed the solution in an instant. No magician willingly shared secrets with his fellows. All of the spells in the forbidden books were complete. But they each contained minor mistakes and glitches that only the original user knew to be false. It was as if they had been published in code, without the necessary key to unlock their power.

Fortunately, Roger owned the greatest code-breaker of all time, a home computer. He had been using it for cracking access codes and breaking into secret files for years. The magic tomes were just another hacker challenge—one that he accepted eagerly. For a change, the payoff would be worth the trouble.

Defining terms and listing proper names demanded time. Patiently, Roger fed all of the necessary data into the machine. He spent a day revising his software, making minor adjustments wherever necessary. The work wasn't very hard. Seven nights after his encounter with the Channeler, he was ready to raise his first demon.

The spell he used came from *The Key of Solomon*, with minor modifications and corrections courtesy of his computer. His magic circle and pentagram followed the instructions of Eliphas Levi, one of the most famous magicians who ever lived. The determination and courage came from Roger.

Slowly and carefully, he recited the summoning spell as reconstructed by his word processing program. Accents were extremely important, and one misspoken word could doom the whole project. Another crucial element in the process was naming a specific demon. Evidently, the summoning spells only worked for distinct supernatural entities. There was no generalized spell to produce a devil. Proper names were a must. Quite handily, the paperback version of *The Key of Solomon* contained an alphabetical appendix of famous demons. For his first try, Roger settled on Astaroth, the lord of Hell most closely associated with the sciences.

Walking *widdershins*, counterclockwise and thus unnatural to the order of the universe, Roger began the spell. Once, twice, three times he read through the entire conjuration. Only then did Roger look up from the computer printout. And found himself staring at a creature of nightmare.

It stomped about angrily in the magic circle drawn on Roger's living-room carpet. Four feet tall, the being resembled a bizarre cross between man and lizard. Along with the proper number of arms and legs, it displayed a multicolored crest that ran down its back from the base of its neck to the end of its spine, where it terminated in a long, sinewy tail some six feet long. Completely nude, it was obscenely male, seemingly in a constant state of arousal.

In contrast to its grotesque torso, Astaroth possessed the head and features of a handsome young man. Long brown hair fell to its shoulders. Its cheeks glowed with good health. Bright white, perfect teeth gnashed in anger, while blue eyes that never blinked surveyed its prison. Only an immense, forked tongue that darted in and out of its mouth made mockery of its seeming humanity. There was no mistaking the devil's identity. It matched perfectly the description given in several of the black magic texts. This horror was Astaroth, demon from the foulest pits of Hell.

"Who dares disturb my rest?" hissed the creature, in a voice sounding like steam escaping from a kettle. Its foul breath stank of sulfur and corruption. "Are you ready to meet thy end, mortal?"

Roger licked his lips, feeling slightly numb. He actually had not expected the spell to work. It took him a few seconds to gather his wits. Meanwhile, the demon peered closely at the lines of the pentagram, searching diligently for any break in the pattern.

"I name you Astaroth," said Roger finally, remembering the necessary binding spell. "And by your true and proper name I command your obedience for one task. Hear me and obey."

Slowly, reluctantly, Astaroth nodded its head in reply. "You know the ritual. What do you want—women, gold, . . . revenge?"

"None of those," said Roger, on firmer footing now. "Women mean nothing to me. Gold or jewels would raise tax questions I couldn't answer. Revenge is for impatient fools."

"Then what do you desire?" asked the demon, sounding curious.

Roger told him. In great detail. Even Astaroth was impressed.

That night saw the beginning of Roger's empire. His scheme was brilliant in its simplicity. Though the demons he raised were limited in their supernatural abilities, all of them possessed enough skill for the task he required. He used the minions of darkness as an unsuspected business fifth column.

Summoning demons wasn't particularly difficult once he got over the initial shock of their unearthly appearance. Like any routine task, it soon settled into a familiar pattern of behavior for Roger. One that paid incredible dividends.

Again and again, he sent the monsters out searching for secret information he could use to his advantage. The diabolical creatures made wonderful spies. Invisible to all but other magicians, they eavesdropped on confidential conversations and reported their findings back to Roger. Nor did classified documents present any more of a problem. Within weeks, Roger knew all of the innermost secrets of the major corporations in the area.

Such knowledge was worth more than all of the gold and jewels that the devils could offer. Quitting his job, Roger went into business as a consultant. Using what he learned through his spies, he built his new firm into a major force in the manufacturing community. Knowledge was power, and the demons provided all the knowledge he needed. However, in the rare instances when insider information wasn't enough to make Roger millions, he used his evil helpers in other ways.

The demons, agents of destruction and chaos, were astonishingly adept at small acts of sabotage. One tiny mistake was usually enough to doom most complex industrial operations. In all cases, the imps cleverly disguised their interference to look like accidents or employee blunders. Again, no one ever suspected supernatural intervention. They all knew better.

Except Roger, who was too busy using his silent, invisible army to get rich. Very, very rich.

Tonight, he planned to try his most ambitious summoning spell ever. It came from the final chapter of *The Lemegeton*, a rare magical text known as *The Lesser Key of Solomon*. According to the book, the conjuration raised one of the High Lords of Hell, a being of immeasurably greater power than any Roger had thus summoned. It sounded risky, but he felt it was worth the gamble. Despite all his newfound wealth, Roger was greedy for more.

One small detail puzzled him. His computer printout emphasized a much different pronunciation of the demon's name from the one commonly accepted. According to the machine, the variation was the correct title of the beast. That explained why most sorcerers had never been able to raise the creature from the pit. For a spell to work, every word and syllable had to be exactly correct.

Roger knew better than to doubt the computer's offering. The machine never lied. Like himself, it was exact in every detail. After all, he had programmed it. Silently, he mouthed the demon's name several times, making sure he had the syllables just right.

One last time, Roger checked the lines on the floor. It paid to be careful. As long as his pentagram and magic circle remained intact, the creatures he summoned could not harm him. Three years of dealing with the powers of darkness had made Roger fearless. Nothing frightened him anymore. Or at least, that was what he told himself.

Taking a deep breath, he began the chanting. Three times he repeated the great spell from *The Lemegeton*. As he spoke, the air trembled with the force of the words pouring from his mouth. There was a feeling of electricity in the air that Roger had never noticed in any of his previous rituals. Though the lights remained unchanged, somehow the room appeared to grow darker. And then the spell was complete.

Roger stared at the being in the center of the pentagram and shook his head in disbelief. This thing did not look anything like the demon prince described in his books of magic. All of his previous summonings had been hideous abominations, warped twisted hideous mockings of life. The being inside the circle appeared human.

It resembled a short, elderly man, crippled and bent with age. The creature stood perhaps five feet tall but was so badly crouched over, like a hunchback, that its hands almost touched the floor. Completely hairless, with skin the color and texture of aged parchment, the being wore a dark blue tunic and wood sandals. A large hook nose and pointed chin gave the creature a vulturelike appearance. Not until it turned and stared at him across the circle did Roger know he had not made a mistake.

Monstrous eyes burned with an inner yellow fire, harsh and unblinking, in the light. Seen directly, the being's face faintly resembled that of a monstrous jungle cat. "Where am I?" the demon whispered, looking around the room. It even sounded human. "*When* am I?"

Roger saw no harm in answering the question. "1997," he said, "just outside San Francisco, California."

Then, remembering the correct procedure, he named the demon and demanded its service.

The creature laughed. "You know my earthly name, mortal. Few dare pronounce it. No matter. Such puny binding spells mean nothing to me. Nations quail at my fury. I am not yours to command."

Roger grimaced in annoyance. He should have realized that someday he would run into this problem. Many demonic titles in the Bible originated in other sources. They were corruptions of names drawn from older civilizations' religions. Instead of raising a devil from the pits of Hell, by using the correct pronunciation of its name he had summoned forth a demigod from ancient history.

All of Roger's magic depended on Christian tradition. None of it meant anything to his captive. It came from a time before Christ walked the Earth. The creature was not subject to the rules of sorcery Roger practiced. Only the magic circle and pentagram, whose origins were lost in ancient prehistory, kept the creature imprisoned.

"Release me," said the crouching man, as if sensing his captor's plight. "Or suffer my wrath. The Lord of the Lions is not yours to command."

The thing waved one gnarled hand in the air. Blue sparks crackled between its fingers. Roger gulped and tried to think of a banishing spell. Sometimes being exact had its drawbacks. He was not very good at improvising.

A minute passed. Roger stood motionless, his thoughts racing through all the mystic lore he had studied in the past few years, trying to come up with a way out of this fix. Meanwhile, the crouching man paced back and forth in the pentagram, softly muttering threats that Roger tried to ignore. It was a stalemate of sorts. Roger couldn't send the demigod back to the outermost dark, but neither could the being escape from the prison in which it was trapped.

Being eminently practical and depressingly materialistic, Roger finally settled on the only possible course of action. He would leave the room and then seal it closed forever. Maybe even fill the outer chamber with concrete for additional security. The creature he summoned would remain trapped inside the pentagram for the foreseeable future, unable to cause any harm. Roger could continue his work elsewhere, exercising a good deal more caution in his selection of demons.

He was turning to leave when the earthquake struck.

It wasn't much of a quake, barely registering on the Richter scale. Dishes rattled, dogs howled, and a few VCRs clicked on for no reason. Other than that, most people looked up from whatever they were doing, hesitated for an instant waiting for worse, then settled back to their normal activities.

In Roger Quinn's subbasement, a little more than a mile from the center of the quake, the concrete floor growled and shifted. It moved less than a hundredth of an inch. Barely enough to send a hairline crack running directly through the center of the magic circle.

Roger blinked in astonishment. The threatening presence no longer stood in the pentagram. Rather, it crouched at Roger's side. Fingers cold as ice clenched him by the elbow.

"Come, my young friend," said the Lord of the Lions, a ruthless edge to his voice. "We have much to discuss."

Unblinking eyes, bright yellow like a cat's, glowed with inner fire. "I want to hear all about this modern world. You have much to tell me—concerning war, plague, pestilence, death, and destruction. And . . . especially . . . about the gods you worship."

∞

1

Standing alone in the elevator, Jack Collins pulled the classified ads from his back pocket. For the tenth time that day, he studied the black-bordered notice he had circled the night before. As the lift silently headed upward to the thirty-fourth floor, Jack carefully searched for the hidden catch in the wording, trying to find a loophole he knew had to exist. There had been too many other ads, too many other disappointments for him not to be suspicious.

> Logical young man with an open mind and active imagination wanted for highly unusual but financially rewarding career opportunity. Some risk involved. Background in mathematics and fantastic literature advised.

Nowhere in the ad was there any mention of the advertiser's name or the exact nature of the job. Still, the clipping did provide the address of a major office building in the Chicago financial district and a suite number. And the high-rent location indicated that the position wasn't in sales or telephone solicitation.

At twenty-seven, Jack was willing to gamble. After nine years of college, he wanted out. Four years spent earning his bachelor's degree, two for his master's, and three more towards his Ph.D. had finally caught up with him. He wanted nothing more than to earn a living in the real world. It was time to break away from university life. Unfortunately, getting a job was proving more difficult than he had imagined.

To his dismay, he found that advanced degrees in pure mathematics meant nothing to most employers. Worse, several companies made it exceedingly clear they couldn't hire him because of his education. According to one painfully honest recruiter, he was overqualified for any entry-level position. Even worse, his advanced degrees could intimidate the other workers.

It was the nineties version of the old paradox of jobs needing experience and vice versa. Now it featured advanced degrees against entry-level positions. The better educated you were, the less chance you had of finding work. In any case, it meant Jack was out of luck.

Weeks of searching for employment had left Jack frustrated and depressed. All his years in graduate school seemed wasted. None of his course work had prepared him for the harsh realities of the everyday world. The only jobs readily available were at fast-food joints, working a cash register and making change.

The spring semester was almost at an end. Over a month ago, Jack had informed his faculty advisor that he did not plan on returning to the university in the fall. Committed to earning a living, after three weeks of searching he was running out of options.

If nothing turned up soon, he would be forced to move back to the East Coast and work in the family import-export business. For that, he didn't need a college degree. Especially one in advanced mathematics and logic. He knew that for the next twenty years, his father would remind him of that fact whenever possible. As would his mother. And his brothers and sisters, aunts, uncles, first, second, and third cousins, all who labored for the Collins consortium.

His relatives never understood why he left home to attend college in Chicago. There was no way Jack could tell them of his need to get away from his close-knit family and make a name for himself in the world. He wanted his own identity, his own life, his own successes to enjoy. Returning to the family business after all these years of school would be admitting defeat. And Jack wasn't ready yet to surrender his independence.

The elevator door slid open, breaking his train of thought. Mentally crossing his fingers, Jack marched into the deserted landing. There were only eight offices on the floor. The one he wanted was at the end of the hallway to the right.

Jack paused a second to straighten his tie and push back his hair with his hands. Six feet tall, slender, with pleasant features and a ready smile, he was better looking than he realized. Gathering his courage, he proceeded down the corridor.

The frosted glass door proclaimed *Ambrose Ltd, Investments* in bold black letters. Etched underneath was the saying, "We Guarantee Your Futures." Jack grimaced in disgust, his high hopes plummeting. He knew nothing about the commodities and futures market. Another opportunity doomed before it started.

For an instant, he considered just turning around and leaving, not bothering to waste his and the interviewer's time. Then, with a heavy sigh, he straightened his tie, threw back his shoulders, and put his hand on the doorknob. No matter how slim the chance, he had to make the effort. Otherwise, it was the import-export business, and his relatives. Resolutely, he pushed open the door and stepped into the office.

The room surprised him. Instead of being filled with massive wood and leather furniture, bustling executives, and a constant din, the reception area was almost empty and absolutely quiet. A few chairs pressed up against the side walls. At the far end of the room, a young woman, engrossed in a paperback, sat reading behind an immense desk cluttered with papers. Beyond her was a solitary door leading to an inner sanctum.

The girl glanced up for a second as Jack approached, then plunged back into her novel. "Be with you in a sec," she said, the words tumbling out in a rush. "As soon as I finish the page."

Shifting his weight nervously from one foot to the other, Roger took advantage of the time to stare at the receptionist. She was stunning, and well worth a second look.

The word "elfin" immediately came to mind. The girl had incredibly delicate features, narrow cheekbones, and long upward-sweeping eyebrows. She wore no makeup and needed none.

Her nose was best described as pixieish, while her thin, ruby-red lips, pressed tightly together, spoke of a hint of sensuality. A fluffy mass of light brown hair fell in immense curls past her back and down her shoulders.

She wore a long-sleeved, multicolored dress that left her golden shoulders bare. Loops of thin gold chain circled her neck and emphasized the healthy glow of her skin. No rings on her fingers, he noted with silent approval, though it was hard to imagine a girl this stunning was unattached.

"Sorry to keep you waiting," she giggled, resting the book on her desk. Dark brown eyes gazed deep into his. "No matter how many times I read *The Lord of the Rings*, I always have trouble putting it down."

"Yeah," said Jack dreamily, still lost in her eyes, "I know what you mean."

The girl smiled, quickening his heartbeat even further. "Can I help you with something?"

Jack inhaled deeply, feeling foolish. "I'm here about the ad in the paper. The one about a job."

"Really?" asked the girl, sounding a bit surprised. She squinted at Jack, as if trying to spot something not seen before. "That's a surprise."

Then, hurriedly, seeing the shattered look that passed across his face, "No, nothing personal about you, silly. When we placed the ad, we didn't expect any responses for a week or more. It just appeared in the paper yesterday. I'm amazed that somebody in the Chicago area answered." Almost as an afterthought, she added, "Actually, I think you're kinda cute."

Jack blushed. He was not used to being called cute—much less by a beautiful young woman. Putting the brakes on his racing hormones, he tried to steer the conversation back in the right direction.

"Then the position is unfilled?"

"You're the first to apply," said the receptionist, rising from her chair. Short and petite, she barely reached up to Jack's shoulders. "I'm Megan Ambrose," she said, flashing her dazzling smile warmly.

"Jack Collins," he replied as they shook hands. Her delicate fingers were surprisingly strong.

Mentally, Jack scratched his head in annoyance. Megan's name struck a chord somewhere in his memory, but he couldn't place it. She looked familiar, though he felt sure they had never met before. He would definitely not have forgotten a woman this striking. He dismissed the notion as a case of wishful déjà vu.

"Pull up a chair, Jack," said Megan, opening one of the drawers of her desk. She pulled out several sheets of paper covered with typing and a red pencil. Brushing aside the clutter, she sat down on the desk top, facing him. "Before we proceed any further, there's a few questions I have to ask you."

Her expression grew serious. "Try your best. The correct answers are very important."

A shiver of apprehension passed down Jack's back. Something in Megan's tone of voice implied that a lot more than a job offer depended on his replies.

"Define a prime number."

"A number that's divisible only by itself and one," replied Jack.

"Explain to me the fundamental theorem of calculus."

They spent the next twenty minutes reviewing the high points of college mathematics. Jack answered all of the questions easily. He had taught most of the material during his graduate assistant days.

Megan listened to his explanations without comment. She rarely consulted her notes and easily followed everything he said. For a receptionist, she knew more mathematics than most of his students. Jack suspected there was more to Megan Ambrose than met the eye.

"A perfect score," she announced cheerfully as he finished describing Cantor's Proof. "Which doesn't surprise me considering your two degrees in mathematics. Let's proceed to the hard part."

Jack blinked. He never mentioned anything about his college studies to Megan. Yet, she seemed to know about them. He again wondered why the girl seemed so familiar.

"Who are the Nazgul?"

"The Black Riders with crowns but no faces," answered Jack automatically, "from *The Lord of the Rings*."

Nodding in agreement, Megan flashed Jack a quick smile. She appeared genuinely pleased that he knew the correct answer.

"In the novel *Three Hearts and Three Lions*, why did the chicken cross the road?"

Frowning, Jack tried to remember the Poul Anderson novel. It had been years since he read it. It took him a minute to recall the correct answer. The next query concerned the use of magic in *The Incomplete Enchanter*. And so it went, with the second half of the quiz proving to be much more challenging than the first.

They buzzed through two dozen questions in little more than an hour. Jack prided himself on his exceptional memory, but several times he was forced to admit that the details of a particular story had escaped him. Megan shook her head with each missed answer, but otherwise made no comment.

In the end, Jack calculated he had answered twenty of the twenty-four questions correctly. Running down the list, Megan confirmed the count.

"An excellent score," she said, grinning. "Though we expected no less from anyone snared by the advertisement."

Pushing her chair away from the desk, she rose to her feet and turned to the inner office door. "Let me pass these results on to Father. I'm sure he'll want to talk to you right away."

Megan disappeared into the other room, carrying the papers with her. Leaning back in his chair, Jack puzzled over her choice of words. "Snared" implied some sort of trap. While "Father" needed no explanation, the casual remark caught Jack by surprise. He should have connected Megan's name with that on the door. Trying to escape his own family business, he had stumbled into another.

"Father will see you now," announced Megan, reappearing from the other room. As Jack walked past her, she reached out and gave him a light squeeze on his forearm, quickening his pulse. "Good luck," she whispered.

The inner office was as sparsely furnished as the reception area. Floor-to-ceiling windows covered the far wall, offering a breath-taking view of downtown Chicago. Dozens of framed and signed photographs of famous people covered the other three walls. In one corner, a huge rubber tree stretched to the ceiling. There were no rows of file cabinets, banks of phones, or any of a hundred other things Jack associated with a major business. He couldn't help wondering what type of investments Ambrose Ltd. handled.

A large ebony desk, devoid of clutter, dominated the room. Behind it, in a huge, black leather and wood chair, sat the only other occupant of the room, a slender, elderly man dressed in a pin-stripe business suit. The harshness of his lean features and weather-browned skin was offset by his twinkling brown eyes. His well-groomed long mane of silver hair matched his sharply pointed snow-white beard.

"Make yourself comfortable, Jack," said the man, casually waving to a chair in front of his desk. "We have a lot to discuss." He patted the test papers. "You impressed Megan with your knowledge, and I can see why. I think you're the man we need."

Jack grinned. Today was his lucky day. Gone were his nightmares of returning to New Jersey and the import-export empire. Chicago was his hometown now.

He sobered almost instantly. There had been no mention of salary. Or exactly what position he was being offered.

"How does a thousand dollars a week sound?" said the bearded man, as if reading Jack's mind.

"A thousand a week?" repeated Jack, stunned. His mouth was suddenly dry as the desert. "For doing what, Mr. Ambrose?"

Jack suspected drug dealing—though performing Mafia-style executions ran a close second. A hundred other possibilities, most of them illegal, stampeded through his mind, while he waited for the bearded man's answer. Seeking to escape his family business, he had stumbled onto something equally threatening. None of his guesses prepared him for what Ambrose said next.

"The forces of darkness and everlasting night are rising in our city. Civilization is terribly threatened. Humanity needs a champion to battle them. You're that man, Jack."

The old man paused, a faint smile crossing his lips. "No reason for you to use the Ambrose alias. I prefer my real name. Call me Merlin."

"Merlin?" asked Jack, still reeling over the bearded man's initial remarks. "Like the famous magician of King Arthur's court?"

The bearded man laughed. "*Like* him? You misunderstand, Jack. *I am him.* I am the legendary Merlin the Magician."

2

"Uh, sure," said Jack, standing. Beads of sweat trickled down his back. The old man was crazy. The sooner Jack got out of the office, the better. "Sure you are. If you don't mind, it's time for me to leave. I just remembered that I'm late for another appointment."

Jack headed for the door. Behind him, he heard the lunatic who thought of himself as Merlin chuckle. "Come back and sit down, Jack," the man said quietly.

In the middle of a step, Jack froze. His brain shouted "Continue!" but his body refused to obey. Horrified, Jack found himself pivoting about, turning away from the door. Moving stiffly, like an automaton, he swung around and marched back to his chair. Unable to do a thing, he found himself back in the seat, facing the bearded man.

"Do you still doubt my identity?" asked his tormentor.

"All I know is that you're nuts," said Jack evenly, surprised to discover he had regained control of his arms and legs. He suspected, however, that a mad dash for the entrance was hopeless. "Anybody can use a mind-controlling drug. Nothing supernatural about that."

"And you inhaled it as a fine mist in the air upon entering the room," said the old man, shaking his head in mock dismay. "Amazing the advances made in chemical warfare these past few years."

Smiling gently, he stretched out his hand. "Perhaps this will change your opinion," he said. Softly, he muttered a few words that Jack couldn't hear. Brights lights flashed, and out of nowhere, a McDonald's cheeseburger—or at least so the wrapper proclaimed—rested on the man's palm.

"Hungry?" asked the magician, tossing the sandwich to Jack. "Go ahead. Take a bite, then explain that away."

Jack drew in a deep breath. If he was hallucinating, this dream was astonishingly realistic. With a shrug, he wolfed down the hamburger. It was still hot. His belief in magic increased with each mouthful.

"Okay," he concluded, wiping his lips, "I'm willing to concede the possibility that you might be Merlin the Magician. But, before I'm fully convinced, there are sure a hell of a lot of questions that I want answered.

"First, though, can you use that same trick to materialize something to drink? The cheeseburger made me thirsty."

Chuckling, Merlin again spoke a few words, and a large McDonald's cup filled with Coke appeared on his desk.

"How do you do that?" asked Jack, reaching out for the drink.

"A simple teleportation spell," said Merlin. "It only works on small objects. There's a fast-food restaurant down the street. I reach out with my mind and snag what I want when no one is watching. A few dollars transported to the cash drawer pays my tab. Merlin of Camelot," he concluded a bit haughtily, "is not a freeloader."

Jack drank the soda pop, his thoughts chaotic. Instead of discussing a fantasy world, he found himself in the midst of one. The notion challenged his sanity. Up until twenty minutes ago, he thought he understood the way the universe functioned. Not so any more.

"I'm willing to listen," he declared uneasily, putting the drink down. "Though," he added truthfully, "I'm not sure I want to hear what you have to say."

"As reasonable a statement as one can make," said Merlin. "I expected no more. Listen closely.

"All my life," the magician continued somberly, "I have been a seeker of knowledge and truth. For nearly a millennium, I investigated the mystery of my origin. First by magic, and then during the past few hundred years, by science. I cannot guarantee what I tell you is the truth, but it is the only explanation I have."

Jack nodded. Better to learn the facts, no matter how unbelievable. He recalled that Harold Shea, in the Incomplete Enchanter series, didn't realize magic actually worked until halfway through the first novel. Thinking about the story, Jack realized why Megan had asked him so many questions about modern-day heroes confronting magic. She had been preparing him for these revelations. But why then the mathematics?

"Ever since the Age of Reason, man has sought to explain away the supernatural. Science has no tolerance for anything that cannot be examined under a microscope. Thus, faeries and elves, demons and devils are dismissed as the foolish beliefs of ignorant peasants. In this modern world there is no room for magic. Yet, it still exists, and with it all of the fanciful beasties and beings of myth and legend."

Merlin paused, dramatically. The old man was not only a magician, Jack observed wryly, but a bit of a ham as well. "Humanity shares a collective subconscious. An overmind of unlimited potential, it has the power to forge dreams into reality. And it has done so for all of man's history. This world-mind is the source of all occult and supernatural beings that have ever existed.

"I sprang into being a thousand years ago, created by the hopes and aspirations of all those who dreamed of a place called Camelot. Originally, wandering bards sang songs of the exploits of a nameless magician in Arthur's court, making them up as they entertained. Soon, storytellers were weaving similar tales of magic, calling this sorcerer Merlin. The simple peasants of the time listened and believed what they heard was true.

"In time, the legend of Merlin the Magician grew famous throughout the land. Mankind's collective subconscious absorbed my history and believed it true. People believed I existed. That evidently was enough. The line between fact and fancy blurred, and I was born."

Again Merlin paused, as if awed by his own story. "Though perhaps 'born' is not the right word, for I emerged from the shadows exactly as you see me today—an old man with flowing white hair and silver beard. I was Merlin the Magician, weaver of spells, companion of kings.

"For hundreds of years, I traveled about the land, practicing my craft, battling injustices whenever possible. During that time, I encountered many others like me, beings created by mankind's dreams and nightmares. Some were good, others evil, but most possessed both attributes, reflecting the dual nature of their creators.

"Gradually, humanity stopped believing in fairies and elves, ghouls and ghosts. Rationality overwhelmed superstition. Yet, though man no longer accepted us, we still survived."

The magician rapped his knuckles on the desktop. "Despite my nebulous origins, I am as solid and real as any man. As is the case with any supernatural being. Once created, we exist independent of humanity's wishes. Moreover, since our bodies are vortexes of mental energy, not flesh and blood, we neither age nor die."

Merlin's pronouncements made an odd sort of sense. Ever the science fiction and fantasy fan, Jack couldn't help but wonder if this vast, collective subconscious mind as described by the magician wasn't actually a manifestation of mankind's latent psionic power. The idea offered all sorts of possibilities. He envisioned a gigantic pool of mental energy tapped upon by an unsuspecting humanity, giving life to its dreams . . . and nightmares.

"How do you explain your magic?" he asked, half-suspecting the answer.

"As a creation of this pool of psychic energy, I, and all those like me, are directly linked to it. When I perform magic, I merely tap into that bottomless well of mental power. It requires little effort on my part. With much greater effort, gifted mortals can sometimes do the same, which explains the occasional human sorcerers."

Jack nodded. It all fit together. One other question disturbed him, though.

"If what you say is true, then where are the rest of these supernatural beings? If all of you are immortal, then the world should be overflowing with mythological creatures."

Merlin shook his head. "We are immortal but by no means invulnerable. Each of us came into being with our specific strengths and weaknesses. The dreams of mankind define us. Thus, a vampire commands terrible powers but one ray of sunlight turns him into dust. And a werewolf is helpless before silver. Over the course of centuries, many of us sank back into the limbo from which we emerged, killed by the very ones who gave us life."

Leaning forward, Merlin looked Jack straight in the eye. "Can't you guess the rest of the answer to your question, my young friend? I am not unique. Thousands of us still survive, living undetected among our creators. As civilization evolved, so did we. We merely changed with the times."

Again, the magician smiled. "In my youth, I was Merlin the Magician. When people turned their back on sorcery and burned warlocks at the stake, I hid my powers behind the title of doctor and pharmacist. Later, when reason became king, I called my magic science to survive. In this day and age, I predict the rise and fall of stocks and bonds. Megan makes sure my forecasts are not too accurate. No one trusts a forecaster who is always correct. Still, we earn a princely sum each month.

"The others are out there, unnoticed by most, still endowed with their original powers. Like myself they have adapted and changed with the times. Magic fills your daily life, Jack, though most humans never realize it."

Merlin reached out, and a cup of coffee magically appeared in his hand. He sipped it slowly, leaving Jack alone with his thoughts.

The cynic within Jack's soul maintained that magic was nonsense and could not exist in a logical world. Unfortunately, that line of reasoning implied that he had slipped over the borders of reality and imagined this whole encounter. And was, therefore, totally nuts.

With a shake of his head, Jack rejected that theory. Ever the pragmatist, he accepted the evidence before him. His parents taught him the necessity of adapting to changing circumstances. Though Jack doubted they envisioned a situation like this, he felt sure they would approve of his reactions.

"I'm convinced," he told Merlin. "But what does it all have to do with my job application?"

"Just one minute and I'll explain," replied the magician. Opening a drawer in his desk, he fumbled around with unseen boxes. Finally, he pulled out a small leather case. "Found them," he announced mysteriously.

"Found what?" asked Jack, his eyes narrowing as Merlin rose from his seat and circled over to Jack's chair.

"Nothing to worry about, my young friend," said the magician, snapping open the container. He held it out so that Jack could see the contents. Inside, resting on a bed of cotton, were two tiny slivers of bright red plastic.

"Enchanted contact lenses," declared Merlin, carefully lifting one out of the case. "Much more practical than the rose-colored glasses we used for centuries. Wear these and you'll be able to instantly distinguish between a real human being and those only masquerading as such."

Jack shuddered. With 20/20 eyesight, he had never worn glasses, much less contact lenses. The thought of anything resting on his eyeball made him queasy. "Uh, I'll pass on those," he said, raising his hands in protest.

"Nonsense," said Merlin, weaving his fingers past Jack's limbs. The lens touched Jack's left eye and vanished. The same happened with the right. "I told you. These are magical. You won't feel a thing."

The magician spoke the truth. Jack's eyes felt unchanged. Only now, he viewed the world tinted lightly pink.

"Look at me," commanded Merlin. "Do you see an aura around my body?"

"No," answered Jack, frowning. "Should I?"

"Look at your hands," replied Merlin, "and then answer your own question."

Jack recoiled in surprise. His arms, his legs, his entire form glowed with a faint golden radiance.

"The rose-colored contact lenses extend your vision into the supernatural spectrum. All humans possess an aura. Supernatural beings do not." Merlin sighed. "I suspect it reflects on that intangible essence called *the soul*."

"You still haven't answered . . ." Jack started to say, but Merlin ignored him. Instead, the magician reached back into his desk drawer. This time, he pulled out a thin plastic card. With a flick of the wrist, he tossed it to Jack.

"Sign it on the back," the magician instructed. He twirled his fingers, and a pen materialized on the desk top. Writing on the casing of the ball point identified it as a free souvenir from a local hotel.

Jack examined the plastic rectangle. Bright gold in color, it appeared the same as an ordinary credit card except for the name. UNIVERSAL CHARGE CARD, proclaimed the logo.

"What is this thing?" he asked, as he wrote in his name. "There's no bank name on here."

"Nor is one needed," said Merlin. "It works by magic, much in the same fashion as the never-emptying purse of folk tales. You use it the same way as an ordinary charge card. Buy whatever you need on credit. The card is universally accepted by any store that accepts charges. It even works in cash machines. And, there's no upper expense limit."

Jack stared at the rectangle suspiciously. "Yeah. But who pays the bill?"

"Round-off charges discharge the debt," said Merlin glibly. "With interest on billing errors, clerical mistakes and overdue refunds filling in the difference. Taken separately, they amount to a mere pittance. Combine the tens of millions of transactions negotiated each month, and this floating pool of resources amounts to a fortune. Don't worry about cheating anyone. They all get paid."

Jack sighed. The magician's explanation sounded too smooth. He came across like a used car salesman, eager to make a deal. The bottom line was what worried Jack.

"Can we get back to the part about the rising forces of darkness?" asked Jack. "And humanity's champion?"

"Of course," said Merlin. "That's why I hired you."

Jack groaned in exasperation. "*Why* did you hire me?"

"Because you answered the advertisement," replied Merlin, his tone benign, as if speaking to a foolish child. He paused. "It was laced with spells to attract the proper individual."

Seeing the bewildered expression on Jack's face, the magician smiled. "Perhaps I should explain things from the beginning."

"What a novel idea," said Jack.

Merlin stood up and walked over to the huge windows. "Businessmen pay me to predict industry and stock market trends. While I carefully avoid being too accurate, I still provide the best service in the field. Needless to say, none of my clients realize my information comes not from analysis of political and social events but from a crystal ball.

"Recently, a major corporation requested I prepare a long-term analysis of employment opportunities in the Chicago metropolitan area. Usually, I turn down such projects, but this time I agreed. Not that I promised much. The future is not set, and the further ahead one looks, the less reliable the prediction. Too many outside factors affect the outcome. At best, I see what *might be,* not what *will be.* Which offers us the faint hope that changing the present will affect the future."

The fear evident in Merlin's voice sent a ripple of apprehension rippling through Jack. "How far ahead did you look?"

"A year," said the magician, barely audible. "They insisted I try, and, to be frank, the challenge intrigued me. So, I cast my spells and gazed into my crystal."

"What did you see?" asked Jack, not sure he wanted to know the answer.

"Death and destruction." Merlin's words rang of despair. "War, famine and plague. An end to civilization as we know it. The beginning of a new Dark Age for humanity."

Jack shivered. "And you think I can change the course of history? One man stop all of that?"

"I *know* you can," replied Merlin. "The world I saw stank of dark sorcery. An evil darkness haunted the land, rejoicing in the desolation. It was fully responsible for what had happened. You must find this monster in the present and destroy it to save the future. You're our only hope, mankind's lone champion. Not that it will be easy. For, though I dread the thought, I suspect one of the Old Ones has returned."

"How do you . . ." Jack began but never finished.

In the outer office, Megan screamed.

"What the hell!" yelled Jack, rising from his chair. Behind him, the door crashed open. A half-dozen bikers, dressed in black leather and chains, crowded into the room. A metal-studded glove slammed into Jack's head, sending him sprawling to the floor.

Struggling desperately to get up, Jack sensed rather than saw the kick aimed at his face. It smashed into his forehead with mind-numbing force. He collapsed to the carpet, blackness overwhelming him, with Megan's terrified shrieks echoing through his mind.

3

Groaning, Jack opened his eyes. It hadn't been a nightmare. He was still in Merlin's office. Everything looked the same. Except the magician was no longer there. Not expecting an answer, Jack called out Megan's name. No one replied.

Gingerly, he touched where his skull throbbed with pain. He jerked his head away in agony. Nothing felt broken, but he worried about a possible concussion. Dizzily, he forced himself to his feet.

The room spun about, then steadied. He rubbed his eyes in annoyance. The colors seemed wrong. There was a pink tint to everything. Then he remembered the rose-colored contact lenses.

The thought sent his mind reeling. He barely glimpsed the invading bikers, but he felt sure they hadn't possessed auras. Merlin and his daughter had been kidnaped by supernatural foes.

Jack toyed with calling the police. He rejected the idea instantly. That path led straight to the mental ward. His own initial reaction to Merlin's identity made that clear. And Jack couldn't back up his claims with magical powers. The authorities were out. If anyone was going to save Merlin, it had to be him.

That the bikers worked for the mysterious evil power described by Merlin, Jack had no doubts. Somehow, the force had discovered the magician posed a threat to its plans and had sent its minions to kidnap the mage and his daughter. Why the gang hadn't just killed the pair, Jack didn't know. He knew for sure it wasn't out of any feelings of mercy.

Fortunately, their unseen enemy was not omniscient. It failed to realize that Merlin had recruited Jack for the struggle. The bikers had treated him as a minor annoyance to be swatted out of the way, nothing more. Unless, he concluded gloomily, his efforts meant nothing and were doomed to failure. At present, that seemed extremely likely.

Merlin's rambling discourses left too much unsaid. Jack had no idea how to find, much less defeat, the evil that threatened the future. A mere graduate student in mathematics, he still had not a clue as to why the magician felt he was qualified for the job of saving mankind. Solving equations, not slaying demons, was his specialty. But, he had to try.

Jack wondered if perhaps that was the reason he had been chosen. All his life, he had faced every challenge in his path, no matter what the odds. He never shirked his responsibilities. He attacked his problems with a single-minded determination that ruled out failure. Defeat was not part of his vocabulary. A relentless streak ran through him, making him a much more dangerous foe than anyone ever guessed.

Wobbly, he staggered out of the office, carefully closing the door behind him. His fingerprints were all over the place. That could cause trouble if anyone noticed Mr. Ambrose and his secretary were missing. Jack suspected supernatural entities left no such marks.

Waiting for the elevator, he suddenly remembered the Universal Charge Card. He fumbled through his pockets for a few seconds before finding it. With a sigh of relief, he slipped the rectangle into his wallet. Perhaps he could use the card to track down the missing magician. It wasn't much of a plan, but at least it provided a starting point for further ideas.

Reaching the ground floor, Jack straightened his shirt and dusted off his clothes before confronting the security guard stationed in the front hallway. He needn't have bothered. The grizzled police veteran didn't even look up from his newspaper when Jack coughed.

"Whatcha want?" the officer mumbled.

"You didn't happen to notice a gang of bikers leaving here a short while ago?" Jack hesitated, realizing how foolish he sounded. "Accompanied by an old man and a young lady?"

The guard squinted over the paper at Jack. Dark eyes peered around warily. "No gangs allowed in my building, sonny. That includes bikers. Now go away and quit bothering me. Can't you see I'm busy?"

A talkative newspaper vendor across the street confirmed the officer's claim. "Ain't their territory," the old man declared in a high-pitched voice. "They steer clear of the Loop. Too many cops around for them to try anything."

Jack shook his head in annoyance. The kidnapers had somehow managed to enter and leave the office building unseen. Merlin claimed the teleportation spell only worked on small objects, so that was eliminated. Perhaps the gang knew the secret of invisibility. With magic real, anything was possible. Anything at all. It was not a comforting thought.

4

Despite all that had taken place in the past few hours, a few lingering doubts troubled Jack. He needed to prove to himself that Merlin had been telling him the truth, the whole truth, and nothing but the truth. There was only one sure way to find out. He decided to test the Universal Charge Card.

It didn't take him very long to find an outdoor cash station. They were scattered all over the Loop. Even the local McDonald's had one.

Gingerly, Jack put the plastic rectangle into the ATM. Without a flicker of hesitation, the machine sprang to life. "Please enter your four-digit identification code" appeared on the video monitor directly in front of him. Gulping, Jack typed in the special code listed on the back of the card he had memorized earlier. No alarms sounded. So far, so good.

Following the instructions on the screen, he entered "withdrawal" when asked what type of transaction he wanted to perform. Up to then, everything followed the usual routine for cash stations. Then magic took over.

Normally, the next screen should ask where he wanted the money taken from—his savings account, checking account, or as a cash advance against his credit card. Instead, large block letters merely asked, "How much, Jack?"

Licking his lips, he typed in "$250." Jack found it somewhat unnerving to have a machine address him by name.

"Small bills okay?" flashed the new message.

"Yes," typed in Jack.

With a hum, the machine closed up tight. When it opened a few seconds later, there was $250 in fives and tens in the money drawer. Along with Jack's card.

"Take care" flashed across the video screen as Jack scooped up the cash and stuffed it in his pockets. There was no receipt nor did Jack ask for one.

After three more withdrawals at different machines, Jack was convinced. He had remained cautious, never taking out more than $250 at any one machine. Not that the automatic tellers questioned the amount. As far as he could tell, they would have given him as much as he wanted. Thousands at least, if not more.

At least he had been smart enough to ask for big bills when prompted by the other machines. Even then, the wad of cash bulging in his pocket made him slightly paranoid. And, he had to admit, feeling terribly tempted.

Hundreds, if not thousands, of cash machines dotted the city and surrounding suburbs. Finding them wouldn't be difficult. It might take a few days to reach them all but he could do it. Especially considering the reward. If he withdrew a thousand bucks from each ATM, he would end up with over a million, tax free, cold cash, dollars. Enough pay to make his most decadent imaginings come true. The thought of that much money his for the taking gave him the shakes.

Jack shook his head. It was a seductive idea, but he was much too honest to do anything more than dream. Merlin obviously knew the power of the card, and yet he had still given it to Jack. There was no way he could betray the magician's trust. Besides, a fortune wouldn't mean much if Merlin's ominous forecast of the future came true.

That thought in mind, Jack started walking down the street to the El. If he was going to save the world, it was time to stop daydreaming and do something. Always methodical—the mark of a good mathematician—Jack planned his next moves.

First and foremost, he needed to return to the university and get some medical attention. After that, dinner would be nice, and some time to reflect carefully on what little Merlin had told him. Then, hopefully, working from that information, he could formulate a plan of attack. Though, he suspected preventing the destruction of civilization might prove to be a bit more of a challenge than his usual routine.

Reaching the entrance to the subway, Jack hesitated. He wondered if taking the underground back to campus might be a bad idea. Money in his pockets put a new twist on things. A rash of muggings, many of them taking place near the Elevated station, had plagued the college for the past month. Walking the three blocks from the train to the school might be tempting fate. As far as he was concerned, one beating a day was more than enough.

Fingering a crisp new twenty-dollar bill, Jack contemplated taking a taxi back to campus. This was entirely different from his daydreams about spending the money on wild living. A cab ride was a perfectly legitimate expense. Merlin had given him the Universal Charge Card and told him to use it whenever necessary. Or, at least the magician seemed to imply that when he gave Jack the card back in his office. Jack couldn't actually remember Merlin saying anything about the card one way or another.

Stifling the last few twinges of guilt, Jack flagged down a cab. One of the prerequisites of saving the world, he decided, was staying healthy long enough to get the job done. And if that meant spending some money not his own on a few luxuries, so be it.

Settling back in the backseat of the taxi, Jack breathed a sigh of relief. Everyone he knew said he spent too much time making decisions. He had to admit they were probably right. On the other hand, it might be the reason Merlin hired him.

"Ain't it somethin' about those girls disappearin' in the Loop?" the cabdriver asked, breaking through Jack's reverie. "Real mystery, huh?"

"Sure," Jack answered, his mind on other things. Then, the meaning of the words gradually sank into his consciousness. "Exactly what disappearances are you talking about?"

"Been talking about it on da radio all day," said the driver. "Big story. Surprised you ain't heard the news."

"Too busy working, I guess," said Jack. "Tell me all about it."

"Seems dat bunches of women, office workers mostly, been vanishin' from Loop buildings durin' the past week. Police been trying to keep the story quiet, but one of the relatives squawked to the news. Caught the cops with their pants down. I heard the chief of police three times today, claiming they expected a big break in the case anytime now. You know what dat means. They ain't got a clue what's happenin'."

"Bunches of women? Disappearing?" asked Jack, frowning. He wondered if the story tied in some way with Merlin and Megan's kidnaping. A cold chill ran down his spine. Coincidence only stretched so far.

"Forty or fifty of them, according to the radio. Missin' without a trace from offices all over the Loop. They just vanish—leavin' work, goin' ta the ladies room, comin' back from lunch. It's damned spooky."

"Only women?" asked Jack.

"You got it, boss. Just babes. Funny thing, though. Ain't only the good-looking ones missin'. According to the news, the dames range in age from twenty to sixty. No ransom notes, no dead bodies, no nothing turned up as of yet. Watcha think? White slavers or somebody like dat? Grabbing the women and shipping them overseas or somethin'? Maybe dose rich Arab sheiks are behind the whole t'ing?"

"I don't know," said Jack. Nor did he. "I truly don't know."

Jack grimaced in frustration. It seemed safe to assume that Merlin's kidnapers were the same gang behind the other abductions in the Loop. But, if the police, with all of their resources and manpower, were baffled by the crimes, how could he expect to solve the mystery? He was a mathematician, not a detective.

I guess if I'm going to save the world, he thought to himself, *I'll have to be both.*

Somehow the thousand-dollars-a-week salary Merlin mentioned no longer seemed that outrageous. Jack had a feeling that before too long he would be feeling underpaid.

5

With a curse, Roger Quinn slammed down the telephone. Life was bad enough these days serving a bloodthirsty demigod without having to deal with incompetent employees. Sometimes he wondered how the world continued to function as well as it did. He paused for a second, then decided he had answered his own question.

For years, he had known that most people were incredibly inept. Now, to his dismay, he was learning that the denizens of the supernatural plane were no better. If anything, considering the fact that they were creations of mankind's dreams and desires, they performed even worse than their makers. Grinding his teeth in annoyance, Roger set off to find his master, the Crouching One, Lord of the Lions. He shuddered to think of the demigod's reaction to the news. There would be hell to pay. Literally.

As usual, Roger found the Crouching One in the library, scanning another volume of the encyclopedia. The ancient god had an insatiable thirst for knowledge and could absorb information at an incredible rate. In the past month, it had gone through dozens of history and anthropology texts, and now was working its way through Roger's reference shelf. Needing neither sleep nor food, the demigod spent all of its time reading or scheming to take over the world. It did not like being disturbed while involved in either activity.

Dressed conservatively in a dark wool suit, black tie and white shirt, the Lord of the Lions appeared to be nothing more than a distinguished elderly gentleman. It seemed remarkably unremarkable, until you saw its eyes. They glowed startling yellow with an inner fire. On its infrequent trips from the mansion, the demigod wore dark glasses.

"Yes?" it hissed, clearly not pleased by his presence. "What do you want?"

"The call came in from Chicago," said Roger nervously. "They got the girl. And her father too."

The demigod's eyes blazed a little brighter. It nodded, looking pleased. "Exactly as I planned. I told you nothing could go wrong. The modern world cannot cope with ancient sorcery."

The Crouching One waved one hand in dismissal. "Now, go, and leave me alone. I do not like being disturbed while I am reading."

Licking his lips, Roger cleared his throat. "Uh, I'm afraid that wasn't all the news."

"What do you mean?" No mistaking the creature for human now. Its voice was like ice. "Tell me."

"When the Border Redcaps broke into Merlin's office, there was another person there. A human."

"So?" said the Crouching One. "That was nothing surprising. You told me the magician was a seer. That he was meeting with a client is no concern of ours."

Roger exhaled, his eyes gaze flickering around the room, trying to avoid the yellow glare of the demigod's eyes. "At the time, the Redcaps thought the same thing. They knocked the man unconscious and left him there. They had specific orders not to kill anyone unless absolutely necessary."

Blue flames crackled above the Lord of the Lions's brow. "Enough wasting time. Get to the point."

"The visitor never reported the attack to the police. Nothing unusual in that. Most people don't like to get involved if they can avoid it. But, according to our spies, he questioned both the guard in the lobby and a news vendor outside the building about the Redcaps." Roger's voice cracked as he reached the point of no return. "And, we've since learned that he's carrying a talisman of great power."

"A talisman," said the Crouching One, its voice a bare whisper. "The magician gave him an enchanted token. You are sure of this fact?"

Roger nodded glumly. "He's displayed it four times already. We're not sure exactly what it did, but each time it was used, the charm emitted a powerful burst of magic. Our sensitives recognized the discharge immediately."

"A lone man, armed with a talisman," said the Lord of the Lions, sounding curious. And slightly worried. "You think the old wizard summoned him to stop us?"

"*I'm* not the god here," said Roger stiffly. "You're the one who answers all the questions." His tone left no doubt what he thought of that arrangement. "I do remember you telling me that every time a challenge to order arises, so does a champion of the status quo. This guy could be the opposition."

"Quite possible," said the Crouching One. "Did the Huntsman question the magician, or his daughter?"

"That's not been possible," said Roger. "They've been unconscious since their abduction. Despite all attempts to wake them, the pair have remained asleep. Von Bern suspects a reflexive spell, one that takes effect immediately on captivity. It prevents the prisoners from revealing any secrets. And, torture is singularly ineffective when the victim is comatose."

"Bah," grumbled the Lord of the Lions, sounding disgusted. "In my day, things were a lot easier. None of this sneaking around in the shadows nonsense. I was a god. My followers worshipped me. They treated me with respect. When I spoke, the world trembled. *I was feared.*"

"I know, I know," said Roger, shaking his head. He was tired of listening to the demigod's complaints. Over the past few weeks, the Lion God had repeated its catalog of woes hundreds of times. It took very little to start its complaining. *No more virgin priestesses. No more blood sacrifices. No more holy wars.* The list went on and on. God or not, the Crouching One was a colossal bore.

"Well, best that we assume the worst," declared the Lord of the Lions. "I remember how all of us gods laughed at that character, Gilgamesh. What a pest he turned out to be. And then, of course, there was Moses. Nobody expected that sanctimonious busybody would cause such trouble."

"Moses?" repeated Roger, his mouth open in astonishment. "You knew Moses?"

"All of the Immortals knew Moses," said the Crouching One. "He was our bane—the first link in the chain of events that banished me and all those like me from the face of the Earth. Damned Hebrew was a lot more dangerous than he looked."

The Lord of the Lions smiled its special smile, the smile that gave Roger the shakes every time he saw it. The catlike smile, ancient and mysterious, without a trace of humor—or humanity. "But now I am back, and I won't be fooled so easily a second time. Not at all."

Blue sparks flashed as the demigod rubbed its hands together. "Call back our allies in Chicago. Let them put out the word to all those who roam the night. This mortal champion must be found and destroyed. He must be crushed before he can interfere with our plans. I want him dead. Now."

"They might not be able to locate him so easily," said Roger, edging back to the door. When the Crouching One started playing with hellfire, it was time to leave. "And, if he's this champion like you think, he might not be a pushover."

"Perhaps," said the Lord of the Lions. "Perhaps. But, he can be traced by the talisman in his possession. Von Bern will know how to do that at least. Night will soon fall in Chicago. The forces of darkness are strongest in the midnight hours. The German and his allies will not fail me." The demigod clenched its hands into fists. "They *dare* not fail me."

"Yes, sir," said Roger, scurrying out of the room. "Yes, sir."

He dashed for the telephone. For the moment, he was in the clear. Von Bern and his stooges had let this champion escape. He was their responsibility.

Roger shivered. Dealing with the Lord of the Lions always left him shaken. He had raised the entity by mistake and was stuck paying for his mistake. Only death could sever his ties with the evil demigod.

Like an echo, that thought reverberated through his mind. Carefully, analytically, Roger reviewed his conversation with the Crouching One. According to the basic principles of science, the final result of any operation was guaranteed if the initial conditions of the experiment were duplicated exactly.

Roger smiled. It was time for him to do some reading. About Moses.

6

"Well, doc," said Jack, only half in jest, "will I live?"

"That depends entirely on whether you learned anything from this unfortunate experience," replied Doctor Nelson seriously. "You were lucky, Jack. Next time, you might not escape with just a few bruises and a bad headache."

A tall, thin, middle-aged man, Nelson was the campus physician. Though he rarely smiled, he had a droll sense of humor. His bland features concealed a razor-sharp wit and a keen mind that rarely missed anything.

"There won't be a next time," said Jack. "I'm not that stupid."

"I hope not," said Nelson. "Though I can't entirely blame you. No one expects to be assaulted during broad daylight. Not even in this neighborhood."

The university was located in one of the worst sections of Chicago's south side. An imposing metal fence supposedly sealed the campus off from the streets, but no one really believed it provided any real security. Campus police did their best to maintain order, but it was a no-win proposition.

"Tell me about it," said Jack, tenderly rubbing the bump on his head. "I've warned my students for years about the problem, but it never occurred to me that I might be the one assaulted. Can I get dressed now, doc?"

"Of course," said Nelson. "You know I have to report this incident to security, Jack."

"Sure," said Jack, pulling on his clothes. "I was going to head over there right after leaving here. But I won't argue if you want to fill out the report. Facing Benny Anderson won't make my headache feel any better. I'd rather wander back to my apartment and lie down for a while."

"You could use the rest," said Nelson. Anderson was chief of campus security. An ex-marine, dealing with him was always an effort.

Reaching into a file drawer, the doctor pulled out a police report form. "I keep a stack of these handy," he said, almost apologetically. "You can't imagine how many of my patients need one of them."

Careful of every detail, Jack retold the story he had concocted to explain his injuries. There was more than enough truth to the recital to make it believable.

"A motorcycle gang," said Nelson, sighing. "As if we didn't have enough trouble around here already. You didn't, by any chance, notice anything special about their jackets? Many gangs sport distinctive colors or emblems. It might provide the police with a clue. Not that they'd be able to do much anyway."

Jack shook his head, causing him to wince in pain. "They jumped me from behind, doc. The only thing I saw was a metal-studded glove that hit me in the face. And a boot that finished the job."

"Funny that they didn't rob you," said Nelson, scribbling down notes on the police form. "You're positive, Jack, that these hoodlums had no reason to rough you up?"

It took Jack a minute to realize what the physician was thinking.

"Hey, I'm innocent, doc. I'm not into drugs and never have been. I don't use them, and I definitely don't sell them. And you're crazy if you think different."

Nelson raised his hands in protest. "Sorry. I had to ask. If I didn't, you can be sure campus security would. Anderson is obsessed with drug dealers. It's the nature of the times."

"Great," said Jack, standing up. "Talk about guilt by associa-tion. I get mugged for no reason by a bunch of lunatics and that means I'm a dope pusher. Meanwhile, logic takes a holiday."

The physician shrugged his shoulders. There was an odd expression on his face. "I'm only doing my job, Jack. No reason to get upset. Take it easy for a few days. Use the whirlpool bath in the gym whenever you can. It'll help those bruises. If the pain bothers you too much, give me a call and I'll prescribe something. Otherwise, check back with me in a week. By then, you should be back to normal.''

Still fuming, Jack left the doctor's office. Nobody ever accused the hero of any fantasy novel he ever read of dealing in drugs as a sideline. Nor, for that matter, did he recall any of those heroes experiencing any real aches and pains other than an occasional hangover or arrow wound. Most of them shrugged off anything less than a life-threatening injury.

Head throbbing, Jack shuffled down the street towards the student union building. He needed food. It was nearly six o'clock and all he had eaten since the morning was the cheeseburger and Coke at Merlin's office. The college cafeteria stayed open till nine. Once he grabbed a bite, he intended to head back to his apartment and collapse. Jack smiled wistfully. So far, his career as a world-saver was not progressing very well.

With evening classes already underway, there weren't many graduate students in the student union. Which suited Jack fine. He wasn't in much of a mood to talk with anyone. Loading up his tray with a hot turkey sandwich, potatoes, a Coke and a piece of cake, he shuffled to the cash register.

It wasn't until Jack reached for his wallet to pay for his dinner that he remembered his pockets were crammed full of greenbacks. He wondered if Doctor Nelson had noticed the cash. That would explain the physician's questions about drug dealing. The more he thought about it, the more obvious it became. Unfortunately, knowing the reason was not a solution. The money suddenly weighed very heavy in his jeans.

Cautiously, he looked around for the campus police. If Nelson relayed his suspicions to the security officers, they could be searching for Jack right now. And explaining how he obtained all that money would be awfully difficult.

Feeling extremely paranoid, Jack marched to the far end of the cafeteria. Dinnertime had the place packed with underclassmen. Finally, after a frantic survey of the room, he spotted a small table isolated from the flow of traffic. With his back to the cafeteria wall, he could keep a watch on the whole room.

With a sigh of relief, Jack sat down and started eating. Hungry but worried, he wolfed down the food without tasting a thing. The sooner he hid the money, the safer he would feel.

Gulping down his Coke and gobbling the last bite of cake, he pushed back his chair, ready to leave. And found himself surrounded by a half-dozen undergraduates, all talking at once. To him.

Preoccupied with his troubles, Jack had not noticed them approaching. Four women and two men, the group consisted of his extra-help class in Freshman Calculus. Escaping them was not going to be easy. Groaning, he settled back in his seat.

Tutoring was something new at the university and one of Jack's least favorite chores. Unfortunately, as a Ph.D. graduate assistant, he had little choice in his teaching assignments. He did what he was told. Needless to say, graduate assistants were always given the courses none of the regular professors wanted.

All freshmen attending the school were required to take at least one math course. Calculus 101 was the bane of the mathematics department. Though they had mandated the requirements, the Board of Regents had made it quite clear that they would consider it quite disturbing if very many of the incoming students, paying tuition that the university desperately needed, flunked the course and dropped out of school. Thus, not only did graduate assistants teach an extremely watered-down calculus course, they also conducted extra-help classes after normal class hours for those students who were so bad at mathematics that they needed a continual shove to keep them even with their classmates.

Jack, born with a gift for calculation and logic, found the tutoring sessions incredibly depressing. All his life, he had labored under the impression that anyone could learn mathematics if taught correctly. The calm, precise nature of the subject seemed as natural as breathing. He never imagined people existed who were unable to perform even the simplest of calculations without breaking into a cold sweat. Until this semester, when he encountered his extra-help group.

Not that they were stupid. The six students were among the brightest young men and women in the university. They all wanted to learn. They struggled desperately to understand. But they were incapable of solving basic equations, much less genuine calculus problems.

In desperation, Jack finally followed the lead of several other graduate assistants struggling with the same headache. Before the most recent exam, he reviewed the entire test with his tutorial. Step by step, he dissected each question, proceeding through it to the correct solution. Though he balked at telling his charges that these were the same problems they would face the next day, he strongly hinted to them that knowing how to solve these practice equations would make the test a snap. And, despite everything, all six flunked the exam.

"You weren't in your office this afternoon, Professor Collins," Sandra Stevens declared angrily, yanking Jack back to reality. The co-ed had a voice like chalk scratching over a blackboard. "We waited for over an hour."

"Yeah," said Gil Neumann. An architecture major, Gil could not grasp the fundamentals of trigonometry. Some time back, Jack had made a sacred vow that in the distant future he would never enter a building designed by Neumann.

"Quite boring," added Simon Fellows. An exchange student from England, Simon's voice betrayed only the slightest accent. Of all Jack's extra-help students, Fellows was the most frustrating. An English major, he scored phenomenal grades in all of his other courses. But, though he could recite the most difficult facts without blinking twice, Simon seemed incapable of understanding basic logic.

"Sorry," said Jack. "I had a job interview that took a little longer than I expected. Then, afterward, I wasted more time by allowing myself to be mugged."

"Mugged?" said Sandra, her voice so loud that half the cafeteria turned to see what was going on. "You were mugged?"

"You do look a little more worse for wear than usual," remarked Simon, eternally cheerful.

Nothing ever bothered the exchange student. He laughed at misfortune, though Jack wasn't sure if it was from sheer bravado or abysmal ignorance. Though handsome, intelligent and charming, Simon was not a very popular person on campus. He was just a bit too weird for most of the students.

Jack never realized how weird until he glanced at the Brit while scanning the hall for campus security. Jack's eyes narrowed in amazement. He shook his head, not sure he believed what he was seeing. Or not seeing. Simon had no aura. The exchange student wasn't human. He was magic.

"Uh, Professor Collins, is something wrong?" asked Sandra. "You look kinda . . . funny."

Jack squeezed his eyes tightly shut, then opened them again. Nothing had changed. The other five students had auras. Simon did not. It was definitely time, Jack decided, to have a word with the Brit.

"I am feeling a bit dizzy," said Jack. "The doctor warned me to take it easy for the next few days. Why don't you all attend Professor Gleason's extra-help classes for the time being. They're scheduled the same time we held ours, so it will fit right in with your free time. If you explain the circumstances to Pat Gleason, I'm sure he won't mind you sitting in."

Gleason would have a fit, but too bad. Jack felt no remorse. Based on Gleason's conduct at the faculty Christmas party last year, the other graduate assistant deserved to suffer.

"Do you need some help getting back to your apartment?" asked Gil Neumann, his tone of voice making it quite clear he wasn't overwhelmed with the idea.

"I'll be fine," said Jack. Then, as the students turned to leave, he quickly added, "Simon, would you mind sticking around for a few seconds more? I wanted to ask you something."

"No problem," replied the Brit.

The others departed, casting suspicious looks at both of them. Jack was at a loss as to what chicanery they might imagine. He couldn't be supplying Simon with test answers. He had done that for all of them to no consequence.

Tomorrow, if things continued on their present course, they would probably assume it had been a drug deal. He had to get back to Dr. Nelson and explain all that cash. Somehow.

"If it's about that last test," said the Brit, "I can explain everything. . . ."

"Forget the test," said Jack, not exactly certain how to begin. Then, before he could say another word, he spotted two campus security officers on the other side of the cafeteria. Beads of sweat popped on Jack's back. The policemen were probably just there for a coffee break, but he dared not risk it. Not with the cash still crammed in his pockets.

"Let's go for a walk," he said, rising quickly from the table. "We need to talk about things. Like auras—or the lack of them."

A startled look passed across Simon's face. For the first time in

Jack's memory, the student looked terribly unsure of himself. "Auras, you say? A walk?"

The two security officers were nowhere in sight. It was time to go. Hastily Jack grabbed Simon by the arm and steered him to the exit. "Magic," he said quietly as he pushed open the door to the outside. "Let's talk about magic."

7

Anxious to get as far away from the Campus Center as possible, Jack hurried Simon along the walk leading to the humanities building. At this time of the evening, there were only a few classes in session and they had the path to themselves.

Not more than a hundred feet from the Center, Simon came to an abrupt halt. Turning, the Brit put both his hands on Jack's shoulders and stared intently into his eyes. After a second, the student pursed his lips in a low whistle of astonishment.

"Rose-colored contact lenses," he said. "I heard rumors that such things existed, but I never expected to encounter anyone actually wearing them. Especially not my mathematics professor."

"Tell me about it," said Jack, sighing. "Then you don't deny you're a supernatural being, some sort of magical creature?"

"Creature?" replied Simon, grinning. "I may not be human, Professor Collins, but I do have feelings. Simon Goodfellow, of the kingdom of Faerie, at your service, my esteemed teacher."

"Call me Jack," said Jack. "I don't mind the 'professor' bit from students seven or eight years younger than I am. But, from a being who has been around for a couple of hundred years, it sounds kinda pretentious."

"Seven hundred and twelve years, to be exact," said Simon. "But then, who's counting?"

They resumed walking down the path, conversing in low tones, appearing to be nothing more than a student and his teacher discussing classwork. Simon seemed quite nonchalant about the whole affair.

"If you told anybody about this," he declared, "they'd think you'd gone daft."

"I've devoured too many fantasy novels to even consider that possibility," said Jack. "Nobody believes the hero, and it leads to all sorts of dreadful complications. The last thing I need at present is more complications.

"For the record, though, what kind of magical being are you? I don't remember reading any specifics on supernatural exchange students."

Simon laughed. "That's because you're thinking too much of our traditional roles, Professor. Oops, sorry—Jack. We faeries have changed with the times. Like all the rest of the supernatural beings that still inhabit this wonderful world. I'm a changeling."

"Merlin did say . . ." began Jack.

"Merlin?" interrupted Simon. "You mean to say that Merlin the Magician is in America?"

"That's who gave me the contact lenses," said Jack. "I gather he's been living in Chicago for quite some time." Casually, Jack added, "Along with his daughter, Megan."

"Daughter?" said Simon. "I never recalled stories about Merlin having a daughter. There was Morgana, of course, but I thought she was his sister."

The Brit shrugged. "That's the trouble with living so long. Fact and fancy get mixed up, and after a while you don't know what's true and what's not. Merlin's in Chicago, though? I'll have to look him up. We share a bunch of memories that go way back. Way, way back."

"That might not be so easy," said Jack. "But before I describe that mess, explain to me this changeling stuff."

"If you insist," said Simon. "A lot of it Merlin explained to me. I don't know how much the old boy told you, but his theories covering our creation are pretty much accepted fare among the supernatural kingdom. So pardon me if I summarize and condense things somewhat.

"You humans are always trying to cover up your own faults by blaming somebody else. These days, it's society or peer pressure or a hundred other excuses. Nobody likes to admit maybe they're the ones responsible for the problems of the world.

"Well, not surprisingly, things weren't that different seven, eight hundred years ago. In those days, the peasants didn't have pop psychology to fall back on. There wasn't this horde of apologists to offer feel-good explanations for aberrant behavior. So, instead, the local populace did the next best thing. They blamed everything on us, the supernaturals."

"I'm not sure I follow what you're saying," said Jack, frowning. "Lots of people accept full responsibility for their actions."

"Sure," said Simon, "but a lot more search for a convenient scapegoat. And their more imaginative solutions created beings like me."

His voice grew caustic. "Got a problem, neighbor? Your young son refuses to plow the field? And he runs away whenever you ask him to shovel the manure? Well, friend, that doesn't sound like the actions of a well-bred, obedient child. Obviously, it can't be any fault of yours. As God-fearing folk, you did your best for him. The only logical explanation is that the boy isn't really your son."

Simon's face crinkled with amusement. In the twilight, his eyes glowed amber. "Blame those damned faeries. Free-spirited, mischievous imps love causing trouble for the hard-working good folk of the earth. They replaced your true son with a shiftless, no-good changeling. Sure, he looks just like the boy, but that's part of the spell. Mark my words. Queen Titania's spoiling your offspring with sweets while this trickster wreaks havoc on your farm. He'll never admit it, but you know the truth."

Solemnly, Simon passed a hand over his face. For a brief instant, his features wavered, grew hazy. Then, an astonished Jack found himself staring at a mirror image of himself.

"Impressive, huh?" asked Simon, in Jack's voice. "You should see me after one of the 'Freddy Krueger-fests' at the Student Union movie theater. I scared a half-dozen co-eds into swearing off beer for a year."

"I'm still not sure I see how this changeling business ties in with exchange students," said Jack. "And switch back to your own face. Life's complicated enough without talking to myself."

"Your wish is my command," said Simon with only the slightest tinge of mockery in his voice. With another pass of his hand, he returned to normal.

"Exchange students?" prompted Jack. Keeping Simon focused on one subject was a full-time job.

"Sorry. My thoughts tend to wander a bit."

"I noticed," said Jack.

"Well, to give credit where credit is due, when you humans dreamt up explanations, you did a thorough job of it. It wasn't enough that changelings replaced human children. There had to be some reason for it. Despite all the talk of faeries acting by different rules of behavior, that actually was never the case. After all, we were created in your image. Your myths always provided us with motives that sounded suspiciously human.

"Anyways, Titania became the villainess. Poor Queen of the Faeries never stood a chance. First, some of your more eloquent bards brought her and Oberon into existence, as the romanticized ideals of pure love. Unfortunately, that meant never getting fat and pregnant. No matter what she did, the Queen remained radiantly beautiful.

"However, most of the peasants were far less noble and wholesome. They visualized faeries as much more . . ." Simon hesitated, and grinned. "Shall we say, earthier. She and Oberon used to make the satyrs blush, and that wasn't easy."

"Exchange students?" repeated Jack, with a heavy sigh.

"Like I said, the Queen got blamed for the changelings. According to popular belief, she desired kids to mother. She never let circumstances stand in her way. So, when the maternal instincts overcame her good judgment, she stole away some poor mortal child and replaced him with a changeling. Then, when the urge left her, we were switched back."

Simon chuckled. "Life was hectic but entertaining. You envisioned me and my kind as good-natured pranksters. And, so that's how we acted. Though there were a few of us not so pleasant. The dark side of the dream if you catch my meaning."

"*Pickman's Model*," said Jack, without thinking. "In the story, the narrator described a group of paintings dealing with the offspring of ghouls replacing normal children in a Puritan family. They all sounded pretty ghastly."

Simon cleared his throat. "Lovecraft got it right. I'm not sure what Merlin told you, but we supernaturals are true reflections of the dual nature of humanity. Among us can be found both good and evil entities. And all possible shades between the two."

He smiled. "Most faeries fall into that middle ground. We're neutral unless forced to take sides. Usually, when provoked we stand with humanity. Though most people find that hard to believe. They confuse mischief with deviltry.

"Even changelings have their purposes. If I drove my foster-parents to drink, it was for a purpose." He laughed. "An obscure purpose at times, I will admit. But for their own good, nonetheless. You have the word of Simon Goodfellow on that."

"Goodfellow?" said Jack. "The name rings . . ."

"Robin," replied Simon. "My cousin of sorts. He's the famous one. Nicknamed Puck by Willy Shakespeare."

"Willy?" asked Jack, but Simon was continuing with his story.

"Times changed and so did we. Like all supernatural beings, we evolved with the changes in civilization. It's our nature to adapt. Take the King and Queen of Faeries, for example. A few years back, they moved to Las Vegas and opened up one of those quickie honeymoon chapel and hotel combos. I got a Christmas card from them last winter.

"From what I hear from my cousins, the Queen is still quite a looker. Now, though, she blends right in with the local scenery. Half the tourists in town think she's a retired hooker or porn queen. Word is that she and Oberon plan to write a sex manual. Probably title it *A Thousand Years of Pleasure*. Boy, that would be a book hot enough to scorch your fingers."

"Exchange students," said Jack.

"Oh, sure. There's not much room for changelings in the modern world. We're impostors by definition. More than that, our basic nature dictates that we have to be disruptive and annoying as well. Which makes us less than welcome wherever we go.

"For a time, I played the role of the long-lost relative. That was fun, though repetitive. After a while, it was like living in one of those 1940's screwball comedies. Maybe you've seen a few? They're the ones where the husband everyone thought dead turns up the day of his wife's remarriage?"

Simon rolled his eyes. "Fortunately, we supernaturals are hard to kill. Otherwise, the two of us wouldn't be talking tonight. I've been shot, stabbed, and electrocuted more times than I like to remember. It was a lot worse, *a lot worse*, when I assumed the role of the long-lost heir who turns up the morning the will is scheduled to be read. Wow! Talk about imaginative ways to eliminate people."

"Then posing as an exchange student . . . ?" began Jack.

". . . is just another variation on the theme," said Simon, completing the thought. "Among us faeries, it's called the 'know-it-all gambit.'

"Each year, I transfer to another university. Using a magical interface, it's easy to fool the school computers into accepting my phony credentials. Ditto for issuing me thousands of dollars in credit for room, board and tuition. Fortunately, nobody in the admissions office ever bothers doing background checks on foreign exchange students."

"This 'know-it-all' role also explains your smug, superior attitude, I take it?" asked Jack.

"You got it, Jack," said Simon. "It's my duty to get on everyone's nerves. I'm here to shake things up a little bit on campus. People need an obnoxious, 'too-damned-smart-for-his-own-good' character to despise. It's healthy for the soul. Or so I've been told, since I don't have one."

"What about your popularity with the fair sex?" asked Jack. "I don't remember that being covered in any stories about change-lings I read."

"Titania and Oberon aren't the only ones with lust in their hearts, Jack," said Simon, his grin widening. "I can't help it if you humans created me with a surplus of roguish charm. And a wild streak that prompts me to use it whenever possible."

The changeling paused, the smile disappearing from his face. "I've answered all your questions. Each and every one. It seems only fair to me that you do the same."

Simon shook his head. "Rose-colored contacts and Merlin the Magician? The implications of that combination worry me. Actually, they scare the hell out of me. What's going on, Jack?"

Jack told him.

∞

8

"Hand me another beer, would you?" asked Simon a half-hour later. The changeling gulped down the contents of the bottle with one swallow. It was his fifth, and as far as Jack could tell, the beer had not affected the supernatural being in the least. Jack suspected it would take a tremendous amount of alcohol to dent Simon's inhuman metabolism. A lot more than he had in his refrigerator.

With a loud burp, the changeling handed Jack back the empty bottle. After Jack's summary of the day's events, they had retired to his nearby apartment to puzzle out the complexities of the situation. Simon looked ready to cry. Or burrow under the cushions of the sofa and hide.

Jack's apartment consisted of a parlor, tiny dining room and kitchenette combination, and a bedroom. A short, narrow corridor linked the rooms. Right in its middle was the door leading to the building hallway. At present, man and changeling sat on a battered old blue sofa situated in the center of the living room.

"You want to explain to me why you're trying to drink yourself into a stupor?" asked Jack. "Things can't be that bad."

"They can't?" retorted Simon. Rising to his feet, he stalked over to the icebox and retrieved another beer. Hooking the cap between his teeth, he twisted his jaw sharply, pulling the metal cleanly off the glass. "Wanna bet?"

"Would you care to be more specific?" said Jack, opening his bottle of beer with an opener. He had a feeling that he was going to need a drink. Probably several. "I'm not very good at reading minds."

Simon shrugged his shoulders. "Don't take this the wrong way, Jack. You're a nice guy and a really good math teacher. Unfortunately, neither of those traits strike me as qualifications for a champion of humanity. No offense, but you're not the hero type. I mean, I knew St. George, Professor Collins, and you're no St. George. His accountant maybe, but no dragon slayer. You catch my drift?"

"But Merlin said I was the only one who could save the world," said Jack defensively. "Right before he was kidnapped he told me that straight out."

"Then," said Simon somberly, draining his beer bottle and handing it to Jack, "the world is in deep, deep trouble. Assuming of course that the old geezer hasn't lost a few screws in this prediction business."

The changeling's tone brightened noticeably. "What do you think? Any chance the famous wizard might have bitten off more than he could swallow? Maybe we're worrying about nothing."

"I don't think so," said Jack. "Merlin struck me as being pretty well grounded. There was no hint of senility in anything he said. Besides, that ignores the supernatural motorcycle gang who grabbed him and Megan."

"Damn," said Simon, his expression souring. "I hate when you humans use logic. I much prefer wishing and hoping myself."

The changeling wandered back to the refrigerator and latched onto another beer. "You're running low on brew. Better buy some more. You got any chips? Beer always tastes better with chips."

"Try the cabinet over the sink," said Jack. All of Simon's worries had obviously not damaged the changeling's appetite. "I figure the first thing we should do is search for the kidnappers. They're our only lead."

Simon, his mouth full of potato chips, gasped, almost choking. "We?" he managed to sputter out. "Uh, who volunteered me? I'm a poor faerie, not a companion of heroes. Remember the mischievous elf, good-natured trickster, I spoke about? Nothing in that description covers saving the world."

Jack smiled. "On the other hand, you mentioned that all supernatural beings reflect man's dual nature — good versus evil. You squarely lined yourself up with the good guys. Well, it's time to stand up and be counted, my friend. I need your help."

The changeling groaned. "You're crazy, Jack. Absolutely, totally crazy. We can't defeat one of the Old Ones. You have no concept of how powerful those monsters are. He'll chew us up for an afternoon snack. A small snack at that. I might be on the side of the angels, but I prefer staying alive. And challenging the overwhelming forces of the dark isn't a way to remain that way."

"Merlin selected me," said Jack stubbornly. "That much I understood. He thought I could handle the job, and I fully intend to try. With or without your help."

Simon pulled a box of cereal out of the cabinet. "I didn't say I wouldn't help. Just give me a little time to consider my options. In the meantime, I'll continue thinking you're nuts. Do you mind if I nibble on this?"

"Go ahead," said Jack. He frowned. "Don't they feed you in the dorms?"

"Sure," said Simon, munching on a handful of frosted corn flakes. "Three meals a day. Normally, I don't eat anywhere near this much in the cafeteria."

"Then why," asked Jack, gritting his teeth, "are you acting tonight as if you haven't had a bite of food in weeks?"

"Annoying, isn't it?" replied Simon, grinning. "Which is exactly the reason I do it. I'm only being true to my nature, Jack. If, after a while whenever we're together, you're not angry with me, then something's wrong. My whole purpose for existing is to drive people nuts. Even my friends."

"Fair enough, I guess," said Jack, squeezing his eyes shut in frustration. Then, as a new thought struck him, he stared directly at the changeling.

"Why don't we follow that line of reasoning one step further. By your own admission, you *know it all*. That's another part of your character. Well, then, I think it's time for you to share some of your wisdom. Let's discover how much information you really possess. Like, for example, who or what is this Old One and why are you so terrified of him?"

Simon paused in the midst of crunching a mouthful of cereal. "That's a good idea," he said. "Wonder why I never thought of it."

The changeling swallowed the rest of the flakes. "I'm filled with knowledge, Jack," he declared. "Not everything in the world, of course, but an awful lot. My mind is like an encyclopedia. Ask me the right question and I'll provide you with the correct answer. But I can't extrapolate on pure guesswork. I need to be pointed in the right direction."

"I understand," said Jack. "It's no different than working with a computer. They're great at retrieving tons of relevant data. But only if you know what you're looking for. I think I can manage."

He drew in a deep breath. Maybe now he would get some answers. "Shall we start again with the obvious question? Who or what is this Old One and why is he such a threat to modern civilization?"

The changeling closed his eyes, as if pondering his reply. It took him a few seconds to answer. There was a note of quiet desperation in his voice.

"What Merlin told you about the lifespans of supernatural beings wasn't absolutely true, Jack," said Simon, his expression serious. "We don't grow old and die, nor can we be killed by most conventional methods of murder. However, we all have our weaknesses and vulnerabilities. Even in its dreams, mankind wasn't foolish enough to make us invulnerable. Except for one tiny segment of our population. The Gods."

"The Gods," repeated Jack, beads of sweat breaking out on the back of his neck. "The Gods?"

"Humanity envisioned its own creators as omniscient, omnipotent, and immortal," continued Simon. "They weren't supposed to die. That worked fine for the early, small civilizations of prehistory. They rarely encountered other cultures. But think of the problems that arose once empires started forming. Gods, as well as civilizations, clashed.

"Fortunately," continued Simon, "what man can imagine, he can unimagine. Or consign to limbo. And so it was with the ancient Gods."

"Huh?" said Jack, totally confused.

"If enough people believed in a supernatural entity, their thoughts brought it to life. Even if all those believers later died, their creation remained. Such was the case with my race, the faeries. Humanity stopped believing in us long ago. Instead, you no longer gave us any thought. So we survived, adapting to the changing world. But that was not the case with the Old Gods."

"Mankind disbelieved them out of existence," whispered Jack, the truth unfolding in his mind. "They were destroyed the same way they were created. By pure thought."

Simon nodded. "Judaism, then Christianity, wiped the Old Ones away. People not only worshiped one God, they firmly rejected the possibility of any other. They denied them. 'Thou shalt have no other God before me,' the Bible commanded, and so it was. All of Jehovah's rivals were *unimagined* out of existence. The ancient Gods disappeared. But disbelief proved to be a lot more complicated than creation.

"The only way to completely vanquish the Old Ones is for no one to believe they exist. *No one.* Need I remind you how often all humanity has agreed on anything? You can count the times on no fingers. Blame the lunatic fringe. Feeding on their doubts, the earliest Gods of civilization, the pagan, bloodthirsty Gods of prehistory, maintain a tenuous grip on this world. They lurk in the outer dark, waiting for an invitation to return. And, from time to time, some utter fool manages to summon one of them back."

"How?" asked Jack.

"Beats me," said Simon. "Who cares? The important fact is that an incredibly powerful supernatural being, one with Godlike powers, has returned to the Earth. And that spells trouble with a capital T."

"Then this sort of thing has happened before?" asked Jack. "Often?"

"Ever hear of the Thule Society in the 1920's?" replied Simon. "They resurrected the dark Germanic God, Wotan. Then along came Hitler. And the Second World War. Talk about cause and effect, Jack. It took all the witches and warlocks in England working together to banish the Norse deity back to the outer darkness. We don't have the manpower or the time to match that feat. Not if the forces of night are already on the move."

"I'm still not clear . . ." began Jack when the lobby intercom buzzed.

"You expecting company?" asked Simon.

"Not really," said Jack, glancing down at his watch. It was nearly midnight. By now, he had dismissed his fears about the campus police as groundless. But none of his friends ever visited this late.

The intercom buzzed again, loud and insistent. It kept on ringing.

Slightly nervous, Jack pressed the transmit button. "Who is it?" he asked. "What do you want?"

"Bernard Walsh, from the IRS, Mr. Collins. I'm investigating a series of suspicious withdrawals made today at several cash stations throughout the Loop. You seem to be involved with the transactions. Mind if we talk?"

All of the muscles in Jack's arms and legs tied themselves into knots. "It's awfully late, Mr. Walsh," he managed to say after several false starts. "Couldn't we discuss things in the morning?"

"Sorry, Collins, but it can't wait till then. The IRS believes counterfeit credit cards are quite serious matters. If you prefer, I can return shortly with a search warrant."

"Uh, no," said Jack. "That won't be necessary. You can come up."

"Thanks," said Walsh. "That's all I needed for you to say."

"Odd choice of words," said Simon, as Jack sank down onto the sofa.

"I didn't notice," said Jack. "At least the money isn't hidden here. That was a good idea, stashing it in your room."

"Great," agreed Simon sarcastically. "Brand me as your accessory. At least, you'll have company in jail."

A heavy fist pounded on the door to Jack's apartment. Man and changeling looked at each other in astonishment.

"That was awfully quick," said Simon, "considering that you're on the fifth floor."

"He must have caught the elevator the second I hung up," said Jack, hurrying to the entrance. "Hopefully, I can talk my way out of this mess."

"All he needed for you to say?" repeated Simon. "As if he wanted you to recite a certain formula. Oh, hell," he gasped. "Jack, he tricked you. Walsh is a . . ."

The changeling's warning came an instant too late. Jack pulled open the door to his apartment. Standing there, white-faced, red-eyed, stood a creature dressed entirely in black. Tall and stately, with a satanic smile and big, big teeth, Walsh was no IRS agent. But he was a bloodsucker all the same.

". . . vampire," concluded Simon, unnecessarily.

9

Jack scrambled back into the kitchenette. Walsh leisurely followed, slamming the door behind him.

"You can't cross the threshold to my home unless invited," declared Jack, his mind racing furiously. For the first time in his life, he regretted not reading *Dracula*. His knowledge of the undead was limited to their infrequent appearances in humorous fantasy novels, and several Christopher Lee film festivals he had attended as a teenager.

Jack had no doubt about Walsh's identity, even without Simon's warning. The bogus IRS agent's lack of an aura branded him supernatural. His glowing eyes and inch-long fangs proclaimed his grisly heritage.

"A mere matter of semantics," said Walsh. He spoke quite well, considering the size of his incisors. "This is the twentieth century, not the eighteenth. The entry hall to an apartment building serves as a common threshold for all the individual units. And you did invite me in."

Straining, Jack shoved the kitchen table in the vampire's path. With an amused shake of the head, the monster grasped the formica top with one hand and squeezed. The hardened plastic exploded into dust. Vampires, Jack remembered immediately, were much stronger than ordinary mortals.

"What do you want, Walsh?" Jack asked, retreating behind the kitchen chairs.

"Information," replied the vampire. He appeared in no hurry to catch Jack. From time to time, his gaze flickered over to Simon, standing motionless by the sofa. He seemed puzzled by the changeling's presence. "My master wants to know all about you, Mr. Collins. And how you came to possess the talisman you carry."

"It was a gift," said Jack, sliding around the last of the chairs and darting into the living room. Grasping at half-remembered solutions, he began reciting the only prayer he could remember.

"Our father, who art in Heaven, hallowed be thy name. . . ."

"Please don't strain your memory," said Walsh cheerfully. "That superstition died out a long time ago. Ditto, the cross thing. I departed this world an agnostic. None of those religious remedies affects me in the slightest. Why not be a good boy and just answer my questions? After all, we already know all about Merlin and his daughter."

"Oh yeah," said Jack, pushing the sofa into the vampire's path. Simon remained frozen in place. He had not said a word since Walsh had entered the apartment. "If you're that well informed, what do you want from me?"

"Mine is not to reason why," replied the vampire. Reaching down, he latched onto the sofa with both hands. Effortlessly, Walsh wrenched it out of Jack's grasp. Chuckling, he tossed it against the living-room wall. The whole apartment shook when it hit the floor.

"Why did the old wizard give you the talisman?" Walsh demanded. "And what did he tell you about my master?"

"Your master?" said Jack, backing up to the windows. He was out of running space. "Since when do vampires work for the Old Ones?"

"A matter of professional courtesy," answered Walsh. "Besides, doing a favor or two for a God never hurts. He promised me New York for finding you."

The vampire smiled, making him look even more ghastly. "So, you do know about the Old Ones. How very interesting. Please tell more."

He stepped closer, edging around a still motionless Simon. Walsh frowned, swirling his cape dramatically.

"Don't interfere in matters that are none of your concern,

faerie," he ordered, glancing at the changeling. "This affair isn't any of your business."

"That's your mistake," said Simon unexpectedly and wrapped his arms around Walsh. Jerking his body around, he wrenched the vampire to the floor.

"Run, Jack!" he shouted. "I can't hold him long."

Caught by surprise, Jack froze. He wanted desperately to help Simon, but he had no idea how. Already, the vampire was pulling free from the changeling's grip. He would be loose in seconds.

Crosses and prayers no longer worked, but there were other ways to hurt a vampire. Struck by inspiration, Jack darted past the struggling supernaturals into the kitchenette. Wildly, he pawed through the bottles on his spice rack.

Hissing like a locomotive, Walsh broke Simon's hold and shoved the changeling hard into the far wall. The faerie collapsed to the floor in a daze.

"I'll deal with you later," he growled at the Brit. The vampire turned to Jack, his red eyes blazing. He snarled, showing his huge yellow fangs. "No more Mr. Nice Guy. Talk or suffer the consequences."

"Take a bite of this," yelled Jack and flung the contents of the spice bottle in Walsh's face. A gritty powder caught the vampire across the cheeks.

The monster shrieked in agony. His skin sizzled like bacon on a griddle. A hundred black burns dotted his features. He staggered back, hands clawing at his eyes.

"Time to leave," said Jack, grabbing a groggy Simon by the arm. Behind them, Walsh howled like a wolf. "Definitely."

Hastily, they scampered down the fire stairs. Jack had no idea how long Walsh would be out of action. Waiting for the building's notoriously slow elevators was out of the question.

Huffing and puffing, he and Simon tumbled out the emergency exit located at the side of the complex.

"Where to?" asked the changeling. "He'll be after us in a minute. And this time, he's not going to be so polite."

"The gym," said Jack, pulling in one deep breath after another. "If we can make it there, I think we can arrange a surprise or two for Mr. Walsh."

"Forward the Light Brigade," declared Simon. "Etc., etc."

Wearily, Jack set off towards the athletic center. Moving was an effort. It felt as if there were lead weights attached to his arms and legs. The day's activities were wearing him down. He needed to rest. But first he had to deal with a vampire.

"Sorry for hesitating," said Simon, as they ran. "Damned monster scared me witless. We faeries weren't raised to be heroes. Vampires are out of our league."

"No need to apologize," wheezed Jack. "You acted when it mattered. That's what counts."

The changeling laughed. "Simon Goodfellow to the rescue. By the way, what was that stuff you threw at our toothy friend? I didn't know they made anti-vampire powder."

"Not exactly, but close enough," answered Jack. "According to the legends, vampires can't stand garlic. So I emptied a container of garlic salt on Walsh. It worked better than I expected."

Simon whistled in admiration. "Pretty quick thinking. Maybe Merlin picked the right guy after all."

"You better hope so," said Jack as they ran up the steps to the athletic complex. "For both our sakes."

10

It took Walsh twenty minutes to find them, which didn't give Jack the time he needed to prepare his trap. He and Simon were still moving equipment when they heard the fire doors slam open upstairs.

"That sounds like a pretty pissed-off vampire," said Simon. "Those doors are reinforced with steel. They weigh a ton."

"Close enough," agreed Jack, licking his lips apprehensively. "If I can stall Walsh for a few minutes, will you be able to finish setting things up? We won't have a second chance."

"No problem," said Simon. "It's a piece of cake. The big question is whether or not he's actually vulnerable to your surprise."

"There's only one way to find out," said Jack, pulling off his clothes. Naked, he slid into the pool of hot water at his feet. "We have to gamble I'm right. Unless you prefer trying to drive a stake through his heart?"

"Not tonight," said Simon. "I was never very good at that sort of stuff. You ready?"

"As ready as I'll ever be," said Jack. "Better turn on the jets. The switch is in the coach's office."

"Yeah, I know the spot. The staff worries that some enterprising students might otherwise use the equipment as a hot tub." The changeling leered. "As if a lock or two could stop me."

Another door slammed, this time on their floor.

"Hurry up," said Jack. "If that water isn't running by the time he arrives, I'm vampire chow."

"I'm gone," said Simon, and he was. Thirty seconds later, the whirlpool tub roared into life.

Sighing with relief, Jack immersed himself in the swirling water up to his neck. The massaging effects of the whirlpool worked wonders on his sore muscles. The humming of the motor soothed his jangled nerves. Closing his eyes for a second, Jack relaxed and let the tension drain out of his body. It felt terrific.

The door to the training room crashed open, destroying Jack's moment of serenity. Walsh strode into the chamber, head held high, lips curled back in a snarl of rage.

"It's the end of the line for you, Collins," declared the vampire. Gnashing his teeth together, he approached the huge whirlpool tub. "You think taking a bath will protect you from me? I'm a vampire, fool, not a dust devil."

Trying to stay calm, Jack watched the monster draw close. Walsh looked terrible. A hundred tiny puncture marks dotted his face and hands. It looked like he had been on the losing end of a fight with a sewing machine. The garlic salt had hurt the vampire, but not enough. The trick had merely enraged the monster. Walsh was hungry for blood—Jack's blood.

Jack prayed that his memory of the legends concerning the undead was accurate. If not, he was in big trouble. And the world was doomed.

Mouth open to reveal his immense fangs, Walsh reached out with both hands to pull Jack out of the tub. Then stopped abruptly, as if encountering an invisible shield rising up from the bath.

"What the hell?" said Walsh angrily and tried furiously to push his hands forward. They didn't budge. Snarling with rage, the vampire flung himself at the whirlpool. And bounced back as he smashed into the same transparent barrier.

"Running water," said Jack, releasing the breath he hadn't realized he had been holding. "Vampires can't cross it. In the legends and folk tales it means streams and rivers and such. But, I guess the definition includes whirlpools as well. Even ones in a bath or pool."

"Stupid trickery," said Walsh angrily. As if testing the power of the spell, the vampire lunged savagely at Jack. With the same lack of success.

"Stalemate," said Jack. A flicker of movement behind Walsh caught his attention for a second. Making not a sound, Simon was setting up a row of lights behind the vampire. "You can't touch me, but I can't leave the whirlpool. We're deadlocked."

"I'll tear out one of these lockers and smash you flat," declared Walsh. "Maybe it won't be as much fun, but it'll get the job done."

Jack licked his lips. He hadn't thought of that. "I'm sure your boss would be thrilled by the publicity," said Jack. "Especially with the plans he has for those kidnapped women."

The last remark was a stab in the dark, but it hit the target. "How do you know what's planned?" asked Walsh suspiciously. "The ceremony won't take place for nearly a week."

"Two can keep a secret," declared Jack solemnly, "if one is dead. There's a lot more than two in your motley crew."

The vampire grimaced, distorting his features into something barely human. "I warned von Bern that his inept band of halfwits would ruin everything. Idiots, all of them, in their fancy motor-cycle jackets and studded boots. I should have been put in charge of the operation, not that dumb German. Only reason he got the job was his fancy sword and title."

Walsh's eyes narrowed. "I'm talking too much. Way too much. Not that it matters, 'cause you'll never tell anyone."

Behind the vampire, Simon raised a hand, signaling all was ready. Jack muttered a silent prayer to Bram Stoker. And to modern science.

"Ever go to a tanning salon, Walsh?" he asked casually.

"What?" snarled the vampire. "WHAT!"

"I didn't think so," said Jack, half-rising from the whirlpool. "Maybe since they use . . . *sun lamps*?"

Walsh whirled around, but it was too late. Simon flicked a switch and a half-dozen bright lights blazed. The vampire shrieked and raised his arms trying futilely to block the rays. But, there was no escape.

Simon had arranged the sun lamps in a semicircle, with Walsh at the center. The whirlpool blocked off his only avenue of retreat. With a cry of despair, the vampire sunk to his knees.

"I'm baking," he screamed, "I'm baking."

Jack gulped and fought to hold down his dinner. Walsh wasn't lying. The vampire's skin blackened and cracked like paper in a

fire. And turned to ash. In seconds, the monster's face and arms
had disappeared into a cloud of soot. As if in slow motion, Walsh's
clothing collapsed in on itself, like a balloon suddenly deflating.
All that remained was a small pile of fine, black powder.

"Think if we mix this stuff with a batch of plasma it would bring
him back to life?" asked Simon, smirking. "Dehydrated vampire."

"I have no desire to find out," said Jack, splashing the dust with
water from the whirlpool. He stepped out of the tub. "I want my
clothes. Another minute in that spa and I'd be a size smaller."

Simon held up the vampire's black cape. "What should we do
with this thing? And the rest of his clothes?"

"Burn them," said Jack, remembering a Robert Bloch story
about a vampire's cloak. "The sooner the better. After which, we
put the lights away and straighten up this place."

Jack yawned. "Then, maybe, we can get some sleep."

∞

11

Jack woke with a splitting headache. It felt as if someone had been using his head as a kettle drum all night. Groggily, he blinked his eyes several times trying to clear his vision. Hovering at the fuzzy edges of his mind was the image of a girl. A slender, good-looking young woman with pixieish features, he vaguely remembered her haunting his dreams. She had been desperately trying to tell him something, but he couldn't recall a word she said.

"Damn it," he muttered, sitting up in the bed. He hated waking up feeling this rotten. First in the office building, now in his apartment. Not that he had much choice the time before, when Merlin and Megan had been kidnaped. *Megan!* With a start, he recognized her as the girl in his sleep.

Anxiously, he tried to grasp the fleeting figments of his dream. Jack felt sure that Merlin's daughter had been trying to contact him. Perhaps she even had a message from her father. Or wanted to pass along some clue to where they were being held. The literature of fantasy was filled with tales of dream messages. Unfortunately, the stories never dealt with the specifics of such communications.

Under normal circumstances, Jack slept fitfully, and rarely remembered a thing when waking. Today was no exception. No matter how hard he concentrated, he couldn't recollect a thing about his dream. If Megan had told him anything, it had been lost on awakening.

Yawning, he padded into the kitchenette and made himself some breakfast. Originally, he had balked on returning to his rooms after his encounter with the vampire. If Walsh had been able to locate him there, so would any of the monster's allies. Simon considered the apartment a death trap. Which ultimately was the reason Jack decided to spend the night there after all.

"They know the location," he had told the changeling after they had finished cleaning the gym. "And they know that I know that they know the location. So, understandably they know that I know the place isn't safe. Continuing that chain of logic, they therefore accept the fact that I would never risk staying in the apartment. Since they're convinced I would never use it, that makes it the perfect spot for me to hide. It's elementary games theory. Besides, I'm tired, I don't have any other place to go, and the bad guys all probably think I'm dead."

"You left me way behind on the 'I know, they know' routine," said Simon, shaking his head, "but you're right about them thinking you dead. Most supernaturals, particularly those dedicated to evil, hold humans in pretty low regard. The notion that you could possibly defeat a vampire on your own would strike them as sheer lunacy. Until one of their sensitives finally notices Walsh's gone, you're safe."

"All I want is a good night's sleep," said Jack. But even that had been denied, due to Megan's unsuccessful attempt to contact him through his dreams. Chewing on a Pop-Tart, Jack wondered why the heroes of all the novels he consumed never worried about what to do next. They always had such nice, clear-cut plans of action to follow. Or stumbled about the scene until they discovered what to do. He didn't even know where to start stumbling. Life was unfair.

After a few minutes of feeling sorry for himself, Jack perked up. While the world might be doomed in a few months, he had held his own last night against the forces of darkness. Even Simon had been impressed by his handling of Walsh.

Jack grinned. The garlic powder and the sun lamp caught the vampire completely by surprise. The trick was applying modern logic to legendary beasts. The supernatural beings of long ago had evolved through the ages. It made perfect sense to Jack that the methods of dealing with them would change as well. Cause and effect never went out of date. The only problem was deducing the new rules before it was too late.

Jack still was at a loss why running water and artificial sunlight had affected the vampire while prayer and a cross had not. As a mathematician, contradictions like that bothered him. They bothered him *a great deal* until he figured out the logical structure behind them. Which, he decided cheerfully, might have been the reason Merlin selected him as mankind's champion.

Feeling quite satisfied with himself, Jack stepped to the front window of his apartment. April in Chicago was usually a bizarre month for weather. Either the temperature hovered slightly above freezing and it rained for weeks, or it was near sixty every day with bright sunny skies. Jack's first year in Chicago, six inches of snow had fallen on Easter, only to melt three days later in eighty-degree heat. To the delight of everyone this year, especially the weather forecasters, spring had arrived in fine fashion, with beautifully balmy afternoons and comfortable temperatures.

Raising the curtains, Jack let the sunshine bathe him in its warmth. Raising his arms over his head, he stretched for the ceiling. Lazily, his gaze swept across the edge of the campus and to the street beyond. And froze.

Slowly and carefully, he backed away from the glass. His eyes remained fixed on two figures barely visible in the shadows of a deserted building a hundred yards distant. Neither gave an indication they had spotted him. Jack wanted to keep it that way.

Once he edged past the last possible angle of visibility, he immediately dropped to the floor. Scrambling on his hands and knees, he crawled back to the window. Cautiously, he raised his eyes above the window ledge, positioning himself so that the center frame hid his forehead.

Squinting, Jack searched nervously for the unholy duo he had glimpsed seconds ago. It only took an instant to locate them. As far as he could tell, they had not moved. He breathed a sigh of relief. His enemies evidently knew approximately where he was located, but didn't have a precise fix on his whereabouts. He was safe, though not for long. Even now, companions of the two across the street might be searching the building for him.

At the precise instant that thought passed through Jack's mind, someone knocked on his apartment door.

"Hey, Jack," called a familiar voice from the hallway. "It's me, Simon. Open up."

Cursing slightly, Jack scurried over to the door and opened it. "Get inside," he commanded softly, urgently. "Quick."

"Now what?" asked Simon, stepping into the apartment. He looked around anxiously. "The forces of darkness are at low ebb during the daytime. We're safe till night."

"Glad to hear that," said Jack. He pointed a finger at the rear window. "Want to tell our buddies across the street the news?"

Moving with inhuman grace, Simon positioned himself at the glass. The changeling's features shifted to a bland, innocuous face resembling neither his nor Jack's. Only then did he risk a look out the window. After a few seconds, his skin turned a delicate but definite shade of green. Jack licked his lips uneasily.

"You recognize them?" he asked.

"Unfortunately," said Simon. He slipped back to the center of the parlor, rearranging his visage with each step. Jack closed his eyes, unable to watch. He found the process unsettling. It reminded him of a Gumby cartoon, but with a real person instead of a clay image.

"A young punk and a big dog, right?" asked Jack, wanting to be sure there was no mistake. "They were lounging in the doorway of the deserted store down the block. Neither of them possesses an aura."

Simon's face was still green. There was no humor in his voice when he spoke. "And you thought a vampire was bad news. Walsh was a pushover compared to those two watching this place. We're in real trouble now, Jack."

"How cheering," said Jack, noting that Simon included himself in the danger. At least there was no more waffling on the faerie's part. "Care to tell me who that character really is, and why that dog gives me the shivers?"

Simon edged back to the window. He beckoned Jack to follow. "Notice anything unusual about him?" the changeling whispered, as if speaking aloud he might be heard by those below.

Jack stared intently at the young man across the street. Tall and lean, he was dressed in faded blue jeans and a black leather jacket. Arms folded on his chest, he appeared half-asleep. Skin the color of old leather, his mouth was a thin red gash curled in an unchanging sneer. On his head, he wore an old red baseball cap, turned back to front in the prevailing style. Except for the fact that he lacked an aura, he could have been exactly what he appeared—a shiftless thug with nothing to do.

"He looks like a typical gang member," replied Jack softly. "Complete with his colors."

"A red cap?" asked Simon.

"According to the lecture given by campus security to all staff members," said Jack, "hat and scarf colors are the usual identification marks for street gangs. Though I don't recall any mention of an organization sporting red caps."

"He belongs to a different gang than most," said Simon, his lips curling in a sneer of disgust.

"Originally, his kind lived in the British Isles. That's where I met them first. Many of us living here now emigrated from there during the Great Wars. We were a gentle folk, and fled the violence engulfing our ancestral home. But not them. They came much later. Not until your cities started to decay, and death walked the streets. That's the type of surroundings they desired. That's when they arrived, like a blight descending on the land."

"They're faeries?" asked Jack.

"Of a sort," said Simon. "Among us, his kind are called the Border Redcaps. They're a mixed breed, part faerie, part troll, part ogre, part who-knows-what else. The only certainty is that they are absolutely evil."

"Border Redcaps?" asked Jack. "I never heard of them."

"Few have," said Simon. "They are not the type of character that populates the novels you favor. There is none of the romantic antihero so popular among current writers. The darkness within them is not a seductive, tempting sort. They are not rebels but cold-blooded murderers. The Redcaps kill without emotion, because it is what they do best. They are butchers of men.

"Their red caps are dyed red from the blood of their victims. They live in high towers along the border between the haves and the have-nots and prey on both. In Chicago, they inhabit the deserted upper floors of the high-rise public housing tenements.

"The police treat them like any other gang, not realizing the true extent of their wickedness. Each year, hundreds upon hundreds of runaways and the homeless disappear without a trace. They vanish into the night, never to be seen again."

"The Border Redcaps?" asked Jack, for a second time. "But why?"

"As I said, it is their nature to kill. And," added Simon, "they need a steady supply of fresh blood to keep their caps red."

"What about the dog with him?" asked Jack, not sure he wanted to hear the answer. A big, black Doberman, the hound waited patiently beside its companion. Looking at it gave Jack the chills. There was something terribly wrong with the beast, something unnatural.

Simon drew in a deep breath. He swallowed hard several times before answering.

"The Redcap worries me," he said, "but he's no great surprise. From the story you told me, I suspected that his sort were involved in the kidnappings. They serve as the devil's footsoldiers. However, the fiends are mere rank-and-file troublemakers. Add them all together and they have the brains of a halfwit. The fools are incapable of anything more than casual brutality and skull smashing."

"Which indicates someone else is directing their activities," said Jack. "Who?"

"Their lord is chief among the followers of the dark in Chicago," answered Simon. "A merciless coachman, he rides the night winds with a pack of jet-black dogs at his side."

The changeling lowered his voice, as if afraid of being heard. "The howling of his terrible hounds paralyzes any beast that hears it with fright. A once mighty leader whose sins were so great that after his death he was reborn in legend as an Archfiend. In olden times, the beasts he commanded were called the Gabble Ratchets, the 'Corpse Hounds.' One such monster waits and watches below. It loyally obeys only one master—Dietrich von Bern, the Lord of the Wild Hunt."

As if summoned by the mention of that name, a heavy fist pounded on the door of Jack's apartment. Caught by surprise, and overwhelmed by Simon's rhetoric, Jack went numb all over. Ghastly visions of a devilish huntsman and his baying hounds raced through his head. Again came the pounding, this time accompanied by a gruff, loud voice.

"Open up, Collins. We know you're in there. It's campus security. We want to have a talk with you. Right now!"

∞

12

Jack peered through the peephole in the door before opening it. He had no desire to learn the hard way that the Border Redcaps were masters of mimicry. A feeling of relief washed over him as he recognized Benny Anderson, chief of the college police force. Bald except for a fringe of white hair, with flat ears, puffy red cheeks and diamond-hard blue eyes, Anderson resembled a kewpie doll on speed. Then, paranoia struck back as Jack remembered Simon's amazing chameleonlike powers.

"You have any identification?" Jack called out nervously.

Turning a brilliant shade of crimson, Anderson hammered on the paneling. "Identification!" he roared. "You open this blasted son-of-a-bitch door in one second, Jack Collins, or I'll smash it to splinters. And you—you two-bit butthead—with it! Enough of this bloody stalling."

Nodding, Jack fumbled with the lock. It was definitely Anderson. An ex-marine drill sergeant, he possessed a style uniquely his own. And a vocabulary to match.

"Sorry, chief," said Jack, stepping side to let the security chief enter. "Don't blame me for being careful. I was mugged yesterday. I've been seeing shadows ever since."

"Sure," said Anderson, swaggering about the living room

casually. His sharp eyes flickered back and forth, as if mentally photographing everything for later appraisal. His gaze rested for a second on the smashed formica of the dining-room table, but he said nothing. "I understand."

He nodded to Simon. "Nice to see you, Fellows. You have business with the Professor?"

"Business?" replied Simon, shrugging unconcernedly. "You might say that. I'm enrolled in Professor Collins's tutorial. I missed the last few classes. He was nice enough to let me stop by and find out what I missed."

"Sure," said Anderson again. He turned to Jack. "Naturally, I heard about the attack. Dr. Nelson submitted a report on it. Nasty business, getting booted in the head and all. No motive for the attack, according to your statement. You sticking to that story?"

"Yes," said Jack, fearing the worst. "Why shouldn't I? It's the truth."

"Yeah, that's what they all say," declared Anderson, his voice cold. "Nelson mentioned you were flashing a big roll of bills. A lot more money than most graduate students carry in their pockets. Especially ones supposedly knocked around by a motorcycle gang."

Jack flushed. "What are you leading up to, Anderson? You accusing me of drug dealing?"

The instant after he made the remark Jack was sorry he mentioned drugs. But by then it was much too late.

"Drugs?" said Anderson, his lips curving in a sinister smile. The security chief looked like a rattlesnake ready to strike. With Jack as his prospective dinner. "I never once brought up drugs."

"I found a new job," said Jack, the words rushing out. Panic sent his mind into overdrive. "You know I've been looking for one for weeks. My new boss advanced me a week's salary to pay off some of my bills. That was the money Nelson noticed. If he had asked, I would have told him just like I'm telling you. And that's the truth."

The chief frowned. "No reason to get riled up, Collins. You can't blame me for doing my job. That's why the Dean pays my salary. It was an honest mistake. I'll even apologize—once I check the story with that new employer of yours. Got a phone number I can call?"

Jack's mouth went bone dry. "Uh, that won't be possible."

"No?" Anderson's voice was ice cold again. "Why not?"

"He . . . she . . . they left town for the week," said Jack. "That's why I was paid in advance. Mr. Ambrose asked me to watch the office while he's gone. No one's there at present. It's a small consulting firm in the Loop."

"Sounds awfully strange to me," said Anderson. "A boss hires a new worker and then leaves town the same day. Putting the fledgling employee in charge of an empty office, no less. You ain't planning any sudden trips yourself, are you, Collins?"

"No, nothing," said Jack.

"Good," said the security chief. "I'd hate for you to leave campus before I could verify your story. 'Cause if you did, I'd have to report my suspicions to the Chicago police. And they might not be so trusting of our grad students as me."

"I'm not going anywhere," said Jack.

"I hope you're not lying, Collins," said Anderson, his voice growing progressively softer. "I hate drugs and I hate drug dealers. They make me sick. And, when I'm sick, I get angry. Real angry. Angry enough to break all the bones in a man's fingers and toes, one at a time."

Inside his shoes, Jack's toes curled. "I'm telling the truth. Nothing but the truth."

"We'll see," said Anderson, heading for the door. "We'll see."

The officer gone, Jack collapsed to the sofa, his body drenched in sweat. "Our friends still outside?" he asked Simon.

"Haven't moved an inch," reported the changeling. "If they stand any stiffer, they'll grow roots. Like I said, during the day they're weak. Tonight is when to worry."

Jack sighed. The day was not off to a good start. He had an uneasy feeling things were not going to get any better.

"You planning to stay on campus like you told the chief?" asked Simon.

"That depends on our buddies across the street," said Jack. "Anderson's paranoid and mean. No question he's a problem I've got to face sooner or later. But he's only human."

"And the pair watching this building aren't," said Simon.

"Exactly," said Jack. "Give me a minute to think."

While Simon cheerfully rummaged through the kitchenette, preparing a second breakfast, Jack contemplated the dilemmas facing him. Merlin and Megan were in terrible danger. The world needed to be saved from an ancient God. His enemies, including Border Redcaps, Corpse Hounds, and the Wild Huntsman, knew where he lived. Benny Anderson suspected him of dealing in illegal drugs. And there were tests from last week still ungraded.

After ten minutes of mental juggling, Jack finally settled on a schedule of attack. Sort of.

"Today's Friday. Thank god for that. I shifted my tutoring classes to Gleason. So I don't have to worry about handling them. But the other two courses I teach require my presence today. I owe my students that much. Then, there's Professor Winston's class at seven p.m. that I grade the papers for. So I have to attend his lectures. Once that's finished, I'm free for the weekend.

"Say we meet at my office in the mathematics building at eight-thirty? That's when we'll plot out our strategy for dealing with this von Bern character."

"Meaning," said Simon, polishing off a piece of toast, "you don't have the foggiest notion what to do, and you're praying the extra hours will give you a glimmer."

"That's about the size of it," admitted Jack. "You got a better idea?"

"Nope," said the changeling. "But I'm not the one supposed to save the world."

For that remark, Jack had no answer.

∞

13

"The vampire failed," said Roger, nervously shifting his weight from one foot to another. "He's gone without a trace, and Collins remains alive. Somehow, this unlikely champion defeated one of our most powerful allies."

The Crouching One, sitting in a huge armchair that dwarfed its small features, bent its head slightly in reply. The demigod seemed strangely pleased by the bad news.

"As I expected," it replied, a brief smile of satisfaction drifting past its lips. "No ordinary mortal could defeat one of the night spawn in combat. Walsh's death merely confirmed my suspicions. His loss matters little otherwise. The magician, Merlin, obviously prepared this young man as mankind's champion.

"Once he is eliminated, none will stand before us. Collins is one frail mortal against the hordes of darkness. The time has come for our allies to put an end to this annoyance. The night of blood approaches. Soon, very soon, my unconquerable spirit shall envelop the world in eternal darkness."

Roger yawned. The Crouching One rarely had anything brilliant to say. It was obsessed with ruling the Earth. Though immensely more powerful than any of the other supernatural creatures Roger had ever encountered, the demigod was no different in character.

All of its actions were governed by a basic set of desires that seemed programmed into its personality. The Lord of the Lions lacked motivation. It acted in certain ways not because it wanted to, but because it had to.

While no student of psychology, Roger recognized a fatal flaw when he encountered it. The Crouching One could be controlled by its needs. Though it commanded astonishing powers, the demigod had the personality and instincts of a spoiled child. Given enough time, Roger felt sure he could subtly gain absolute mastery of the creature. And then the world would be his plaything.

"I want you to contact von Bern on that magical telephone device you use," said the Crouching One, breaking into Roger's daydreams. "Tell him to use whatever force is necessary to kill Collins. He can offer any reward, enlist any ally in this task. As long as the German does not jeopardize our master plan, he can do anything he wants to accomplish my desires. No half-measures this time. The human champion must die. Without any more delays."

"You said that yesterday," remarked Roger casually. "Are you confident the Huntsman can handle this situation on his own? He hasn't shown any sign of competence so far. Chaos Sword or not, he's not particularly bright. You need someone with real brains on the scene. Maybe I should fly to Chicago and personally oversee the operation. That way there would be no mistakes."

"And leave me to fend by myself?" said the Crouching One, slowly shaking its head from side to side. "I would be lost without you, my faithful servant. Lost and alone. Helpless in this confusing, modern world."

Not particularly superstitious, Roger found himself involuntarily crossing his fingers for luck. Sarcasm by the Crouching One usually preceded fireworks.

"It was only a suggestion," said Roger. "I was merely trying to be useful."

"Useful," repeated the demigod. "How considerate. The thought of escaping my power never once entered your thoughts. You know that my strength wanes with distance. In Chicago, you would be free of my grip. And filled with the secrets learned from me."

"I-I-I would never do that," stuttered Roger, knowing his life was on the line. The Lord of the Lions was not a forgiving god. "I'm loyal to you. I swear it."

The Crouching One nodded. "A wonderful thing, loyalty. It can be bought by many things—gold, jewels, love, even hate. But the strongest bond is fear."

The demigod pointed to the book it had been reading before Roger had entered the library. "Do you see that small black spot on the cover of that volume, my loyal servant?"

Roger glanced at the hardcover. "Yes," he answered, trying to keep his voice from trembling.

"Watch it," said the Crouching One. "Watch it closely."

Roger stared at the mark. A tiny, dark blemish, less than a half-inch in diameter, it looked like a fingerprint. With a sudden flash of insight, Roger realized that it was exactly that. The fingerprint of the Crouching One.

Staring intently for a minute started his eyes burning. He blinked to clear the tears, then blinked again, this time from bewilderment. The spot appeared larger. And darker. Much darker.

After a few seconds, Roger realized what was taking place. The circle consisted of crumbling black ash, as the leather binding aged hundreds of years in seconds. Like a slow but relentless blight, the mark continued to grow. The breath caught in Roger's throat as within a minute the volume turned into a pile of dust.

"Look at your arm," said the Crouching One. "You know where."

Trembling, Roger gazed at his elbow, where the Crouching One had touched him after its escape from the magic circle. Barely visible were five tiny black spots. Choking back a scream, he looked at the smiling demigod.

"The touch of my hand is legend," said the Crouching One. "Pestilence and plague are my servants. Death and decay are my children. Remain true to me and your rewards will be beyond number. Betray me, and the blight will claim you."

Roger's gaze jumped back and forth from the pile of dust to the fingerprints on his elbow. His face was white as chalk.

"I'll contact von Bern now," he finally managed to whisper hoarsely. "No more suggestions. Whatever you say, goes. You're the boss."

"A wise choice," said the Crouching One. "A very wise choice."

∞

14

The day crept by at a snail's pace. Jack expected no less. Under normal conditions, he was not a patient person, and these were definitely not normal times. He hated waiting. All his life, he had tackled problems head-on, attacking trouble before it had a chance to develop. He believed in getting things done, never procrastinating. Enforced idleness drove him crazy.

By eight that night, he was experiencing extreme difficulty staying awake. Professor Winston was a school institution. Which, in college jargon, meant he should have been forced to retire ten years ago. Nearly blind, hardly able to walk, he spoke in a voice that rarely rose above a whisper. Seventy-eight years old, with tenure, he insisted on teaching one course each semester.

In a rare flash of wisdom, the chairman of the department assigned the professor an elective course in Advanced Topologic Design. Along with the esoteric and difficult subject matter, the class was further handicapped by scheduling it on late Friday evening. No one felt any sympathy for the six brave students who enrolled in it.

Jack handled all the paperwork for the course. Winston lectured, assigned homework, and prepared tests. Jack graded the papers and calculated the students' grades. Unfortunately, to keep up with the material, he was forced to attend the class each week. Though he tried dutifully to remain awake through Winston's discourses, he rarely remembered more than a few words of the professor's rambling monologues.

Tonight, as if sensing Jack's impatience, the elderly teacher was in rare form. He spent the evening solving problems on the blackboard, speaking directly to the wall. Not a word of his lecture escaped to his students. Jack, sitting in the back row, stared at the ceiling and drifted off into daydreams. Involuntarily, his eyes closed as boredom overwhelmed him. He was not entirely awake or asleep but in a region between—one that was well known to students of all ages.

"Jack," a young woman's voice whispered in his thoughts. "Can you hear me?"

"Megan?" he asked, not using words but instead instinctively thinking the reply. A mental image of the young woman's elfin features materialized before him.

"Yes, it's me," replied the girl, her voice echoing in his mind. "I tried contacting you in sleep last night, but deep slumber made communication impossible. It's a lot easier when you're barely conscious but still nominally awake."

"You can thank Professor Winston for that," he projected back to her. "Where are you? What's going on? Are you and your father safe?"

"We're unharmed," she stated, answering his last question first. "I'm not sure of my location. Father cast a sleep spell on the two of us right after we were captured so we couldn't reveal any information to our enemies. Unfortunately, it made it difficult for me to learn anything either. The Border Redcaps, under the command of Dietrich von Bern, kidnaped us, but I sense from your thoughts that you know that already. They're holding us prisoner along with a whole bunch of hysterical women in a vast dungeon somewhere in the city. Sorry I can't be more specific."

"That's all right," thought Jack, trying to focus his thoughts clearly. "Why didn't your father contact me this way? I need to ask him a million questions. Maybe more."

"Merlin can't enter the dream world," replied Megan, offering no further explanation. "And there's no time for chatter. You're already drifting away from me. This link can't last much longer."

Megan's astral voice sounded frightened. "You're in danger, Jack, terrible danger. Von Bern and his cohorts plan to kill you tonight. They're already on campus, waiting for you in ambush. For some reason, they can't enter the building you're in, otherwise they would've attacked already."

"Huh? How did you learn all that? You're asleep."

"It's part of Merlin's spell. Our senses continue functioning even while slumbering. I overheard two of the Border Redcaps discussing your murder. Evidently, word had come from von Bern's master that you were to be killed no matter what the cost.

"I failed to contact you last night, but I had to try again when I learned their plans. Either your daydreaming state or the urgency of my message made communication possible."

"What should I do?" he asked. In this dreamlike state, the threat hardly worried him. "Any suggestions?"

"Don't leave your present location," said Megan, her voice growing faint. "As I told you, von Bern and his men can't enter the building. Something about the place frightens them. You're safe inside it. Stay there till morning."

"In the math building?" said Jack. "What makes this place so special?"

"I don't know," came Megan's reply. Her voice was fading fast. Jack could hardly hear what she was saying. "No matter what, don't let them force you outside."

"Megan?" Jack called, but there was no answer. "Megan?"

"Did you have a question, Mr. Collins?" asked Professor Winston, turning away from the blackboard. Held tightly in one hand was a piece of white chalk. He pointed it like a gun at Jack's forehead. "I thought I heard your voice."

"No sir," said Jack, straightening up in his chair. "Just clearing my throat."

"Oh, well." The elderly professor looked down at his watch. "No one ever seems to have a question. Not in my classes, at least. That's all for this week. Students, don't forget to pick up your homework assignment sheet on the way out. Assuming I remain functional, I will see you next Friday."

Cautiously, Jack sauntered over to the windows that covered one wall of the room. He glanced outside, searching for Redcaps. High above street level, his location afforded him a bird's-eye view of the campus. Classrooms were located on the second, third, and fourth floors of the math building. Needless to say, Winston's class met on the top floor. At the end of the hall. If possible, the faculty would have put the course in a closet.

Housed on the main level were the department offices and the college's computer labs. The first floor was the only one in the building that was air conditioned. The machines needed their environment kept cool all year round. No one cared if the students roasted, but the computers required pampering. During the summer, the lab was the most popular spot on campus.

Jack whistled softly as he counted eleven red caps in the moonlight. Though they were invisible at ground level, he had no trouble spotting the gang members from forty feet above the street. Megan hadn't exaggerated. The bad guys were out in full force tonight. Jack smile ruefully. It was nice to know they considered him that dangerous.

"Spot any good-lookin' women, Jack?"

The sound of Simon's voice, only a few inches away, caught Jack completely off guard. Sweat froze into icicles on his back. Slowly, he turned and faced the faerie. His hands gently circled the changeling's neck.

"Don't ever sneak up on me again," he said quietly. "Or I will strangle you."

"Sorry," said Simon, with a wan smile. "I warned you. It's my nature. I can't help yielding to temptation. You weren't at your office, so I came searching for you. Old Winston told me you were still here. What's so fascinating outside?"

Silently, Jack released his friend, then pointed. Simon's eyes bulged in shock.

"And you accused me of scaring you," said Simon. "That's the second time today I made the mistake of looking out a window at your prompting. Remind me not to do it anymore."

The changeling sighed. "I walked right past them and didn't see a thing. Obviously, the devils were waiting for a bigger prize. Lucky you caught sight of them first."

"Luck had nothing to do with it," said Jack, and he proceeded to tell Simon about his dream conversation with Megan.

"Incredible," said Simon, "absolutely incredible. Despite all the talk about psi powers, wild talents and ESP, thought communication is extremely rare. The effort requires an incredible amount of mental energy. Merlin's daughter, huh? And you conducted an actual conversation with her? Very interesting."

"It never happened to you?" asked Jack.

"Nah," said Simon, dismissing the idea with a wave of the hand. "Faeries don't dream. You say this Megan is beautiful as well as talented? She sounds like a very special lady. One certainly worth a bright grad student's pursuit."

"She's *extremely* beautiful," said Jack wistfully. "Smart, too. Unfortunately, being Merlin's child, she's probably seven hundred years old. I don't mind dating older women, but one the age of a giant redwood would be stretching things a bit."

"But she's . . ." Simon began, then clamped his mouth shut. Eyes twinkling, he patted Jack on the back. "The path of true love never runs smooth, my young friend. But, remember, affairs of the heart usually work out in the end."

"Oh, yeah?" said Jack sarcastically. "Like Samson and Delilah? Or Tristan and Isolde? Or Romeo and Juliet? Or . . ."

"Enough," interrupted the changeling. "I concede the point. Still, I have a feeling the future holds a few surprises for you. Supposing, of course, that we survive the night."

"Good point," said Jack. "It seems to me our best course of action is to remain here till tomorrow. If the Border Redcaps can't enter the building, and that appears to be the case, I don't see any way they can drive us out. No reason for us to suffer in the meantime. Let's order a pizza and relax in the faculty lounge. I have a key."

"We won't have problems with campus security?" asked Simon.

"There shouldn't be," replied Jack. "The guard locks up the computer lab early, but the rest of the building stays open all night. It's not uncommon for grad students to remain till dawn in their offices grading papers or studying for finals. Friday evening, we should have the building completely to ourselves."

"Let's hope so," said Simon. "Fighting the forces of evil is enough trouble without having to worry about innocent bystanders as well."

"Agreed," said Jack. "There's a pay phone in the hall. I'm ready to place that order for pizza. Which do you prefer—deep dish or thin crust?"

∞

15

"What's the time now?" asked Simon nervously.

"Five minutes later than before," said Jack irritably, not bothering to look at his watch. "Ten minutes later than the time before that. And so on back for the past hour. You've asked me that question at least a dozen times tonight. It's made reading this novel awfully difficult."

"Sorry," said Simon. "I'm a mite nervous, that's all. No reason for you to snap at me."

With a sigh, Jack dog-eared the page he had been trying to finish for the last twenty minutes and closed the book. Grunting with the effort, he laid the volume on his desk. An immense historical novel entitled *With Fire and Sword*, it weighed nearly five pounds. The first of a trilogy dealing with war and rebellion in 17th-century Eastern Europe, the book was considered the national epic of Poland. Jack had been reading it in his spare moments for much of the spring term. Well over 1200 pages, the novel read like Robert E. Howard's swords-and-sorcery adventures crossed with *War and Peace*. Jack originally harbored vague hopes of finishing the book before he finished school. Now he hoped he would reach the conclusion while still alive.

"I understand why you're worried," said Jack, rising from his chair. "But there's no reason to be scared."

He peered out the window of his office. The Border Redcaps had emerged from hiding once the security guard left the building. Nearly fifty of them crowded the plaza in front of the mathematics complex. An equal number waited at the rear entrance. Silently, they watched and waited, never once making any effort to approach the doors of the building.

Cookie-cutter monsters, Jack mentally noted, studying the features of the evil faeries. Each Redcap was a virtual duplicate of every other. They were all a little over six feet tall, big and bulky, with swarthy features, and skin the color of old leather. Each of them had a pushed-in pug nose, flat ears and greasy black hair that poked out in wild disarray from beneath their identical red baseball caps.

The rest of their outfit consisted of metal-toed motorcycle boots, faded blue jeans, and shiny black leather jackets cluttered with studs and chains. All of them wore dark leather gloves. Jack suspected they all spoke with the same accent. Their gathering resembled a Hell's Angels clone convention.

"I wonder if the school founders built this complex on top of an old Indian burial ground or someplace like that," said Jack. "Maybe that's the reason the Redcaps can't enter."

"Not very likely," said Simon. "No reason Indian religious beliefs would effect Old World Faeries. Maybe they hate mathematics."

"Placing them squarely in tune with a majority of Americans," said Jack, chuckling. "I can't see how the subject, no matter how distasteful, could prevent a supernatural being from entering a building. Besides, you're inside."

"I'm good. They're evil," said Simon. "That's the one big difference between us."

Jack's brow furled in concentration. "If mathematics actually bothers the forces of darkness," he said thoughtfully, "it would partially explain why Merlin chose me. . . ."

The ringing of the campus church bell halted Jack in mid-sentence. Nine, ten, eleven, twelve, the clapper chimed loudly, announcing the hour.

"Midnight," said Simon softly. "Evil's hour."

As if in response to the changeling's remark, a huge black limousine pulled up on the street a hundred feet from the math complex. The automobile glowed with an eerie white light, the sight of which gave Jack goosebumps. The car exuded dark, supernatural menace.

A low moan escaped the crowd of Border Redcaps. Hurriedly, they scrambled away from the entrance of the mathematics building, leaving a clear path from the limo to the door.

A massive form circled the car from the driver's side to the sidewalk. Dressed in a chauffeur's uniform, the figure moved at a slow, dignified pace. Jack stared curiously at the being. A solemn, almost-sad face topped a body seemingly carved from solid, unyielding stone. A thick, unkempt beard merged with shoulder-length gray hair, giving the figure the appearance of great age.

"Who's that?" he whispered to Simon, lowering his voice as if afraid to break the silence.

"Charon," replied the changeling. "Amazing how many centuries he's managed to survive. He's been in the transportation business for millennia. Probably because he maintains a low profile. He's neutral, neither good nor evil. Nice enough fellow, though not much of a conversationalist."

"It's a long way from the River Styx," remarked Jack.

"Last I heard, he was working on the Staten Island Ferry," said Simon. "I guess von Bern made him a better offer. Charon always was a greedy bastard. He sold Cerberus to the circus for a handful of silver."

The ancient Greek boatman opened the passenger door of the limo. As if shot by a cannon, a half-dozen jet-black Dobermans erupted from the car. Six pairs of blood-red eyes glared at the mathematics building while six jaws parted in silent snarls, revealing gigantic yellow fangs. The Gabble Ratchets, hungry for life.

"In olden days," said Simon solemnly, "the Wild Huntsman drove across the moors in a black coach drawn by six headless horses and followed by his pack of corpse hounds. One of the arch-fiends, he sought souls for his infernal master, and woe be the luckless mortal out of doors on the night of the Wild Hunt."

"He didn't need to adjust much for the modern world," said Jack cheerfully, trying to fight the feeling of impending doom. "Only now the coach is manufactured in Detroit, the horses are under the hood, and the dogs ride inside on the cushions."

Jack punched Simon gently in the shoulder. "Calm down, buddy. Megan said we were safe as long as we remained inside the building. That sounds easy enough. We refuse any rides tonight in that big black limo."

"I hope you're right," said Simon. Raising a hand, he pointed at the car. "Here he comes—Dietrich von Bern, Master of the Furious Host."

Even from a distance, Jack could see that von Bern was a giant of a man, standing nearly seven feet tall. Towering over the Border Redcaps, he marched forward, the Gabble Ratchets darting in circles about his feet. He wore an elegant black tuxedo, with gray cummerbund and matching bow tie. A gigantic velvet cape swirled behind him in the wind. Striking the only discordant note to his otherwise perfectly matched outfit was the sheathed saber bouncing against one thigh.

A black goatee, pencil-thin mustache, and thick mane of dark hair gave the German the good looks of a matinee idol. His dark gray eyes smoldered with an inner fire. Only twin scars, one on each cheek, marred his otherwise perfect features.

"Wounds inflicted by the devil himself," supplied Simon, as if reading Jack's thoughts. "Legends claimed that von Bern challenged Old Nick to a swordfight, gambling his immortal soul against an offer of eternal life. A proud, arrogant man, the German was the greatest bladesman of his age. However, Satan, taught by the greatest fighters in history, easily matched the German's skill. Toying with von Bern, the devil marked him on both cheeks before finally administering the coup de grace. Yet, in a fashion, von Bern achieved his goal of eternal life. Satan condemned him to roam the earth forever as Master of the Wild Hunt, searching for the one prize he can never find. Humility."

"Nice story," said Jack. "Any truth to it?"

"I doubt it," said Simon. "But my opinion doesn't matter. Enough people once believed the tale fact and thus brought the fiend to life. Leaving us to deal with him."

The giant had reached the door to the math building. Standing there, on legs the size of small tree trunks, he drew his saber. Resting the point of the blade on the sidewalk, the German leaned on it like a walking stick. His gaze swept the front of the building until it came to rest on the window of Jack's office.

"Truce, Professor Collins," he called out in a clear, deep voice. He spoke perfect English without a trace of an accent. "I declare a truce. Come down to the entrance so we can discuss our problems face to face. I have some important information that I must tell you. We cannot enter that cursed place so you are safe enough. And I swear on my sacred blade, the Sword of Chaos, that you shall not be harmed in my presence."

"What do you think?" Jack asked Simon.

"It could be a trick," said the changeling. "But he did swear on his sword. That's pretty strong stuff for a guy like von Bern. Honor is important even to fiends."

"I agree," said Jack. "After all, this joker is holding Megan and Merlin prisoner. We can't ignore the possibility he might be willing to make a deal. Who knows what he has on his mind? If it's important enough for him to offer a truce, we should at least find out what he wants to discuss."

It only took a few minutes for Jack and Simon to reach the entrance to the building. Pushing open the door, Jack stared at the huge German. Up close, von Bern was awe-inspiring. Like some vast supernatural dynamo, his body burned with raw, untamed power.

"All right, von Bern," said Jack. "I'm Jack Collins. What did you want to say to me?"

"Truce's over!" shouted the giant and dropped like a sack of wet cement to the ground.

Instinctively, Jack leapt for a nearby coat closet, dragging Simon with him. Behind them, the glass doors of the entrance exploded in a hail of gunfire as fifty Border Redcaps blasted the portal with automatic weapons.

"I thought faeries couldn't handle cold steel," said Jack, huddled behind a stack of metal chairs in the cloakroom. "Not to mention .357 Magnums."

"That geas phased out around a hundred years ago," said Simon. "Nobody was exactly sure why, but one day the touch of iron no longer bothered any of us. Sorry for not mentioning it sooner, but you didn't ask. It never occurred to me they might be carrying guns."

"So much for von Bern swearing on his sword," said Jack, disgusted with himself for believing the German. "Remind me not to be that naive again. There's no honor among fiends."

He paused, frowning. "In the meantime, why isn't this place swarming with cops? After all, it does sound like World War Three outside. We should be knee-deep in police."

"Von Bern probably enveloped the whole area in an amnesia spell before he arrived," said Simon. "It's pretty powerful magic.

Anyone coming too close forgets why he was heading in this direction and returns to his starting point. The spell effectively cuts off the location from outside interference. Nobody will notice anything wrong here until morning."

"An amnesia spell?" repeated Jack, pressing closer to the chairs as several bullets ricocheted into the cloakroom. "No visitors? No interruptions? What great news. I gather that means we're stuck here until his flunkies get tired of shooting."

"Or run out of ammunition," offered Simon, remaining true to his character.

∞

16

Twenty minutes later, the gunfire ceased. Fifteen minutes after that, Jack risked a look outside. The Border Redcaps remained clustered on the plaza outside, but their guns were holstered. Von Bern was gone, as were the black limousine and the Gabble Ratchets. Leaderless, the evil faeries stood in small groups, laughing and smoking cigarettes. Not one of them stirred when Jack and Simon sprinted down the main hallway to the teacher's lounge.

"That was too easy," said Jack, huffing and puffing as he tried to catch his breath. "Von Bern must know we weren't killed by the gunfire. From what you told me, he didn't strike me as the type that gave up easily."

"I concur," said Simon. "He probably returned to his hideaway to conduct the attack from there. No reason for him to remain close to the action. He directs the Redcaps by simple telepathic orders. They're too dumb to understand complex commands."

The changeling paused, the color draining from his features. His complexion turned white as chalk.

"What's wrong?" asked Jack.

"Another possible explanation for von Bern's departure occurs to me. The amnesia spell works on both mortal and supernatural beings. It's impossible to summon mythical beasts from within its boundaries. The German might have left the area to call upon some grisly monster to force us out of the building. He has the reputation as a master sorcerer."

"But if he couldn't enter the mathematics complex," said Jack, "how can whatever horror he summons?"

"Most legendary creatures are morally ambiguous," replied Simon. "They act in accordance with their own nature. A few, like werewolves and ghouls, fall into the evil category. Likewise, unicorns are basically good. However, a vast majority owe loyalty to neither side. Thus, whatever geas prevents the forces of darkness from entering this place will not affect them."

Wearily, Jack slumped into a plush chair. "Nothing we can do to stop him, right?"

"Right," said Simon. "Fortunately, only creatures in the immediate vicinity will obey his call. Pray that nothing particularly dangerous roams the streets of Chicago tonight."

"I'll keep my fingers crossed," said Jack. "Meanwhile, my body needs rest. I'm taking a nap. Wake me if anything exciting takes place."

Less than an hour later, Jack's eyes popped open. Simon was desperately shaking him by the shoulders. It wasn't hard to understand why.

All around them, the lights in the lounge flickered on and off wildly. In one corner, the portable TV clicked through channel after channel, turned off then turned on again. The radio beside it blared loud then soft, spinning through a dozen stations in an instant.

Candy bars spewed like bullets out of the vending machine. A puddle of burning hot coffee soaked the carpet nearby, while the microwave sandwich maker started then stopped, started then stopped. It was as if electricity had gone mad.

"What the hell is going on?" Jack shouted.

"I'm not entirely sure," shouted Simon, his mouth next to Jack's ear. It was the only way he could be heard over the racket. "I was half-dozing myself and not paying much attention to anything. This whole mess only started a minute or two ago. I heard a sizzling noise, and right afterward, the overhead lights started blinking."

"It's a massive power surge," Jack yelled back at Simon. "An enormous jolt of electricity that's fried all the circuits in the machinery."

His jaw dropped in astonishment. *"What the devil is that?"*

A minuscule ball of white fire, less than an inch across, floated out of the candy machine's coin return. Tiny bolts of lightning snapped and crackled across its surface. Waves of hot air rippled around the sphere as it drifted towards the soda pop dispenser. Emitting a soft, sizzling sound, the fireball disappeared into the machine. Instants later, a dozen soft drink cans exploded off their racks and into the lounge.

"It's a will-o-the-wisp," cried Simon, ducking beneath one of the projectiles. "Damned imp must be working for von Bern. In olden times, the little buggers were a minor nuisance leading superstitious travelers astray. Amazing how well they adapted to the modern era."

"We can't stay here," said Jack, beckoning to the door. "Let's retreat to the hall and see if it follows."

It did. Sizzling merrily, the will-o-the-wisp attacked the corridor lights. One after another, the bulbs exploded, showering Jack and Simon with tiny shards of glass.

"Well, at least now I know the truth about those unexplained power surges the electric company never can explain," said Jack, shaking glass fragments from his hair. The words resonated through his brain, setting bells ringing.

"Come on," he said to Simon, pulling the changeling by an arm. "I have an idea."

Using his master key, Jack opened the door to the main computer lab. Outside, the electrical imp happily exploded the remaining fixtures.

"Don't turn on the lights," said Jack, moving confidently into the room. "I spent enough hours teaching here that I know my way around in the dark."

"I don't like this place," said Simon nervously. "Something's wrong here. It gives me the shakes."

"Nonsense," said Jack with a laugh. "You're uncomfortable because the machines handle numbers better than you. Stay by the entrance if you prefer. We'll know in a minute if my hunch is correct."

Groping around on one of the desks, Jack located the necessary switch. "Here goes nothing," he declared and pressed the button turning on the power bar for one of the computers.

Instantly, the amber glow of the monitor filled the room. Jack quickly stepped back from the machine. Impatiently, the screen prompt blinked, asking for the correct date.

Like a shark sensing blood, the will-o'-the-wisp floated into the lab, the air around it crackling with energy. Straight as an arrow, it shot to the computer. At the last instant, the fireball seemed to hesitate, as if sensing something wrong. But it was too late for the imp to stop. Sizzling, it disappeared into the console.

The monitor went berserk, a hundred bizarre images flashing across the screen in a miscrosecond. Jack blinked in amazement. It was like watching a high-speed photo montage. He caught a glimpse of a thousand surprised faces—a thousand victims of the will-o'-the-wisp—spread out over five centuries. Then, with a snap loud enough to be heard throughout the lab, the power bar clicked off.

"Surge suppressor," said Jack, his eyes intent on the dead screen of the monitor. After a minute, he grinned in satisfaction.

"It's designed to shut off whenever a major energy fluctuation threatens the system. Which, I believe, in rather general terms defines our friend the will-o'-the-wisp."

Jack tapped the metal bar fondly. "Ain't technology wonderful? That annoying little imp is trapped in the computer, unable to power it up. Of course, his presence renders the machine inoperable, but that won't be for long. Some bright student will realize there's a defect in the surge suppressor and remove it. That will release the pest. By then, I strongly suspect it will be happy to escape this place."

"Me, too," said Simon shakily. "Let's leave."

They returned to the hall. Glass crunched under their shoes as they walked. "It might not be a good idea to be discovered here in the morning," said Jack. "Explaining this mess could prove to be awfully difficult."

"Not to mention the bullet holes in the entrance," added Simon. The changeling looked immeasurably better since leaving the computer lab. "I'm an expert at concocting excuses, but this disaster presents a major challenge even to someone of my talents."

"Maybe a localized . . ." began Jack, then stopped. "You hear something?"

"No," said Simon. "Not a thing."

"Funny," Jack replied. "I swear I hear rock-and-roll music playing. The noise sounds like it's coming from somewhere in the building. But we're the only ones here."

"I have spectacular hearing," said Simon, frowning. "And I can't hear a note."

"That's strange," said Jack, stepping over to the wall. He pressed his head against the plaster. "Listen. It's that song by Quiet Riot, the one about 'the noise.' Remember? They filmed the piece as a music video with the walls exploding from the sound."

"I avoid music videos if at all possible," said Simon. "They're not aimed at my age group."

"I'm surprised you don't hear it," said Jack. "The bass has the walls vibrating."

"Is it getting louder?" asked Simon. The changeling bit his lower lip, his expression thoughtful. "Much louder?"

"The noise is growing," admitted Jack. "It's not loud enough to shake the foundation—yet."

Jack put his hands over his ears. That helped, but not much. "What's happening? Overwhelming sound requires amplifiers like they use at rock concerts. That's not normally the type of equipment housed in the mathematics department."

"I've got it," said Simon, snapping his fingers. "It's a banshee. Von Bern's using it to force you outside."

"A banshee?" said Jack. "I thought they were Irish spooks."

"They migrated," said Simon. "Not many castles left to haunt these days. Chicago's large Irish population attracted them to the Midwest. Besides, the girls enjoy singing too much to remain in old stone towers. Now, they live in big apartment buildings, driving the tenants crazy.

"Using their powers, they create the phantom music you hear lying in bed at night. They're the stereo playing upstairs or from the next apartment, just loud enough to keep you awake, but that's never on when you go to complain. Plus, they're the ones responsible for the loud, giggling noises you hear coming from the bathroom grate at three a.m.

"No question that a banshee has targeted you for its attentions. They can focus on one person if they wish. That's why I can't hear a thing. Usually they tire after a few hours. But, in the meantime, there's only one sure way to stop them."

"What's that?" asked Jack, pressing his hands tighter. "My teeth are starting to ache."

"The old-fashioned solution," said Simon mournfully. "A banshee quits singing when its victim dies."

"That's not an answer," declared Jack. "I am firmly against suicide. Especially my own." He cursed. "If this was the dorms, we'd padlock the bastard responsible for the noise in his room all night and see how he enjoyed life without the convenience of a bathroom."

"Not very pleasant, I'm sure," said Simon. "How did you get offenders to turn off the stereo?"

"Usually, it took them a couple of hours to understand their predicament," said Jack. "Until then, we survived by drowning it out with our own systems."

Jack laughed wildly.

"That's it," he yelled and rushed for the stairs leading to the second floor. "Follow me."

He located what he was searching for in the third office he searched. It rested on the desk of another graduate assistant. Triumphantly, Jack held his prize aloft.

"A portable CD player," he declared. "Complete with headphones."

Fumbling through the desk drawers, Jack pulled out a CD case. "*A Question of Balance* by the Moody Blues," he said cheerfully. "One of my favorites. I especially like 'The Minstrel's Song.' It should do the trick nicely."

Jack hooked the player to his desk and fitted the receiver on his head. Grabbing several rubber bands, he snapped them over his skull, forcing the ends of the headphones tight against his ears. Grinning, he turned on the device and programmed the seventh song on continual repeat. In seconds, his face relaxed in an expression of total bliss.

"I don't understand," said Simon.

"Sorry," answered Jack loudly. "I can't hear a thing you're saying. That's the beauty of headphones. If the ear pads are positioned properly, the music sounds like it's coming from inside your head. It drowns out anything. The banshee's powerless as long as I'm using this unit. And, unlike the ghost's thumping, I find this music very soothing."

Yawning, he flopped onto the nearest chair. "Hopefully, the

banshee is the last of von Bern's surprises. I doubt if I can sleep wearing this thing, but at least I can rest."

He yawned again, stretching his jaw wide open. "Damn. Being a hero is exhausting business. And so far, I haven't done much."

Sighing, he shook his head, thinking of Megan. "Not much at all."

17

No other spirits disturbed them that night. A few minutes after the sun rose, the Border Redcaps disappeared, as did the amnesia spell. A short interval later, a band of bewildered janitors warily approached the mathematics complex. It soon became clear they had been wandering about in a daze for the past hour, trying to find a building they cleaned every morning.

Surveying the wreckage that covered the floor, Jack concluded that discretion was the better part of valor. He and Simon exited through the rear doors as the maintenance men cautiously entered through the bullet-riddled front entrance.

"Wait till your buddy Anderson learns you were the last one seen in the place," said Simon, as they hurried across the stretch of lawn leading to the street. "I'd advise staying off campus for a few days. Or years, depending on the chief's temper. He did not strike me as the forgiving type."

"Funny, I received the same impression," said Jack, laughing. He sobered immediately. "I'm dead on my feet. We both need sleep and plenty of it. Let's head back to your dorm room and rescue the money I hid there. Using some of it, we'll rent a motel room off campus and sack out for a day."

"What then?" asked Simon.

"I'm not entirely sure," said Jack. "However, von Bern is our one definite link with whatever deviltry the Old One is planning. We've got to locate the Huntsman's hideout and rescue Merlin and Megan. And free all those other women as well."

"There's a group of supernaturals living on the north side I visit when life on campus wears thin," said Simon. "They're cousins of mine. Maybe they know where we can find von Bern."

"Fine," said Jack. "Time for us to get that cash and scoot."

Twenty minutes later found them at the front entrance to the Hideaway Motel and Lounge. Located a mile off campus in one of the less respectable areas of the city, the bright red neon sign overhead proudly proclaimed, "Three Hour Rates, Nap Attacks, Adult Cable TV, Waterbeds."

"I'm not terribly convinced about the wisdom of staying here," Jack said to Simon.

"Nonsense," declared the changeling, grinning. "You're letting puritan morality blind your judgment. No one would ever think of looking for us in a place like this. It's one of the few spots in town we can rent a room without luggage. And the manager definitely guarantees the privacy of his guests."

"Okay," said Jack reluctantly. Digging into his pockets, he pulled out a wad of cash, which he handed to Simon. "But you check in for the two of us. I can't."

The Brit chuckled. "No problem. Stick around and I'll demonstrate the joys of shapeshifting."

The changeling passed a hand over his face. As before, his features wavered, shifted, and reformed in the space of seconds. Jack gasped at the transformation. Simon's visage was gone, replaced by the snarling mug of Benny Anderson.

"Like it?" growled Simon, his voice a perfect copy of the security chief's. "I've wanted to do Benny for a long time. He's got personality."

Simon in the lead, they marched into the motel office. A heavyset woman, in her forties, with bleached blonde hair and black roots, sat at the desk, her attention riveted on a portable TV mounted on the rear wall.

"Be withcha in a minutoo," she said in a shrill voice. "Soon as dey run a commershill."

"Well," said Simon loudly, "hurry it up. I ain't waiting all bloody morning for some crap TV show."

Smiling broadly, the clerk swiveled around and faced the

changeling. A nametag on her blouse proclaimed her to be Mona. "Benny, my love," she said cheerfully, "I didn't expect you today. It ain't Tuesday."

"No it ain't," said Simon, casting a surprised glance at Jack. He winked, then turned back to the clerk. "I had a bad week at the school. I needed a break today."

"Sure," said Mona knowingly. She jerked her head at Jack. "Who's your friend?"

"None of your friggin' business," said Simon. "We got some business to discuss. Private business."

"My lips are sealed," said Mona. "You want me to round up a few of da girls? Cheri and Lola ain't busy this early in the morning. For the right price, they'd hop right on over."

The clerk laughed coarsely. "You remember Cheri," she said, wiggling her hands six inches in front of her chest. "She's the one with the huge . . ."

"Not today," interrupted Simon hastily. "I don't want any visitors. Anybody asks, I'm not here and you never saw me."

"Yeah, yeah," said Mona, "just like always. Your regular suite, 11-B, is free. Take that." She pushed across a room key. "I don't know nothing."

"How much?" asked Simon.

"Usual rate," said Mona, "minus the courtesy discount. You want me to put it on your tab?"

Jack coughed loudly before Simon could answer. Using the security chief's identity was bad enough, but making him pay for it as well was too much.

"Not today," said the changeling, sounding mildly disappointed. He pulled out Jack's roll of cash. "Write me out a bill, would you? In case I need a receipt for taxes."

The clerk chuckled. "Entertaining clients, huh. Two C-notes will cover it."

Simon peeled off ten twenties, paused, then added another. "Don't forget. I said Privacy, with a capital P."

"Your wish is my command," said Mona, stuffing the extra twenty into a back pocket.

She winked at Simon. "Enjoy yourself, boys," she said, turning back to the TV.

Neither Jack nor Simon said a word until they reached room 11-B. Once inside, the changeling exploded with laughter.

"You see the look she gave me?" he asked Jack, tears of mirth running down his cheeks. "Especially after I turned down the girls. She thinks you're my new boyfriend. Won't that do Anderson's reputation a world of good."

"Huh," replied Jack. "Boyfriend? You lost me. Besides, she swore not to reveal a thing."

"And the moon is made from green cheese," said Simon. "As soon as we leave today, you can bet your last dollar that Mona will be burning the phone lines with news that our buddy Benny has come out of the closet."

"But, but," stuttered Jack, "that's despicable."

"Welcome to the real world, compadre," said Simon. "You're incredibly naive for a graduate student. It must be that mathematics background."

The changeling surveyed the motel room. A low whistle escaped his lips. "Don't worry too much about Anderson's reputation. Judging by this setup, a guilty conscience is the last thing on his mind."

Leather and handcuffs dominated the suite's decor. An umbrella stand full of whips stood next to an oak bar stool with padded black leather seat. Several pairs of fuzzy white wrist and ankle restraints dangled from the headboard of the king-size bed. Looking up, Jack observed without much surprise that a huge mirror covered much of the ceiling.

Gingerly, he sat on the edge of the bed. "Silk sheets," he declared. "Nice quality, too."

"At two hundred bucks an afternoon, they should be," replied Simon, rummaging around behind the bar at the back of the room. "The refrigerator's well stocked. Want a beer? Or a bottle of champagne?"

"Nothing," said Jack. "Just five or six hours of uninterrupted slumber."

"There's a whirlpool tub in the bathroom," added Simon.

"Nothing," said Jack, stretching out on the bed. Kicking off his shoes, he folded his arms behind his head. "Don't you need sleep?"

"Very little," said Simon, munching on a bag of chips. "It's one of the benefits of not being mortal. We rarely sleep and when we do, we never dream."

"To sleep, perchance to dream," murmured Jack wearily. Simon's words bothered him for some reason he could not fathom.

"One of Willy's best lines," said the changeling. "He had us faeries in mind, of course, when he wrote it."

Simon headed for the door. "I'll walk back to campus and see what's up." Anderson's features dissolved and reformed into the changeling's own. "To be on the safe side, I'll lock the door and take the key. You rest."

"Rest," repeated Jack groggily. He was asleep before the faerie left the room.

18

"Hello, Jack," said the woman in red, her voice deep and seductive. "My name is Crystal."

"Uh, hi," said Jack, frowning. Sitting in the midst of the black silk sheets, he had no memory of waking up. Or of letting anyone into his room. And Crystal was definitely not someone forgotten easily.

She stood at the edge of the bed, dressed in a bright red sheath dress that could not be any tighter. A lycra knit, the outfit hugged her body like a second skin. A micro-mini, it barely covered the tops of her thighs. Long-sleeved and low-cut, the dress revealed an astonishing amount of cleavage. Crystal was extremely well endowed, and her taut nipples pressing against the thin material proclaimed she was not wearing a bra.

Wavy red hair coiled down across her milk-white shoulders. She had an oval face with a pert nose, beautiful blue eyes, and the whitest teeth imaginable. Her full lips curled in a sensual smile.

"Like what you see?" she asked in the same throaty tones. The sheer, undisguised desire in her voice set his whole body trembling. Crystal was too good to be real. It was then that Jack realized the truth.

"I'm asleep," he said sadly. "You exist only in my dreams."

Crystal nodded, setting her delightful breasts jiggling. Jack's mouth went dry. Dream or not, the girl was having an astonishing effect on his body.

"That's me," she replied. "A dream girl. I'm merely a figment of your unconscious mind."

"I never guessed my subconscious was so gifted." For the first time since his dream began, he noted he was completely naked under the sheets. "Hooray for figments."

"Mind if I make myself comfortable?" Crystal asked coyly. "These clothes are so . . . constricting."

"Jack," whispered another woman's voice, so faint it could barely be heard. With a shake of his head, he banished the sound from his mind.

"I hate to see a beautiful young lady suffer," he declared righteously. "Go ahead. Make my day."

Reaching down, Crystal took hold of the bottom of her dress and pulled upward. In a matter of seconds, it was off. With a flip of the wrist, the dream girl tossed the outfit in the corner. Clad in the tiniest possible thong bikini, she ran her tongue slowly over her upper lip. "That feels a lot better. Thank you so much."

"No," said Jack, his throat dry. "Thank you."

Grinning mischievously, Crystal hooked her thumbs underneath the straps of her panties. "Last but not least," she said, giggling, and slid them down and off.

Completely nude, she slid onto the bed. Despite his lack of clothing, Jack's temperature soared. Playfully, Crystal twirled a finger in the silk sheets.

"I love being naked," she said, her gaze roaming across Jack's chest. "It makes me think wicked thoughts."

"Uh, what kind of wicked thoughts?" asked Jack, gulping. He was not accustomed to aggressive women, even in his dreams.

"You know," said Crystal, crawling closer. Her huge breasts swayed with her every motion. "The very wickedest ones."

Reaching over, she cupped his chin with one of her hands. Crystal's skin burned hot against his flesh.

"You're a handsome man, Jack. A very handsome, *very desirable* man."

"Jack," whispered the same familiar voice in his mind, louder this time. Angrily, he forced it away. Crystal needed all of his attention. She demanded it.

The dream girl was very close now. Her body exuded warmth.

She radiated pure, unadulterated lust. Bending forward, she covered his mouth with hers.

The kiss seared his lips. Crystal's tongue slipped between his teeth and darted about like a snake. One hand caressed his cheek while her other searched anxiously through the sheets. Crystal moaned passionately when she found what she wanted.

"I need you, Jack," she whispered huskily, pushing him back on the bed. "I need you right now."

Jack was in no position to argue. He had never felt so aroused in his entire life. Crystal's naked body covered him like a sheet. She straddled him, her thighs pressed against his, her breasts jammed to his chest, her hot lips inches from his own.

"No more talk," she declared, her eyes glowing with passion. "I'm ready for action."

"Protection, Jack," whispered the persistently annoying voice in his mind. "Protection."

Hundreds of hours of TV ads, flyers, health lectures, and stern parental warnings worked their own sort of magic. "I need protection," muttered Jack. "Can't take chances with disease."

Instinctively, he wriggled an arm free from Crystal's embrace and over to the nightstand. Groping about, his fingers touched the familiar metal foil of a condom. Jack howled in unexpected pain. It felt as if he had grabbed a live electrical wire.

"Drop it," snarled Crystal, lips pulled back from her teeth in a grimace of hate. "It's not necessary."

Jack squeezed his eyes shut. He never experienced pain before in his dreams. Nor was he able to pause and reflect on what was happening. Things were not as they seemed.

Opening his eyes, he stared at Crystal's face. Even with her features contorted in anger, she was beautiful. Much too beautiful to be true. And, dream or not, she had no aura.

Swinging up his arm, Jack poked the dream girl in the hip with the condom.

With a shriek, Crystal sprang completely off the bed and onto the floor. Catlike, she landed on her feet. Eyes fixed on the foil package in Jack's hand, she hastily backed towards the door.

"Stay away from me," she said, her voice ice cold and barely human. "I'll scream."

"Go ahead," said Jack. "Scream all you want."

He pinched the flesh of his neck. It hurt. "I'm awake," he

declared, sighing. "This wasn't a dream. You're real. And working for Dietrich von Bern."

"Crystal doesn't work for anybody," the woman declared angrily. "Word's out on the street. Ten thousand in gold for your head, attached or not. I saw you come in and thought I'd earn myself a quick bit of change."

"What are you?" asked Jack, holding the condom in front of him like a sword.

Crystal snapped her fingers. Instantly, she was fully clothed, the red dress smooth and unwrinkled against her skin. "Old habits are hard to break," she said, smiling. "Only now I get paid for sex. Consider yourself lucky you found the one object that destroys my spell. I'm a succubus, Jack."

Snapping her fingers a second time, she vanished. Only a lingering trace of perfume indicated she had ever existed.

"Thanks, Megan," murmured Jack, finally recognizing the voice who had brought an end to the seduction. "I think."

He was sitting on the edge of the bed, wondering what would have occurred if Crystal hadn't been stopped, when a key grated in the lock. It was Simon.

"Feeling better?" the changeling asked.

"Yes and no," replied Jack.

He related his encounter with the succubus. After he finished, Simon smiled and shook his head.

"Yield yourself to a succubus and she controls your passions forever after," said the faerie. "According to most accounts, they possess insatiable sexual appetites. It would be a sweet life, my friend, but a very short one. You'd be dead within a week or less."

"I can believe that," said Jack, remembering the look of raw passion in Crystal's eyes. "She mentioned ten thousand in gold for me dead or alive."

"They're scared of you, Jack," said Simon. "Each time you evade a trap, it frightens them more. That's a nice-size treasure. It tempts me, and I'm on the side of the angels."

"So much for my news," said Jack, starting to get dressed. "What's the scoop on campus?"

"Nothing you want to hear," answered Simon. "The disaster at the math complex has the whole school buzzing. Nobody's saying much, but the word is out that Anderson blames you for the whole mess."

"I was afraid of that," said Jack.

"The hottest rumor circulating the cafeteria paints you as a major drug supplier for Chicago's south side. According to five different co-eds I spoke with, the fracas last night was the first battle between your gang and the Border Redcaps over disputed territory. Neat, huh?"

"They pin the Kennedy assassination on me yet?" asked Jack.

"No," answered Simon, "but give Anderson a chance. He's probably working on that theory right now."

Jack shrugged his shoulders. "No use worrying about school when modern civilization is set to collapse. I'll deal with Benny after we've saved the world."

"That sounds reasonable to me," said Simon. "You prepared to head uptown and meet the relatives?"

Jack checked his watch. "It's close to two o'clock. Thank goodness Crystal allowed me to sleep a few hours before trying her tricks. I'm starved. What's in that refrigerator? No reason to leave before lunch. After all, we paid for it."

Simon rummaged through the icebox. "Along with eight containers of whipped cream in various yummy flavors, three bottles of cheap champagne, and a six-pack of beer, there's hearty portions of roast beef, turkey, and cheese. Mona provides a nice spread for her clients."

"Any bread?" asked Jack.

"Yes," said the changeling. "A packaged rye. If you're willing to take a chance, I also see big bottles of Miracle Whip and mayo. Though who knows to what ungodly and immoral uses they've been subjected."

Picking up a kitchen knife from the bar, Jack waved it in the air. "Lay on, Macduff, and damn'd be him that first cries 'Hold, enough!'"

"I knew him, too," said Simon, stuffing a slice of cheese into his mouth. "Macduff, that is. Rather dull fellow, actually. But a *good* swordfighter—damned good."

∞

19

They decided to take a cab north. Jack experienced no second thoughts about the subway, once Simon described in garish detail a few of the supernatural monsters lurking in the dark tunnels. Worse things than will-o-the-wisps had crossed the ocean in the past few hundred years.

"America's free and open," explained Simon as they waited outside the motel for their cab to arrive. "There's room to wander. Not much of that left in England. Or most of Europe, to be perfectly honest. A majority of supernaturals were created in an age of rolling meadows and untamed forests. We've adapted pretty well to urban life, but we all need the woods. That's why so many of my kind live in Chicago and the Midwest, where nature is always less than an hour's ride away."

"Considering the frequency of my encounters with your kith and kin," said Jack, waving at the taxi cruising towards them, "a hell of a lot of you must reside in the city."

"A goodly number," said Simon with a sly smile as he climbed into the back seat of the taxi. "Several thousand at least. A vast majority of them come from the British Isles and Europe. As I mentioned with the banshees, Chicago's large Irish population drew many of us here. Not to mention the lake, and the wilderness so close to the city.

"Other supernaturals migrated to climates reminding them of home. I've been told that the Las Vegas area is filled with genies and other denizens of Arabic myth. There are Chinese dragons in California and dybbuks in the Jewish sections of New York City. Each kind travels to where it is most comfortable. The world is full of real magic, Jack. Unfortunately, you humans rarely notice it."

Both of them settled comfortably in the cab. Simon gave the driver an address on Chicago's far northwest side. As the driver steered the taxi into traffic, Jack recalled an idea from the night before.

"Head to the Loop first," he directed the cabbie. "Stop at the first ATM we spot. Afterward, I want to find a coin shop. The bigger the better."

"Why a coin shop?" asked Simon.

"Insurance," answered Jack. "I need to buy some insurance."

An hour later, they were once again proceeding north. Along with ten crisp hundred-dollar bills, Jack's pockets clinked with a half-dozen antique coins. His insurance policy.

At five o'clock that afternoon, they arrived at the proper address. The house was located in an old Polish neighborhood of small bungalows and well-kept front yards. Unfortunately, all that remained of the structure was a blackened, burnt shell.

"Dis da right spot?" asked the cabbie. "Looks like dey had a fire here recently."

"It's the right house," said Simon, his face ashen. "Pay the man, Jack. I need to ask the neighbors a few questions."

After dismissing the taxi, Jack carefully inspected the ruined home. A series of police barricades connected by rope cordoned off the site from the street. There wasn't much left to investigate. A few charred timbers pointing skyward gave mute testimony to the fury of the fire.

Simon wandered over, his hands clenched into fists. "The blaze broke out two nights ago. Around midnight, according to the folks across the street. It swept through the entire house in minutes. From the neighbor's description, I suspect von Bern used a salamander. It's been the firebug of choice the past decade for supernatural arsonists."

"Any news of your cousins?"

"Mrs. Studzinski claims nobody escaped," said Simon. "But faeries don't die easy. Hopefully, they'll turn up okay."

Jack rubbed his fingers against his forehead. "Two nights ago was before Merlin hired me," he said slowly.

"Tell me something I don't know," said Simon. "The forces of good and evil live in a precarious truce in the city, my friend. Occasionally, it erupts into battle. They attack a few of our centers. We retaliate and level a few of theirs. That could be what happened here."

"Of course," said Jack, "though stretching coincidence to the breaking point and beyond."

He frowned. "Damn, damn, damn. Those mysterious kidnappings started a week ago. Plug this fire and who knows how many other attacks into the equation, and there's only one possible solution. Merlin stumbled on the Old Ones' plot—but not when it was first starting. Von Bern's scheme is nearly finished. The novel's almost over and I still don't know the plot."

"Oh, shit," said Simon.

"Agreed," said Jack.

"Same expression," said Simon, "but different reason, Jack. We've got company—unwelcome company. Over there."

Four massive figures were headed in their direction. Each one stood well over six feet tall and had incredibly broad shoulders. Big, powerfully built men dressed in tight white muscle tees and faded black corduroy jeans, they shared a common hair style. Or lack of one. Their heads were shaved clean.

Less than a block away, they shuffled forward slowly, ungainly, their huge arms swinging apelike from side to side as they moved. Red, green and black tattoos of snakes covered their exposed flesh—dozens and dozens of snakes with gaping jaws and fangs dripping venom. Etched on their shirts were the words, "Born to Raise Hell." None of the quartet possessed an aura.

"Skinheads," said Jack, backing up a few steps in the other direction.

"Worse," replied Simon. "Trolls."

Anxiously, Jack tried to remember everything he read about the mythical creatures. His subconscious drew a blank, other than the story of the three billy goats and a bridge.

"They're not neutral?" he asked Simon, both of them walking backwards now.

"Far from it," said the changeling. "They serve the dark. Willingly and completely. They hate the sunlight and become stronger as the night increases. Mistletoe destroys them, but all woods hurt them. Creatures of hatred, they are ugly in form and in spirit."

Ugly, Jack decided, barely described the approaching monsters. With sloping foreheads, piglike red eyes nearly buried beneath heavy brows, flat noses, and chalky white cheeks, their faces defined the term "Neanderthal" perfectly.

The lead skinhead grinned, revealing a mouthful of broad, yellow teeth. In one shovel-sized hand, he held a crumpled flyer. The creature studied Jack's features, then consulted the paper. Up and down, up and down the troll's head bobbed before a glimmer of recognition flashed in its beady eyes.

"It's him," the creature growled in a voice so deep Jack's ears hurt. "The one in von Bern's flyer. His head is worth ten thousand in gold."

"Ten thousand," repeated a second troll, unwrapping a length of chain from around its waist.

"In gold," added a third monster, sliding a pair of brass knuckles on each hand.

"For his head," declared the fourth, pulling an immense switchblade knife from one boot.

"Easy money," said their leader. Though he carried no weapon, he appeared quite capable of ripping Jack's head off his shoulders without any mechanical assistance. "Good fun, too."

Jack's gaze swept the area. The cab was long gone. Except for him, Simon, and the trolls, the street was empty of life. "Think the nice people in these bungalows will come to our aid if those monsters start ripping us apart?" he asked Simon softly.

"Are we discussing modern city dwellers?" retorted the changeling. "They might call the police—after the trolls finish the job and leave. Maybe then. Maybe not.

"I think we better retreat," continued Simon. "Those hulks are strong and mean. But they're also dumb and slow."

"South," said Jack, and he started running.

Simon hesitated for an instant, gestured obscenely with one finger at the trolls, then dashed after Jack. Bellowing in rage, the four monsters followed. They ran with the grace of participants in a sack race.

Mathematics majors rarely spent very many hours on the athletic field. Jack was no exception. His track experience consisted primarily of running after a missed bus or subway train. However, his life had never before depended on his speed. He surprised himself by soon outdistancing his demonic pursuers. After five blocks, he slowed down to a fast walk.

Huffing and puffing, he glared at Simon. The changeling seemed hardly winded by the sprint. "Was that necessary?" Jack asked, laboring to suck air into his lungs.

"I warned you," said Simon. "I can't help myself. Mischief is my business. At least, we escaped from those lugs pretty . . ."

Simon swallowed the rest of the sentence. Jack swore. Dead ahead of them, less than fifty feet away, at the next intersection, waited the same four trolls.

"You gave me the finger," rumbled the lead monster. "That wasn't nice. I'm gonna bite your hand off for that."

"Back the way we came," Jack shouted and set off as fast as he was able.

Running hurt, but he managed decent speed for three blocks. Again, there was no sign of any pursuit. Simon, features grim, caught up with him right past the intersection of two streets.

"How did they do that?" Jack gasped, bending over and trying to regain his breath.

"I'm not sure," said Simon. "Nobody knows what powers trolls possess. Unfortunately, that's because . . ."

". . . nobody survives to tell the tale," said Jack. "Any idea what hurts them other than mistletoe?"

"Cold iron?" suggested the changeling.

"I doubt it," answered Jack, "seeing that they carried chains and knives."

"They're back," said Simon.

Jack shook his head in despair. The trolls stood less than twenty feet behind them. They were close enough for him to see the nasty glint in their tiny eyes.

"We know shortcuts," said the troll wearing the brass knuckles. "Lotsa shortcuts. You can't escape us."

"Nobody escapes trolls," added the troll with the chain. "Nobody."

"There's always a first time," said Simon. "Climb on my back and grab hold of my neck, Jack. No arguments. I'm stronger than I look. And you're in no condition to run."

Incredibly, Simon ran for nearly eight blocks carrying Jack piggyback before finally collapsing to the pavement. Lying side by side in the street, man and changeling waited for the inevitable arrival of the trolls.

"One trick left," said Simon, pushing himself up on one elbow. His features wavered and changed. Jack gasped as he stared at his own face for the second time in twenty-four hours. He would never be comfortable with Simon's talent.

"Two Jack Collinses," said Simon. "They won't know which one is real. Seeing double might confuse them long enough for us to escape."

"More likely they'd merely rip both our heads off," replied Jack.

"Good point," said the changeling, letting his features return to normal. "Now that you mention it, I think I'll stick with my own handsome visage."

The air in the intersection ahead of them rippled and twisted as four trolls emerged out of nothingness. Wearily, Jack struggled to his feet, pulling Simon with him.

"That's the secret," Jack declared, astonished. "They cross space through four-dimensional crossroads. Somehow, they mix quantum mechanics and magic. Incredible."

"I get the message," said Simon. "If they use intersections, we won't. Head for that alley."

Narrow alleyways cut through many of Chicago's older neighborhoods. Continuing in straight lines for miles, they provided rear access and limited parking for homes stacked one against another. And served as garbage routes for the city's sanitation department.

Ducking around a large red Dumpster, Jack and Simon wheezed their way past locked garages and high wood fences. After a few minutes, they came to where the alley crossed the next street. No trolls appeared as they darted over the pavement and back into the passage.

"I hear them behind us," Simon declared cheerfully, "moving with the grace of a herd of elephants. It appears that alley openings must not qualify as proper intersections. Twenty minutes and they'll be hopelessly behind us. I can't imagine that crossroad trick works if they have no idea where we are."

Jack nodded in agreement. Their near brush with death had badly shaken his nerves. He wasn't in the mood for small talk.

With darkness falling, they didn't discover their deadly mistake until it was too late. Concentrating on the trolls behind them, they paid little attention to the alleyway ahead of them. Until it abruptly ended in a makeshift barbed-wire fence that stretched from one side of the passage to the other. Invisible from the street, the barrier effectively barred them from continued retreat.

"Hey," said Simon. "Don't these people know it's illegal to block an alley?"

"We'll report them later," said Jack. "If we don't move fast, those trolls will trap us here."

Hurriedly, they backtracked to the mouth of the alley. And found their pursuers waiting for them.

"No more running," said the troll leader, pounding one huge hand into the other. "We kill you now."

"It's against the law to murder people," said Jack. His head turned desperately from side to side, searching for help. "Besides, violence never solves anything. Can't we talk?"

He pulled the Universal Charge Card from his pocket. "I'll pay you double what von Bern offered if you leave us alone. Think of that—double the price for not working."

"Pay in gold?" asked the troll wearing brass knuckles.

"Not exactly," said Jack. "ATMs don't deal in precious metals. But cold cash will buy all the gold you want."

"Nah," said the troll with the chain. "It don't matter what you offer. I like killing."

"Me too," said the leader. He spread open his gigantic arms. An evil grin spread across his face. "I'm gonna twist your head right off your shoulders."

Jack clenched his hands into fists. If he was going to die, he planned to die fighting, useless as that might be.

"Is this a private party?" someone asked calmly from the darkness behind the trolls. "Or can anybody join in?"

20

Ponderously, the trolls turned. The leader of the monsters grunted in surprise when he spotted the speaker. A tall, attractive black woman, she leaned casually against a solitary streetlight. Both of her hands loosely gripped a thick wooden walking staff. Capped with silver on each end, the stick was covered with unusual glyphs faintly visible in the moonlight. The woman smiled and nodded in a friendly fashion at Jack and Simon. She possessed no aura.

"Don't bother me, girlie," growled the troll leader, flexing his sausage-sized fingers threateningly. "This fight ain't any concern of yours. Make trouble and you'll be next."

"Oh, my, my, my," replied the mysterious woman, her voice tinged with sarcasm. "I do believe you intend to commit acts of violence towards my friends. Sorry, but I can't permit that."

"Friends?" whispered Jack to Simon. "You know this woman?"

Simon sighed deeply and smiled. "Indeed I do. She's Cassandra Cole. At least, that's the name she's used for the past few hundred years. Deliverance is at hand, Jack. Think of her as the cavalry, Captain America, Hulk Hogan, and the Force combined into one. Cassandra makes Wonder Woman look like a Twinkie."

Evidently, the trolls were not aware of Cassandra's reputation.

And they were too stupid to wonder why one woman risked taunting four of them. Their original quarry forgotten, the quartet spread out in a line facing their new enemy.

"*You* can't permit it?" repeated the troll with the chain. He swung the metal links in an ever-widening circle over his head. The steel whistled with each rotation.

"She thinks she's tough," said the troll with the switchblade. With the click of a button, the knife opened, revealing an eight-inch blade.

"Real tough," agreed the third troll, smashing together its brass-knuckled fists. Sparks flew as metal hit metal.

"She needs to be taught a lesson," declared the leader of the monsters. "I hate uppity broads."

"Should we try to help her?" Jack whispered urgently to Simon. "There's four of them."

"Relax," said Simon. "Cassandra appear worried?"

"No, but . . ."

"Stop fretting and watch. The odds are unfair." Simon chuckled. "But not the way you think."

The trolls shuffled forward, growling threats. Cassandra waited patiently, feet planted solidly on the ground, hands spread about twelve inches apart from the center of her walking stick.

"Last chance," she stated, sounding almost apologetic. "You goofballs turn around and depart, and I won't hurt you. By Athena, I swear it."

The troll leader snorted. "Screw Athena. Dumb bitch goddess."

"Bad remark," said Simon, grinning. "A very bad remark. It's not a good idea to make Cassandra mad."

"You dare insult the goddess," said Cassandra, her voice flat and menacing. "For that you will suffer. Suffer dearly."

Moving with blinding speed, Cassandra attacked. Like a serpent's tongue, the bottom end of her walking stick lashed out and caught the lead troll in the crotch. Grunting in shock, he doubled over in pain. The grunt turned into a shriek as the stick's top slammed into his mouth, jarring loose a handful of teeth.

Twirling on her toes like a ballet dancer, Cassandra thrust the walking stick directly into the path of the whirling chain. Jerking the wood staff at precisely the right instant, she yanked the metal links right out of the astonished troll's grasp. Snarling, the monster lunged for its weapon, dangling only inches out of reach. With a snap of her wrists, Cassandra whipped the steel off her post and into the troll's face. Bones crunched and blood spurted in fountains as the creature stumbled back, howling in surprise.

Bellowing in mindless fury, the troll with the knife swung the blade in a deadly arc aimed to slice the black woman in half. Effortlessly, Cassandra leaned out of the weapon's path. Off balance, the slasher stumbled past her. Instantly, the wood staff hammered him across the back, driving him to the ground. As he fell, his arms tangled with the walking stick and wrenched it away from Cassandra. For an instant, she stood defenseless.

"Got you," crowed the fourth troll, wrapping his huge arms around Cassandra's chest. More cautious than his fellows, he had circled the black woman and attacked from the rear. Locking his hands together, he squeezed.

"Hai!" screamed Cassandra and drove her left heel into the troll's left arch. The monster ground its teeth together in pain but refused to let go. Eyes squeezed shut with effort, the creature tightened its grip further.

Wedging her skull under the troll's chin, Cassandra jerked her head back sharply. Blood bubbled out of the monster's mouth, but it continued to squeeze.

"Enough of this shit," Cassandra declared angrily. Hooking her own fingers together, she pulled the double fist up towards her breasts. Brute strength battled brute strength. And the troll lost.

The monster's fingers popped apart and Cassandra dropped to the ground. Whirling around, she savagely swung a leg up in a short, lethal arc. Her toes sank deep into the troll's midsection. Coughing blood, the creature collapsed.

The fourth troll's heroics had given its comrades a chance to recover and regroup. Battered and bruised, they rushed Cassandra in a bunch.

Fists flashed faster than Jack could follow. But he had no doubts as to their accuracy. They sounded like jackhammers pounding pavement. The trio of trolls staggered out of the woman's reach, whimpering in fear.

As if by magic, Cassandra once again held her wood walking stick. Her face grim, she advanced on the cowering skinheads.

"Insult the goddess, will you?" she declared angrily. Her staff crunched into the troll leader's side. Ribs cracked. Again, the staff lashed out, catching the monster in the chest. As Cassandra raised her weapon a third time, the troll's courage broke. With a shriek, it turned and ran.

"Don't hurt us," begged the two trolls still standing. "Don't hurt us."

"Get going, and take your buddy with you," said Cassandra, pointing her staff at the unmoving fourth troll. "And if I see any of you goons in this neighborhood again, I won't play so nice."

"Yes, ma'am, yes, ma'am," said the trolls. Gathering up their fallen comrade, they wobbled down the street as fast as they were able. The darkness swallowed them.

"Killing trolls is nearly impossible," Cassandra remarked pleasantly, as if discussing the weather. "But they hate being roughed up. Especially when it's done by a woman. Those four won't be pestering the locals for the next few weeks."

Tucking her walking stick under one arm, Cassandra linked her hands and cracked her knuckles. Brushing traces of dust from her clothing, she walked over to Jack and Simon.

"Well met, Simon Goodfellow," she said with a smile. "Long time, no see."

"Well met, Cassandra Cole," answered Simon, bowing elegantly. Taking one of her hands in his, he kissed her fingertips. "It was in Paris, during the Revolution, I believe."

"Ah yes," she said. "If I recall, it was under remarkably similar circumstances. I saved your butt from a gang of marauding goblins."

Eyes twinkling, she turned to Jack. "Aren't you going to introduce me to your mortal friend? After all, he's the reason I'm here."

"Sorry," said Simon. "I didn't mean to be rude. Cassandra Cole, say hello to Jack Collins. Jack, Cassandra. She's an Amazon. Toughest babe I've ever met. Awfully good-looking for someone well over two thousand years old."

"Pleased to make your acquaintance," said Jack. Up close, the black woman was incredibly attractive. She was also several inches taller than Jack, forcing him to look up when he spoke to her. "That was an impressive display of fighting."

"Thanks," said Cassandra, grinning. "Though it really wasn't much. I'm out of shape. Life's too easy in this century. Back in the Middle Ages, I blindfolded myself to fight troll gangs. It evened out the odds slightly. Not enough, though. Ogres, on the other hand, they were a challenge. Always could count on ogres for a good scuffle."

"Uh, Cassandra," said Simon, "knock it off. This isn't the place for idle chatter. You know if my cousins escaped that fire the other night?"

"Burn a faerie?" laughed Cassandra. "Not likely. Lucky for you. They're the ones who sent me searching for Collins. Them and Witch Hazel. I didn't know you were along for the ride."

"What are you talking about?" Jack asked. "I never met any of Simon's relatives. What do they want with me? And how did you find me?"

Cassandra pulled a crumpled piece of paper out of a rear pocket. "Dietrich von Bern's Border Redcaps started circulating these flyers throughout the supernatural community this morning. They're printed in magic ink, of course, so humans can't read them."

"Jack's equipped with rose-colored contact lenses," said Simon, "given to him by Merlin the Magician."

"Merlin?" said Cassandra. "That old goat is living in Chicago?"

"May I look at the paper, please?" asked Jack.

"Apologies," said Cassandra. "Here."

Jack winced as he studied the flyer. Beneath a large black-and-white photo of his face were the words, "Ten thousand in gold for the head of Jack Collins. No body necessary." Under the headline was a paragraph in small print. Jack's eyes widened in dismay as he silently read the information.

Clutching the paper tightly in one hand, he turned to Simon. "Listen to this," he said softly. " *'Collins can be located and identified easily by the magical talisman known as the Universal Charge Card he carries with him at all times.'*" His voice rose with each word. "Didn't you realize the bad guys traced us because of that stupid charge card?"

"Uh, sorry," said Simon. "The thought never crossed my mind."

"I should have realized it immediately," said Jack, "the way we kept bumping into supernatural villains whenever we turned. Merlin never had a chance to warn me. This damned card acts as a beacon, drawing enemies to me like flies to honey."

"Speaking of von Bern and his cronies," said Cassandra, "we can't stand around gabbing all night. The darker it gets, the stronger the German becomes. I'm willing to fight anybody, but I'm no match for the Wild Huntsman and the Gabble Ratchets."

"You have a car?" asked Jack, mental wheels turning.

"An old wreck, but it serves," answered Cassandra. "I parked it a block from here. Didn't want to warn the trolls."

Jack refused to ask why. He suspected she had worried the monsters would have fled without a struggle.

Cruising in Cassandra's rusty old Chevy, they located five ATMs in the next hour. Jack withdrew two thousand dollars from each machine, building up his bankroll substantially. Finally satisfied, Jack had the Amazon find a 7-Eleven.

While Simon and Cassandra drank Slurpees and reminisced about old times, Jack bought a package of envelopes, a roll of Scotch tape, a pen, and some stamps. Slipping the Universal Charge Card into one envelope, he folded it over and placed it in a second. Securely taping it shut, he addressed the outer envelope carefully and applied the correct postage.

"There's a window open at the main post office in the Loop," he told his friends. "We'll mail the letter there. I can't take the chance of a mailbox. Von Bern's men would zero in on it before the next pickup."

The letter deposited, Jack breathed a sigh of relief. "I mailed it to myself at my parents' home in New Jersey. When any letter for me arrives there, my mother scratches out her address and scribbles down my forwarding address at school. Judging on past performances, the entire trip will take a week or more. That should provide us with a little breathing time to save the world."

"Saving the world?" said Cassandra eagerly. "You mind telling me what this disaster is all about? After rescuing you from those trolls, I feel I'm entitled."

"No argument from me," said Jack, choosing his words carefully. "I appreciate all you've done. But this task is extremely dangerous. I don't want you to feel obligated to help in any way."

"You let me worry about danger, Collins," said Cassandra. "It's a long ride to Simon's cousins. We've got plenty of time. Tell me the whole story. From the beginning."

∞

21

"Well, doctor," asked Roger, his voice quivering, "is it cancer? Tell me the truth."

The physician shook his head. "As far as I can determine, Mr. Quinn, the marks on your elbow are a curious skin blemish and nothing more. I label them curious because of their uncanny resemblance to a man's fingerprints. In all my years in medicine, I've never seen their like. If you're truly concerned, we can run further tests. But, except for the discoloration, I can't find a thing wrong."

Roger stood up and put on his shirt. He shook his head. "That will be enough for the moment. Maybe I'll return in a few days. My . . . uncle . . . is in town and requires constant attention. He dislikes my leaving him for any length of time. Fortunately, I needed to buy some sacrifices—I mean groceries—this afternoon, enabling me to escape for a few hours. If I don't return soon, he'll start to worry. And I definitely do not want him to grow disturbed."

The doctor frowned. "Your uncle sounds like a tyrant. Why do you tolerate such behavior?"

"Relatives," said Roger, suppressing a scream. "It's an old story. Can't live with them. Can't live without them."

"Oh," said the physician. "I understand. Money problems? Well, if anything happens to those marks, give me a call. Otherwise, forget them. They're harmless."

Driving back to his mansion, Roger fought back tears of rage. He should have known better. Even modern medical science was helpless before ancient sorcery. The Lord of the Lions held him in an unbreakable grip. It was not a comforting thought.

The demigod met him at the door. "You obtained the fowls?" it asked, sounding anxious.

"Of course," said Roger. "The cage is in the back seat. Give me a few minutes and I'll haul it to the basement."

"Good," said the Crouching One, "very good. I will reward you handsomely for your devotion, my faithful servant. When I rule your world, this state of California will be your plaything. For I am a generous God."

Roger bowed, not believing a word the demigod said. Talk was cheap, even among immortals. While the Lord of the Lions needed neither food nor drink, it required living sacrifices every few days to maintain its energy levels. After experimenting with various small animals, they discovered that chickens worked best.

Every three days, Roger traveled to a farm outside the city and bought several chickens. The owner eyed him curiously each trip, but with satanic cults, food fetishes, and oddball pet owners thriving in California, Roger's money spoke louder than any suspicions.

"Von Bern called while you were out," said the Crouching One. "I spoke to him at length."

After numerous demonstrations, the demigod had finally learned how to use a telephone. Roger grimaced, remembering the trouble he had had explaining the instrument to the ancient being. The Lion God believed all technology to be modern magic. For the sake of his sanity, Roger agreed.

"Well, what did the German have to report?" Roger asked, hoping for the worst. Von Bern was evil to the core, but he was an incompetent clod.

"The fool failed again," growled the Crouching One, blue sparks flying. "Exactly as you predicted. He had Collins in his grasp and could not kill him. The human escaped."

Elated, Roger tried his best to sound disappointed. "I warned you. Von Bern and his goons are creatures of instinct. They can't deal with a man who thinks instead of merely reacts. In this modern age, old-fashioned methods no longer work. If you want to defeat this champion, you need to use someone who understands him, someone who thinks like him."

"Perhaps," said the Lord of the Lions. "Perhaps. But, he deserves a chance. Remember, his plot had a double edge. Even though Collins managed to - stay alive, he didn't guess the German's other trap. If all goes well, this champion will be rendered ineffective by his own kind. Wouldn't that be a delicious irony? Speaking of delicious, I grow hungry for life."

"I'll bring in the chickens," said Roger quickly.

After his last mishap, he definitely did not want to appear too eager. At present, he was quite happy leaving von Bern in command of the hunt. The German's continued failure only served to promote Roger's aim. Silently, he prayed for Collins's success.

"Yes, the fowls," said the Crouching One, its eyes glistening. When it was hungry, the demigod was almost bestial in nature. At times, Roger expected the Lord of the Lions to drop to all fours and run through the house like a gigantic cat. "Take them to the basement. I will begin the ritual immediately."

Roger shuddered. The demigod conducted the sacrifice behind closed doors, and Roger had no desire to find out what took place during the ceremony. The weird howling and dark smoke that filtered into the rest of the house spoke of things best not questioned. Afterward, nothing remained of the birds other than a few feathers and bloodstains on the concrete floor.

"Von Bern reported that the Border Redcaps kidnaped their final victim," announced the Crouching One as Roger marched to the front door. "She joined the rest in the cavern. At least, in that task, he satisfied my demands. There are ninety-one women waiting for the kiss of fire."

Roger felt a familiar chill of horror race through him. Ninety-one was an occult number of incredible power. The product of the mystic numbers seven and thirteen, it contained both nine and one, the two other major figures of power. If the Lord of the Lions fed on the souls of ninety-one human sacrifices, his strength would be increased a thousandfold. The demigod would become uncontrollable.

The murder of nearly a hundred innocent women mattered nothing to Roger. Their deaths weren't his concern. He worried only about himself. He wanted the Crouching One incredibly powerful, but not until he was the entity's master. Not until then.

Fervently, he prayed that Jack Collins understood what von Bern planned to do next. And that Collins had some plan to stop him.

22

Yawning, Jack rolled over and fell out of bed. With a groan, he sat up and opened his eyes. As usual, it took a few seconds for them to focus on his surroundings. A row of sightless skulls stared back at him from a nearby shelf. Next to them stood several dozen corked beakers filled with unidentifiable potions, each cryptically labeled with a number. Beneath them, held captive in a fragile wire cage, were several large tarantulas. Shaking his head, Jack muttered, "This doesn't look like Kansas, Toto."

Wearily, he crawled back onto the edge of the cot and pulled on his clothes. *The trouble with sleep these days,* he reflected unhappily, *is that I wake up more exhausted than when I retired.*

His head hurt. It felt as if Indians had used his skull as a tom-tom. Frowning, he tried to concentrate on Megan's latest attempt to contact him through dreams. After a minute, a single word emerged. "Beltane." It sounded familiar, but he wasn't sure where he had heard it before. But discovering its meaning wouldn't be hard. Not with the company he was keeping these days.

When he stretched, his hands touched the roof of the trailer. The mobile home belonged to another one of Simon's friends, an ugly old crone named Hazel. She had to be the witch Cassandra had mentioned earlier. By the time they reached the trailer camp last night, he wouldn't have cared if she was a dragon. All that mattered was that Hazel had an extra bed he could use. Simon was quartered with his relatives somewhere else on the lot.

Still feeling hazy, he wandered forward, into the tiny combination kitchen-living room of the camper. His hostess stood in front of a small stove, humming to herself as she worked. Hazel fit perfectly in the camper's cluttered quarters. A thin little old lady, a few inches over five feet tall, with wrinkled skin and stringy gray hair, she looked like she had stepped right out of *Hansel and Gretel.*

The witch was busily stirring a mysterious concoction in a huge pot. Small, unidentifiable black objects floated in a bubbling white glop the consistency of oatmeal. Warily, Jack approached the old woman.

"Morning," she said, not turning. Her voice was surprisingly mellow for one so old. "Simon stopped in an hour ago to see if you were awake. He went out for the Sunday papers. Want some breakfast?"

Jack licked his lips, not sure how to answer. He was hungry, but Hazel was a witch. Swallowing his apprehension, he nodded. "Sure. What do you have?"

"How about some of this witch's brew, dearie?" she asked. "I eat some every day. It's honey nut oatmeal, with raisins thrown in for flavor."

She chuckled. "Caught you by surprise, didn't I? You thought maybe it was stewed lizard with toad tongues? I may be a witch, son, but I enjoy my creature comforts. Grab a couple of bowls from the cupboard, and let's eat."

Jack devoured two bowls of oatmeal along with several slices of cracked wheat bread and a glass of orange juice. "This cereal is delicious," he declared, pushing himself away from the table. "I can't eat another bite. Is it an old family recipe?"

"Probably," said Hazel. "The Quaker family, that is. I buy the ready-made stuff. It tastes a lot better than anything I ever made. Don't believe any of these folks who long for the 'good old days.' Preparing all your own meals from scratch was a pain in the ass. I know. I was there. Give me modern convenience food any time."

Reaching over to the kitchen counter, Hazel pushed a button on the portable radio. Nothing happened. Grimacing, the witch shook the device, but it refused to make a sound. "Batteries must be dead. I'll buy some later."

A large black cat strolled over to the table and rubbed up against Jack's leg. Without thinking, he bent over and scratched the animal's neck.

"That feels great," said the cat. "How about getting the back, too?"

Jack jerked his hand back in shock. Hazel grinned and pulled the animal onto her lap. Immediately, it started licking the remnants of oatmeal from the witch's dish.

"Sylvester's my familiar. When I was created, everybody got black cats. Toads and goats and interesting stuff came later. Like everybody here in the trailer camp, he's magic."

"So I noticed," said Jack. He stared at the cat. For a second, the cat stared back, then returned to its cereal.

"How does he form the words?" asked Jack. "I didn't think cats had the proper vocal cords for human speech."

"They probably don't," said Hazel, "but who cares? Magic functions independent of science, Jack. The rules for one don't apply for the other. Or, if we follow Arthur C. Clarke's logic, maybe they're actually the same and we're just too damned primitive and ignorant to understand the common factors."

"You read Clarke?" asked Jack, astonished.

"Of course," said Hazel. "Doesn't everybody?"

"I guess so," said Jack. He winced as the throbbing in his head increased. "You happen to have any aspirin handy?"

"Headache?" asked Hazel.

"A killer," replied Jack. "A Megan Ambrose special."

Briefly, he related his experiences with dream communication. Hazel nodded knowingly as he described his problems remembering Merlin's daughter's messages.

"A perfect case for recipe number four," said Sylvester, licking its paws.

"My thoughts exactly," said Hazel. Rising from her chair, she bustled into the bedroom. She returned carrying one of the beakers Jack had noticed when he awoke.

Pouring a small amount of a vile yellow liquid into a cup, the witch handed it to Jack. "Drink this," she commanded. "It'll cure your headache in a flash."

"What's it made from?" Jack asked, staring at the fluid.

"You don't want to know," said Hazel. "Drink."

Jack drank. The potion tasted terrible, but he forced himself to swallow every drop. Instantly, an invisible wave of fire engulfed his forehead. He blinked and it was gone. Along with his headache.

"Incredible," he declared. "You could make millions selling bottles of that stuff."

The witch smiled knowingly and recorked the beaker. "You mind your own business and save the world, Jack, and I'll mind mine. The mass market isn't ready yet for witch's brew."

"Hazel worked as a pharmacist once upon a time," said Sylvester, hopping from the table to the floor. "Until they fired her."

"Why?" asked Jack. "Practicing without a license?"

"Nonsense," said the witch. "My credentials were perfect. Supernaturals have a talent for forging documents and manufacturing backgrounds. It's a survival skill necessary to live hundreds of years among mankind. We've learned to blend in, not make waves.

"I slipped and stayed with the same company too long. During a cross-check of employee records, they discovered that according to their files, I was eighty years old. Damned do-gooders forced me to retire. They wanted me to enjoy my golden years."

"Tough break," said Jack. "Been out of work long?"

"Two decades next month," replied Hazel, grinning. "I saved plenty and invested it wisely. After five centuries of struggling, I decided to take a few years off. Bought me this trailer and settled down in the country with Sylvester."

"No desire to return to work?"

"I've been mulling over a few offers," declared the witch. "With all this New Age mysticism around, it's no big deal anymore claiming to be a witch. So, I'm not bound by the same constraints as most other supernaturals. Nobody takes me seriously, but they all want to hear what I have to say. In the past six months, I've lectured at three colleges, a half-dozen feminist rallies, and turned down an appearance on Oprah. It's been a kick. Trouble is, most people involved in the revival are more interested in pagan ceremonies and getting naked than real magic. But, that's pretty much the way it's always been, even during the Middle Ages."

Jack rose to his feet. "The word 'Beltane' mean anything to you, Hazel?"

The witch frowned. "It have something to do with a festival of sorts? The title sounds familiar, but I was never much one on ceremonies. I was a woods witch. Ask Simon. If anyone in camp knows the word's significance, it'll be him. He always does. Simon's a know-it-all."

"So I noticed," said Jack. "He has the right answer, if you ask the right question. That's the trick."

"The newsstand isn't far from here," said Hazel. "I'm surprised he's not back yet."

"I'll go outside and wait," said Jack. "Besides, I want to stretch my legs. Thanks again for breakfast."

"Always glad to help a mortal in need," said Hazel, her bright eyes twinkling. "It's my nature."

The trailer camp consisted of nearly two dozen campers spread out over several acres of woodland. The owner of the grounds was a leprechaun named O'Malley, who Jack had yet to meet. According to Cassandra, the Irish faerie had cashed in his gold hoard years ago and invested the money in real estate. He lived in Illinois because it was one of the few states that still permitted blind land trusts. Rumor had it that O'Malley owned half the real estate in the Loop.

Fortunately, the faerie believed in sharing his good fortune with his fellow supernaturals. He maintained the trailer camp in Chicago's far western suburbs for those of his kind who couldn't afford any other lodging. Or who longed for the company of others like themselves. The ones with money, O'Malley charged a small rental fee; the others stayed for free.

Jack drifted idly through the campgrounds, letting the tensions of the last few days drain from him. The green grass, the huge old trees, and the cool spring breeze combined to form an incredibly restful setting. A child of the city, born and bred in concrete and steel surroundings, Jack had never fully grasped the lure of the outdoors. Now, for the first time, he felt in some small way he understood what Simon meant about needing the woods.

After roving aimlessly for twenty minutes, he stumbled across Cassandra in a small clearing, exercising with her walking staff. Mesmerized, he watched the black woman practice. She moved silently, with an inherent grace and speed that Jack found fascinating. The Amazon flowed from location to location, never resting in one spot more than a few seconds. She handled her wood staff with such incredible skill that it seemed like an extension of her body. Though her arms and legs glistened from a thin layer of sweat, she exhibited no other signs of physical distress. Watching her work, Jack had no doubt that she was the most beautiful and most deadly woman he had ever seen.

"Hey, Cassandra," he called after a few minutes passed and she showed no signs of slowing down, "how about taking a break? I'm getting worn out from watching you."

Twirling her staff around so fast that it blurred, Cassandra slammed the wood stick into the ground. It quivered for an instant, then stopped, one end embedded six inches into the soil. Smiling, the Amazon stepped over to Jack.

"Sorry. I truthfully didn't notice you. When I'm practicing, my mind is totally focused on my art. Nothing distracts me."

She smiled. "Feeling better this morning?"

"Much," he replied. "This place is terrific. It's so peaceful."

Cassandra chuckled. "It's great if peace is what you're looking for."

From the tone of her voice, it was quite clear that peace was not one of Cassandra's top priorities. Her expression grew serious. "I want you to do me a favor, Jack."

"Name it," he replied. "You saved my life, remember? I'm in your debt. Ask away."

"I'd like to join your party," said Cassandra nervously. Voice trembling slightly, she continued. "You and Simon can't defeat von Bern and the forces of night without help. There's too many of them. While most of the supernaturals in this camp sympathize with your goals, they're not fighters. Most of them prefer not to get involved. In many ways, they've adapted too well to modern life. Hazel, Sylvester and Simon are the exceptions, not the norms. Me, too. My kind believe in battling for the underdogs. I would help even the odds."

Jack shrugged. "It sounds like a wonderful idea to me. I'm not proud. If you're crazy enough to make the offer, don't expect me to turn you down." He paused. "Obviously, you thought otherwise. How come?"

Cassandra smiled gently, her eyes misting noticeably. "I've lived an awful long time, Jack Collins. Legends of the Amazons date back to the time of Troy, and thus, so do I. For three thousand years, I've burned with the constant desire to fight. A true warrior maid, I live for battle.

"Most of those centuries were spent living on my own. There weren't a large number of Amazons originally, and we were created with an insidious weakness that rendered many of us vulnerable to the ravages of time. I suspect I may be the last of my kind alive. And being a true Amazon in a man's world is no fun. No fun at all."

Cassandra wrenched her staff out of the ground. "The notion of equality between the sexes never existed before this era, Jack. Men, especially fighting men, have always had a hard time accepting a woman who fought as well, if not better, than themselves. You can't imagine how many famous heroes rejected offers similar to the one I made to you. You truly can't imagine. Thousands of innocents suffered and died because their 'saviors' were too proud to accept the aid of a woman. I appreciate your trust in me. You won't be sorry."

"That's the least . . ." began Jack, only to be interrupted by a loud voice from the woods.

"Hey," called Simon, emerging from the trees, "guess who's back from the 7-Eleven? I heard you were looking for me."

Sighing, Jack turned to the changeling. Interrupting meaningful conversations defined Simon's talent. Jack shook his head, wondering what Cassandra meant by "an insidious weakness." From the Amazon's tone of voice, he felt certain it was not a subject she would broach willingly. He made a mental note to put the question to Simon when they were alone. In the meantime, another more urgent query required his attention.

"The word 'Beltane' strike any chords in that storehouse of knowledge inside your head?" Jack asked the changeling. "I think it's vital to our mission."

"Beltane," repeated Simon, his eyes glazing over, "is the name of the ancient Celtic festival of fire held on the eve of May first to welcome the advent of summer. Its origins are lost in the sands of prehistory. It survives in a much different form today as May Day. As does the winter festival, Samhain, now celebrated as Halloween.

"The Celts believed that along with Samhain, Beltane was a day when Beings of Terrible Power walked the Earth. The Druids considered it sacred. On May Day Eve, the priests sacrificed hundreds, burning them alive in wicker cages to satisfy the hunger of their gods."

"Human sacrifices?" said Jack, blood draining from his face. "I don't think I like what I'm hearing. It's only four days until May first. Is it possible that's what von Bern is planning? On May Eve, he intends to sacrifice the women he kidnapped to the ancient demigod pulling his strings."

"The demon Gods of antiquity thirst for the souls of the living," declared Simon. "If von Bern handles the ritual correctly, it would impart to his master incredible power." The faerie's voice dropped to a whisper. "Godlike power."

"Perhaps provide the monster with enough energy to destroy civilization," said Jack. "I'm convinced. We've got to find von Bern's headquarters and stop this mad scheme before it's too late. For all humanity."

"That's not going to be easy," said Simon. "Particularly considering the headline on today's paper."

"What are you talking about?" Jack asked. He frowned as Simon handed him the front section of the Sunday newspaper.

His eyes bulged as he stared at the bold print. *Drug War on Campus!* Beneath the headline, in smaller type, the story proclaimed, "College Drug Lord Vanishes, Millions in Narcotics Found in His Apartment!"

Jack's picture filled the rest of the page.

"I see what you mean," he said, his hands shaking, as he returned the section to Simon.

23

They convened a council of war in Hazel's camper. One human, three supernaturals, and one magical cat sat around the kitchen table and debated what to do next. Jack, his face white with anger, tightly clutched the offending newspaper in both hands. He appeared ready to rip it to shreds. His voice trembled with rage when he spoke.

"Von Bern and his flunkies set up this frame perfectly. That Border Redcap Simon and I spotted watching my apartment building was there for a reason. He never stirred because he was waiting for us to leave. That's when the goon acted, planting the dope in my rooms. The German used a double-edged attack.

"He tried to kill me at the mathematics building. At the same time, he rigged my apartment, knowing I wouldn't dare return there. When I escaped his one trap, he sprang the second. The newspaper mentioned an anonymous phone tip to Anderson. And I was the one stupid enough to mention dope to the security chief in the first place."

"Don't get bent out of shape, Jack," said Cassandra. "There's nothing you could have done. If it hadn't been drugs, the German would have come up with another scheme. He's a devious bastard. It's built into his character. The important thing is not letting your anger cloud your good judgment.

"Simply put, you've been framed. The Huntsman caught you looking in the wrong direction. Now, not only are von Bern and the Gabble Ratchets hunting you, but the police as well. You're a wanted man, Jack. What do you plan to do about it?"

"Cassandra's right," said Simon. "Von Bern wins this round. He's put you on the run. Score a point for the bad guy. But, winning a skirmish doesn't mean the war's over. Consider the big picture. If we lose, your reputation won't be the only thing in ruins. Remember, according to Merlin, our entire civilization is at stake."

"Merlin the Magician," declared Hazel unexpectedly. She laughed, a high-pitched cackling sound right out of the Saturday morning cartoon shows. "Let him handle your legal problems. He's sneakier than any lawyer. The Old Boy is an expert untangling sticky situations. He snaps his fingers and all the tangled mess falls into place. Or close enough. Look how he managed that King Arthur nonsense. You worry about saving the world. Once Merlin's free, he'll take care of the small stuff."

"That *King Arthur* nonsense?" repeated Jack.

"Another time," said Hazel.

"All right," said Jack reluctantly. Conversations with the supernaturals drove him crazy. They interspersed their comments with tantalizing mentions of past exploits, but they never clarified any of those points later on. Jack wanted to know more about Willy Shakespeare, Cassandra's earlier encounters with heroes, and King Arthur. But that would have to wait. Beltane required his immediate attention.

"At least, we have answers to some of the questions concerning this upcoming apocalypse," continued Jack. "We know *who* locally is in charge of the enemy. We also know *why* von Bern kidnapped the women. Beltane answers the question of *when* he plans to conduct this sacrifice. What we still don't know is *how* he managed to conduct his crimes, and *where* he intends to kill his victims."

"Whatever you say, Jack," said Simon, a blank look on his face. "You're in charge. My relatives will provide whatever support they can. But none of them are willing to take any risks. Von Bern scares them too much. I'm the only one willing to contribute. I'm part of the team."

"Same with me," said Cassandra. "I love a good fight. I'm in this to the end. You can count on me. But don't look at me to offer many ideas. I'm a fighter, not a thinker."

"That's the truth about most of us," said Hazel, nodding her head in agreement. "We act by instinct, not by plan. Which is why humans are always the heroes and we supernaturals make up the troops. Sylvester and I are with you too, Jack. If you'll have us."

"Of course," said Jack. "The more the merrier. I need all the help I can get."

Mentally, Jack grimaced. He had hoped for a few useful suggestions or ideas. By now he should have known better. His friends possessed incredible powers, but original thinking wasn't included in the list. Deductive reasoning was his job. Unfortunately, even Sherlock Holmes couldn't solve a mystery without a few clues. And Jack had absolutely nothing.

"Why not talk to the mall nymphs?" said Sylvester, leaping into Hazel's lap. Purring, the cat made itself comfortable and began cleaning its paws. "They know the answers to lots of questions. It's part of their nature."

"What a wonderful suggestion," said Hazel. "I should have thought of them. The nymphs are neutral, and they love to gossip. Everyone tells them their secrets."

"Of course they do," said Simon, grinning. "You can't make time with a mall nymph unless you tell her a secret."

"Disgusting little tramps," said Cassandra with a sneer.

"They seem to enjoy themselves," said Hazel, cackling again.

Jack winced. The witch's laughter hurt his ears. "Someone want to fill me in?" he asked. "Who are these mall nymphs? And, more important, can they actually help us?"

"Mall nymphs are the genius loci of shopping malls," said Simon cheerfully. "Like our friend Cassandra, they date back to the time of ancient Greece."

"Don't link me with them," said Cassandra angrily. She glared at Simon. "Shameless female spirits, they called themselves dryads during the Golden Age. They lived in forest groves, frolicking naked among the trees. Entirely devoid of shame, the vixens delighted in tempting unwary soldiers foolish enough to camp in their glades."

Jack stifled a grin. With a flash of insight, he realized a basic truth about the Amazon. Cassandra was a prude. He wondered if the trait somehow tied in with her "insidious weakness." Reminding himself to question Simon about Amazons, he focused his attention on what Hazel was saying.

"Immoral or not, mall nymphs love secrets. They pry them out of any male supernatural they encounter. And, since they are among the most beautiful and definitely the most amorous of all our kind, the girls entertain many, many visitors. I'm sure von Bern or his lieutenants have enjoyed their company numerous times."

Jack pursed his lips. "Uh, how do you propose persuading these lovely ladies to reveal what they know? Or haven't you thought about that?"

Simon smirked. "Trust me on this one, Jack. I'm on excellent terms with the girls. They'll tell me anything. I guarantee it."

Jack turned to the old witch and her familiar. "Hazel?"

"Simon is an obnoxious braggart," said the witch, "but he has a certain way with the ladies. If the mall nymphs will speak freely with anyone, it will be with him."

"Cassandra," Jack continued, "any thoughts?"

"Hazel's right," said the Amazon, her expression sour. "Simon possesses a silver tongue. He can talk a bird out of a tree if he sets his mind to it. Let him work his wiles on the nymphs. After all, do we have any other leads?"

"My feelings exactly," said Jack. He stood up. "I'm ready to head off and meet these nymphs."

"You might be," said Simon, "but unfortunately, the malls don't open till noon on Sunday."

The changeling held up the newspaper with Jack's picture. "While I dislike raising the possibility, since the advent of all those 'Most Wanted' shows on television, aren't you taking a big chance going to the shopping mall? I would hate for civilization to collapse because a nosy old grandmother spots your face and calls the cops."

"I didn't think of that," admitted Jack.

Hazel cackled and scurried for the bedroom, sending Sylvester flying to the floor. "I hate when she does that," said the cat. "Hurrying never solves anything. We cats know better."

Hazel scuttled back into the kitchen, holding a half-filled flask in one gnarled hand. "Almost forgot I had this stuff. Potion number ten."

She filled a paper cup to the top with the black fluid. It looked like India ink. And smelled like turpentine. Jack wondered if the old witch made the stuff in the sink. He hoped Hazel wasn't going to ask him to swallow it. She did.

"Bottoms up," she said, handing him the container. Before he could blurt out his question about the ingredients, she shook her head. "The same answer as earlier. You're better off not knowing."

Eyes squeezed shut, Jack swallowed. A jolt of electricity raced through his body, standing his every hair on end. As with the previous drink, the sensation vanished in an instant. Other than a slight tingling to his skin, he felt fine.

"Nice trick," said Simon, grinning.

Cassandra shook her head, smiling faintly. "Witchcraft."

"What are you talking about?" Jack asked, suddenly apprehensive. "What happened?"

Hazel handed Jack a small mirror. "See for yourself, dearie."

Gripping the looking glass with both hands, Jack stared at his reflection. He gasped, as he found himself confronted by a perfect stranger. Or, more exactly, a not-so-perfect stranger.

"My hair is purple," he whispered, "and cut in a Mohawk. My teeth are yellow and my skin is too pink. There's a gold skull earring dangling from my left ear. And I don't have any eyebrows. What did you do to me!"

"Touch your ear," commanded Hazel. "Feel an earring?"

"No," said Jack, watching in the glass as his hand reached up and tugged at the gold skull. "Nothing's there. But, in the mirror . . ."

"It's an illusion," said the witch. "The potion creates a perfect, three-dimensional simulacrum. Beneath the deception, your features haven't changed a whit."

"Thank god," said Jack. "Why purple hair?"

Hazel shrugged. "Why not? These spells work the way they want. Not much I can do to control them. Cheap ingredients."

The witch's tone turned serious. "One word of warning. The spell isn't a particularly strong one. I'm not sure how long it will last. Or if its magic will survive contact with a stronger sorcery. So, beware."

"If that's the case," said Jack, "let's move it. By the time we arrive, the mall will be open. Cassandra, you'll drive?"

"Of course, assuming my car will start. Don't expect me to help you find those mall tramps, though. I'll wait outside."

"Agreed," said Jack.

He was looking forward to meeting the nymphs. They sounded delightful. And not having Cassandra around as a chaperone didn't upset him in the least.

24

Cassandra's car made it to the mall. Barely. Chugging and wheezing, the old wreck collapsed in a parking space. Muttering curses in ancient Greek, the Amazon slammed her door shut and stalked to the front of the auto. Wrenching the hood open, she glared at the engine like a particularly vile enemy.

"You'll run," she spat out, "or I'll rip your innards to nuts and bolts."

"Uh, Simon and I will head into the mall, Cassandra," said Jack, edging away from the car. "We'll be back soon."

"Whenever," said Cassandra, her hands fiddling with the motor. Her eyes glistened with battle lust. "I'll be here."

Jack and Simon hurried to the mall's main entrance. Neither of them said a word until they were inside.

"I'm glad she's on our side," said Jack, letting loose the breath he had been holding since the parking lot.

"Cassandra definitely has a style all her own," said Simon. He glanced around the wide hall. "The nymphs usually hang out in the center of the mall. Let's head there. It might take a while to find them. They tend to walk around a lot."

As they walked through the long gallery, Jack recalled the mystery he had wanted to question the changeling about.

"In one of our conversations, Cassandra mentioned an 'insidious weakness' that doomed most of her companions. You have any notion what she's referring to?"

"Of course," said Simon, smiling. "If you tried, you could probably guess it easily enough. Amazons lived for battle. They possessed none of the usual female longings and desires. But humanity created them with human emotions.

"Amazons are immortal and nearly invulnerable. But they have one fatal flaw. If they fall in love, truly in love, they become human. They metamorphose from deathless warrior to mortal woman.

"That is what happened to Cassandra's companions. Over the centuries, they grew lonely, took lovers, became wives, raised children, died. Surrounded by the temptations of flesh and spirit, they could not resist experiencing life. Only Cassandra stayed true to the Amazon creed. She is the last of her kind, and very lonely."

Jack sighed heavily. Immortality sounded wonderful, but he doubted he would be willing to pay the price. Life without love was not life, merely existence.

"Hazel's spell seems to be working," said Simon, as if sensing Jack's mood and trying to change the subject. "Considering the stares you're getting, it's proving quite effective."

Jack glanced in the window of a nearby shop and nearly collapsed in shock. He was prepared for his features, but he hadn't realized the disguise spell affected his clothing and size as well.

He resembled an outcast from a grade-B teen exploitation film. Skinny as a rail, he stood well over six feet tall—dressed in a tie-dyed multicolored shirt, faded blue jeans with the knees ripped out, and floppy sneakers with the long laces untied. No one walked by him without turning at least once for another glance.

"I'm the center of attraction," Jack whispered to Simon. "Everyone's staring at me."

"Don't complain," said Simon. "No one in their right mind would associate a weirdo like you with Jack Collins. You're safer with this oddball appearance than any regular disguise."

"I'll take your word for it," said Jack, grimacing.

"By the way," he continued, "this grotesque outfit reminds me that I've been wearing the same clothes for two days straight. After we meet your friends, I want to pick up some new duds before we leave. Cassandra won't mind if we do some shopping."

They spent the next thirty minutes wandering aimlessly through the mall. Upstairs, downstairs, through big department stores and little specialty shops, they searched for the elusive nymphs without success. Finally, they rested at an ice-cream shop where Jack ate a cone and watched his friend devour three milk shakes in quick succession.

"You bring money?" asked Simon, gazing wistfully at the empty container.

"More than enough for another shake," said Jack. "I grabbed a handful of twenties when we left. Without the Universal Charge Card, we're stuck using cash."

"A fate worse than death. Maybe one last shake wouldn't be a bad idea. Hey! There's a nymph!"

Jack whirled, his gaze sweeping the crowd. "Where? Where?"

"The tall blonde in the white miniskirt," said Simon, pointing at a young woman already disappearing into the throng. "Hurry up. They move fast."

Simon darted off into the crowd, weaving ghostlike through the hordes of shoppers. Pausing long enough to drop a twenty-dollar bill on their table, Jack followed.

Now his bizarre appearance proved useful. People, seeing Jack coming, scrambled out of his path. He looked like trouble, and no one came to a shopping mall hunting confrontation. The sea of faces magically parted before the running scarecrow with purple hair.

He caught up with Simon at one of the shrub-encircled rest areas that dotted the huge passageways. Dozens of caged birds twittered as Jack approached the changeling and his companion. Seeing him, Simon waved happily. "Jack, come meet April."

The mall nymph reminded Jack of Crystal in blonde. The thought of the succubus set his blood fizzing. Forcing his hormones to behave themselves, Jack held out his hand to the young woman.

"Pleased to meet you, April. I'm Jack Collins."

April smiled, revealing a mouthful of dazzling white teeth. Her eyes were bright blue and her shoulder-length hair platinum blonde. Tall and slender, she was curved in all the right places. A white half-blouse barely covered her full breasts, leaving the bronzed skin of her stomach bare. A matching white miniskirt was equally daring, displaying an incredible amount of tanned flesh. White boots with high heels completed the nymph's outfit.

She was a teenage fantasy come to life—the elusive beauty

spotted from a distance walking through the mall but never actually encountered. It struck Jack that the nymphs' persona had changed little from thousands of years past. The only difference in their lifestyle was the location. April was temptation personified.

"My pleasure," said April, bells tinkling in her voice. Catching Jack entirely off guard, she reached up with both hands, held him gently by the cheeks, and kissed him full upon the lips. "It's a tremendous thrill encountering a real hero."

"The thrill is mine," said Jack dreamily. "Are your sisters equally stunning?"

April giggled. "I'm the ugly duckling of the bunch," she declared. "The others are much prettier."

Twenty minutes later, Jack was forced to agree. April was unbelievable, but her three siblings were irresistible.

Moving with a fluid grace that made Jack painfully aware of the nymph's supernatural origins, April escorted them into the tunnel leading to the mall offices and restrooms. She paused beside the water fountain, watching carefully until no one was in sight. Then, with a quick sidestep, she disappeared into the wall.

"What the . . ." began Jack. Before he could finish the sentence, one of April's hands snaked out and snared his arm. With a quick yank, she tugged him into and through the barrier. A second later, Simon followed.

"Faerie magic," the nymph explained. "Only supernaturals or those in physical contact with them can pass through the magic door. It keeps the riffraff out."

They were outdoors, in a beautiful woodland glade at the center of the shopping mall. Huge trees stretched to the sun, while a bubbling brook flowed lazily past their feet. Not far distant, a young fawn and her mother grazed on bright green grass. It was a dream landscape, impossible, yet real. The one discordant note was four chaise lounges set beneath one of the trees. Three of them were occupied. Jack's jaw dropped with he realized none of the other nymphs were wearing any clothing.

"Hi, girls," called April. "I've brought company. You remember Simon Goodfellow. And this is his mortal friend, Jack Collins, the hero we've been hearing so much about."

Squealing with delight, the trio of nymphs bounded off their chairs and ran over. Clustering around Jack, they each insisted on kissing him in the same manner as April.

"I'm May," declared a redhead with sparkling green eyes. After a very long, intense kiss, she winked provocatively. "I *love* heroes."

"I'm June," said the second, a brunette with flashing brown eyes. Her kiss lingered on his lips. "Think of me as a summer fling."

"July is my name," murmured the last of the three, with jet black hair and matching eyes. She kissed with a passion matched only by her voice. "I'm the oldest, and the best."

"What do you mean by that?" said May angrily. "You're no older than the rest of us. We were all created at the same time. And I'm the best."

"Says who?" asked June.

"Says me," declared May, her slender hands curving into fists.

"Wait a minute," said April, sounding belligerent. "I found them. By rights, they're mine. Especially Jack. I think he's cute."

"Girls, girls," said Simon quickly. "No fighting, please. Consider the possible damage to your exquisite bodies."

"He's right," said Jack. "Besides, each of you is uniquely beautiful. Comparing perfection against perfection is impossible."

May licked her upper lip with her tongue slowly, sensually. "I'd forgotten how nicely you humans turn a phrase. April, June, July, I'm willing to forgive and forget."

"All right, I guess," said April, "though I still think Jack's cute."

"Your apology's accepted," said June.

"Likewise," said July. "Why don't we stroll over to the stream and relax for some refreshment, Jack?"

"A Coke would be nice," he said, trying to keep his wits in order as April and her three incredibly desirable, completely nude sisters conducted him to a chair next to the spring.

"I swear there were only four chaise lounges here when we entered," said Jack, stretching out on the recliner. There were six chairs now, one for each nymph, Jack and Simon. In the plastic cup holder attached to one arm of Jack's seat was a large paper cup filled with ice-cold Coca-Cola. Sipping the drink, he noted without surprise the name of the mall snack shop on the side of the container.

"A teleportation spell?" he guessed, remembering Merlin's trick.

"Of course," said July. "We use it for all our needs. Why pay for something when you can borrow it? We return the furniture to storage when we no longer need it."

"But the forest, the running spring?" said Jack, waving a hand in the air. "Inside the mall?"

"It's an illusion, of course," said May. "But a very, very detailed illusion. One with texture and depth. You can't pick a leaf from the trees or drink from the stream, but otherwise, this world is real. In the summer, we change it to the beach. And in the winter, it snows. Sex isn't our only talent, Jack."

"The mall was constructed with a hollow, doorless courtyard area in the center," said July slyly. "No one ever questioned the architect why he designed it in that manner."

She chuckled. "Silly boy. He was so easy to convince."

Indolently, she turned her head and stared directly into Jack's eyes. "And why have you come to visit us, my handsome young man? Simon never brings company when he comes calling. At least, he never did before."

"Tell me the last time a true hero walked among the fey folk," said Simon. "Jack is the personal protégé of Merlin the Magician. And a close personal friend of mine. I thought you girls would enjoy meeting him before he becomes famous."

Simon lowered his voice, as if afraid of being overheard. "Jack's going to save the world from the forces of eternal night. How often does someone like that come along? Remember all the trouble it was getting to see Arthur?"

April giggled. "It was worth the effort," she declared. The nymph laughed again. "Even with the scandal afterward."

May and June blushed. All over, Jack noted with wide eyes. Hours later, he tried imagining what might embarrass one of the mall nymphs. His mind boggled at the possibilities.

"Dietrich von Bern claims Jack is yesterday's news," said July, arching one eyebrow. "According to the German, in a few more days he's going to be running the whole show. He sounds pretty sure of himself."

Simon sneered. "So did Hitler. And the Kaiser. And Bismarck. All the way back to Charlemagne. Overconfidence is part of the German national character. It's bred into them like beer and sauerkraut."

July stretched her arms over her head, setting the sweat on Jack's back sizzling. But what she had to say cooled his passion instantly. "Von Bern intends sacrificing a bunch of human women to the dark gods. Burning them alive, if I remember correctly. Are you two planning to stop him?"

"Maybe," answered Simon warily. "What's it to you?"

"We hate human sacrifice," said May. "We're creatures of pleasure, not pain. Von Bern's a handsome devil, and usually we enjoy partying with him. But he's stepped over the line with this scheme."

"Then you'll tell us where the ceremony is going to take place?" asked Jack.

"Would if we could," said May. "But von Bern keeps information like that to himself. Now that I think of it, though, I remember Jan saying she heard the German mention something about his hideout the other night."

"Jan?" said Jack.

"Our other sister," explained April. "Jan's short for January. She's off visiting the naiads at the aquarium today. You'll have to return tomorrow evening if you want to talk to her."

"Terrific," said Jack, rising to his feet. They finally had a lead. "We'll be back."

"Oh, you can't leave yet," said May, also rising. "We don't allow our guests to depart so quickly. That would be rude."

"Oh, sure," said Jack, realizing for the first time that without the nymphs' cooperation, he was trapped in the courtyard. "We're not in any rush."

"That's good," said May, running one hand slowly along Jack's arm. "Because what we have in mind might take a while."

25

Nearly two hours later, Jack and Simon stumbled out into the momentarily deserted corridor. "See you tomorrow," April's voice echoed after them.

Gasping, Jack grabbed the water fountain and gulped down what seemed like a gallon of water. Afterward, he splashed several handfuls of the liquid in his face.

"Are they always so . . . enthusiastic?" he finally managed to ask his companion.

"They are incredibly vigorous," said Simon, sticking his face directly into the stream of cold water. "Remarkable girls, especially when you consider they've been around for thousands of years."

"Remarkable," agreed Jack, straightening his clothes. "We should move. Cassandra's probably wondering what's taking us so long."

Simon shrugged. "She knows the nymphs' tastes too well to worry. Though, if I was you, I wouldn't mention what went on in the courtyard to her. Ever."

"It's our secret," said Jack. "Uh, Simon. The games the nymphs played with us . . . and that King Arthur nonsense Hazel mentioned this morning . . . ?"

"Pretty much the same," said Simon. "You understand why Merlin hushed up the whole incident?"

"You bet," said Jack. "My lips are sealed. Permanently. Let's hit those department stores. I definitely have to buy some new clothes. My wardrobe needs replacing. April's nails ripped the back of my shirt to shreds."

Jack soon discovered his bizarre appearance proved no deterrent to his spending money. Though most of the sales people eyed the floor when talking to him, they all readily accepted his cash. Five shirts, three pair of jeans, and several packages of underwear and socks swiftly filled his shopping bags.

"That should do it," he decided, stuffing the loose change back into his pockets. Located a few stores away was the exit to the parking lot. "This has been a very satisfying day. I won't forget our visit to the mall quickly."

Glancing about, his gaze settled for an instant on a Radio Shack a dozen feet away. A window display of radios and CD players caught his attention. A memory from breakfast floated through his mind. Hazel's portable radio needed batteries. "One last errand," he told Simon, handing him the bags of clothing. "It won't take a minute."

Stepping into the store, Jack looked around for electrical supplies. Not finding them, he strolled further back into the shop. And found his path blocked by a huge exhibit advertising the chain's new CD-ROM computer.

"Nice system," said Jack, momentarily distracted by the hardware. He bent over and ran his fingers over the computer keyboard, calling up the tutorial. As he did so, a ripple of cold fire crossed his body.

"Bad move," he said to himself and glanced at his reflection in the monitor. His normal, non-purple features glared out from the glass. "I'm not sure why, but that was awfully dumb, Jack."

Anxiously, he backed out of the store and into the mall. Simon's eyes bulged when the changeling saw him.

"The spell wore off," said the faerie softly as Jack clutched one of the shopping bags up to his face.

"Right you are," said Jack, his voice muffled by the heavy paper. "Maybe our luck will hold and no one will notice. Head for the car."

"I'll steer," said Simon, linking arms with Jack. "Ready?"

"Ready," said Jack and, without thinking, stepped forward—

directly into the path of a tiny, white-haired old lady. The collision sent them both sprawling to the floor.

"I'm terribly sorry," said Jack, scrambling to his feet. Bending over, he offered the woman his hand. "The packages I was holding blocked my view."

"No problem," said the old lady, peering curiously at Jack's face. "My, you look so familiar. Do I know you?"

Before Jack could answer, the woman nodded as if answering her own question. "Help, help!" she shrieked in a voice louder than most air-raid sirens. "Murderer!"

"What the hell?" swore Jack, straightening in shock. All over the mall, people were staring at him and the little old lady at his feet. Out of the corner of an eye, Jack spotted a mall security officer hurrying towards them.

"Drug lord! Drug lord!" the white-haired woman screamed. "Help, help, help!"

"We're trapped," wailed Simon.

"Not yet," said Jack. Reaching with both hands into his pockets, he pulled out all of his loose cash. Though he had spent freely, there were still hundreds of dollars left.

"Free money!" he yelled at the top of his lungs, and threw the bills into the air. "Free money!"

The mall erupted like a volcano. Crowds appeared out of nowhere. People shot out of store fronts as if propelled by cannons. Men and women, children and adults all raced madly for the cash cascading onto the pavement.

"Free money!" Jack shouted again, and tossed the rest of his reserve high over his head.

No one was immune to the siren song. Girls and boys battled over loose change. Men and women crawled on the floor, grabbing at any paper that moved. Even the little white-haired old lady shut up and lunged for a twenty floating past her face. A dozen yards away, the security guard struggled desperately with a teenager for a fifty. No one noticed Jack and Simon sprinting for the exit.

"Never underestimate the power of cold cash," declared Jack as they burst through the doors and into the parking lot. "And, in a showdown between greed and justice, take greed every time. It's a sure bet."

"There's Cassandra," said Simon, pointing down a row of parked cars.

"Get that beater started!" he shouted to the Amazon. "Security's after us!"

The old wreck's motor roared to life as Jack and Simon ripped open the back doors and hurled themselves inside. Not waiting for an explanation, Cassandra backed the auto into the aisle. Foot pressed down on the accelerator, she sent the car roaring past the long row of parked cars, heading for the street.

Ahead of them, sirens wailed. Red lights flashing, a mall patrol car roared into view. Tires squealing, the vehicle sped swiftly towards the end of the aisle, seeking to cut off their escape route.

"No way they're stopping me," declared Cassandra savagely, and she slammed the gas pedal to the floor. "Hang on."

Engine bellowing in pain, black smoke cascading from its tailpipe, the old car thundered forward. Ahead of them, the police car screeched to a halt, blocking all but a few feet of the aisle. Two security officers jumped out of the vehicle, took one frightened look at the massive wreck heading straight at their car, and ran for cover.

"Cowards," sneered Cassandra, and she slammed both feet onto the brake, spinning the steering wheel at the same time. Rubber burned as the auto wrenched sideways. Spinning furiously, it smashed sideways into the side of the security vehicle. The police car groaned in pain as the force of the collision hurled it backwards. Metal screeched against metal as for one instant the two cars remained locked in a steel embrace. Then Cassandra's foot hit the accelerator and sent her car howling through the enlarged opening into the street.

"Easy as pie," she said, laughing merrily. "You boys survive okay?"

"Physically or mentally?" asked Jack, trying to force his fists to unclench. "What about pursuit?"

"Real cops will be after us in a few minutes," said Cassandra. "Not to worry. There's a haunted cul-de-sac up ahead. It's invisible to mere mortals. We can hide there till nightfall."

"Haunted?" said Jack. By now, nothing surprised him. "What about ghosts?"

"Spirits know better than to fool with an Amazon, Jack," said Cassandra. "They'll stay out of sight. Damned spooks are afraid of their own shadows. If they had them."

Jack sighed. Merlin hadn't lied. Magic was everywhere.

"One minor problem," said Cassandra, as she steered the car

onto a dirt road that seemed to appear out of nowhere. Up ahead, he spotted a rickety old wood bridge crossing a moss-covered stream. The haunted cul-de-sac.

"What's that?" asked Jack, envisioning goblins, demons, perhaps even a dragon or two waiting for them in the shadows.

"We need a new car. This old heap is shot. It's fine for smashing police cars. But won't do us much good if von Bern shows up. We'll need some real fire under the hood to give that limo of his a race."

"Even after throwing money to the crowd, I have plenty of cash left back at Hazel's trailer," said Jack. "Tomorrow morning, we'll go automobile shopping. Then, hopefully, at night, January will reveal the location of von Bern's hideout."

He clenched his hands together in frustration. "We're running out of time. Even if we discover where the German has his prisoners, I don't know how to rescue them. And there are only four more nights till Beltane."

26

The rest of the evening proceeded exactly as Cassandra predicted. They left the haunted cul-de-sac shortly after eight o'clock and returned to the trailer camp without difficulty. At ten, Jack suffered through the indignity of watching reports of his appearance at the shopping mall on the Sunday Night News. Each time the reporter referred to him as "the alleged drug kingpin of Chicago's South Side," Jack winced. Merlin would have to be a magician to repair the damage to his reputation.

Channel 9, with an hour news program to fill, devoted a whole section of their broadcast to his exploits. Along with an interview with Benny Anderson, they ran a montage of close-ups made by his students and classmates. Jack slumped lower and lower in Hazel's sofa as he listened to their remarks. The statements painted him as a combination of the Marquis de Sade and Hannibal Lecter. Sandra Stevens, eager as ever to grab the spotlight, assured the unseen newsman that "Professor Collins rarely displayed any interest in his students," and "he often came to class looking as if he was zoned out on drugs."

Jack chewed on his lower lip in disgust. He didn't regret the many extra hours he had spent tutoring Sandra. That was part of his job. What he did regret was giving her a passing grade for trying hard. Getting ready for sleep that night, his only consolation was that at least he didn't have to wake up early for classes the next morning.

Hazel insisted he drain another potion before bed. "It will sharpen your memory while you sleep and when you rise," she told him. "If Merlin's daughter contacts you in dreams, this drink will ensure you remember what she says."

Closing his eyes and holding his nose, Jack gulped down the formula. As before, it tasted dreadful. "Don't you have any potions that taste good?" he asked.

"Lots of them," said Hazel. "Problem is, they don't do much of anything. Only the vile ones work right. It's part of the lore."

"I should have guessed," said Jack. "People expected witch's brew to be nauseating, and thus it was. Belief led to definition."

Worn out, Jack drifted off to sleep as soon as his head hit the pillow. And found himself floating in a featureless, gray void. Megan Ambrose hovered only a few feet away.

"Jack," she said, sounding relieved. "I was beginning to think you'd never arrive. I've been reciting poetry aloud to keep from going crazy. It's incredibly boring having your mind awake while your body remains asleep."

"Sorry," he said. "I've had a busy day."

"Your image appears much sharper tonight," she said. "Maybe you'll retain more of our conversation. Did you remember my warning about Beltane?"

"Not really," he admitted. "However, I've since pieced together von Bern's plans. You didn't, by chance, tell me the location of his hideout the other evening?"

"No," said Megan. "I have no idea where we are. I gather you don't either."

"Not yet," said Jack. "But I hope to find out tomorrow. I'm meeting with a nymph named January who knows something important."

" A nymph?" said Megan, her voice noticeably cooler. "You didn't mention any nymphs in our previous discussions."

"I only met them today," said Jack. "They seem like nice girls."

"So I've heard," said Megan icily. "Why don't you tell me all about your *busy day*, Jack? It sounds . . . fascinating."

"It began with a witch named Hazel," said Jack, launching into a description of his activities for the past fifteen hours. A firm believer in protecting both his reputation and his life, he minimized his encounter with the four nymphs. Though, from a certain glint in Megan's eyes, he suspected she was not so easily fooled.

"Witch Hazel, Simon Goodfellow, and Cassandra Cole," she remarked when he finished reciting his adventures. "I've heard good things about them. You've assembled a fine band of adventurers, Jack."

He nodded. "I almost feel like Jim Phelps on the old *Mission Impossible* TV show. Each supernatural adds a special talent or skill to our team. Hazel has her spells; Cassandra's the muscle; and Simon provides the information."

"Don't forget the most important member of the group," said Megan softly. "Jack Collins. He's the one with the brains. Without you, Jack, nothing would happen. The others aren't leaders, they're followers. They need you to make the right decisions."

Jack grimaced. "That's the problem, Megan. So far, I haven't done a damn thing to justify their faith in me. Or your father's either. If I'm supposed to save the world, civilization is in big trouble."

"Nonsense," said Megan.

She snapped her fingers and was instantly at Jack's side. "Wonderful what you can do in dreams," she said, as she circled one arm around Jack's neck and pulled his mouth to hers.

An eternity or two later, she released him. "Kissing in dreams isn't real," she sighed, "but it's better than nothing."

Jack agreed. Megan's kiss wasn't as fiery or as passionate as the nymphs' embraces, but it touched him in a place the others never came close to. His heart.

"What was that for?" he asked.

"No reason," she replied. "Or every reason. Call it a confidence booster. I have faith in you, Jack. Take my word for it. You're the right choice. I know it."

"I'm not stupid enough to argue with the girl of my dreams," he said. "But making love here isn't going to save you from being burnt alive by Dietrich von Bern."

"You'll stop him," said Megan.

"I wish I shared your confidence," said Jack. "Finding von Bern's headquarters is only the first step. After that, I've got to defeat him and the Border Redcaps somehow. And I don't have a clue to his weakness."

"He must be vulnerable to something," said Megan.

"That's what's driving me nuts," said Jack. "According to the old legends, cold iron defeated the forces of darkness. But I've seen firsthand that's not true anymore. Iron and steel no longer affect the supernaturals. Until I understand why, nothing about them makes sense."

"I'm not sure I follow what you're saying," said Megan.

"There has to be an underlying logical basis to the rules governing the existence of the mythical creatures living on our world," said Jack. "Your father worked out the principles of how you are all created. Again and again, I've witnessed the truth of his deductions. Every supernatural entity obeys the specific beliefs, the particular legends that brought it to life. Though they've evolved over the centuries, Simon and Hazel and the nymphs and all the rest are still true to their original nature. The universe requires consistency. There has to be cause and effect. But, if that's true, why isn't cold iron deadly to von Bern and his unholy crew?"

Megan shrugged. "Modern times?"

"Uh-uh," said Jack. He tapped his fingers together in frustration. "Rules are rules, no matter when they are applied. Consider, for example, Walsh the vampire. He still couldn't cross running water. And sunlight killed him."

"But didn't you tell me that the cross didn't harm him?" replied Megan. "Why should one method work and not the other?"

"I don't know," said Jack. "But there must be an answer."

"Maybe you're approaching the problem from the wrong direction," said Megan. "What about the other monsters you faced? You defeated them with unconventional methods of attack."

"That's true only in a manner of speaking," said Jack. "In those cases, I had no choice other than to experiment with new approaches to the old solution. The creatures had evolved with the times, and the old versions of eliminating them no longer applied to their new forms. I merely updated the answers to fit their modern states. The rules hadn't changed, only the representations."

He paused, as the meaning of his own words vibrated through his mind. "Maybe that's it. Walsh wasn't harmed by the cross because it personally meant nothing to him. It no longer represented what it did a hundred years ago."

Jack grinned. "As the monsters evolve, so do the icons affecting them. That's the law I've been searching for. The solution is a symbolic one. A century ago, the crucifix stood for the triumph of good over evil, light over darkness. It was a unique symbol, the embodiment of a specific principle deadly to creatures of the night like the vampire. More important, people believed in its power. And that belief made it work.

"However, as civilization changed, religion fragmented into a thousand different beliefs, with none of them holding sway over mankind's psyche. A symbol sacred to one group meant nothing to another. Walsh was unaffected by the cross because it was no longer the proper icon. In our modern world, the crucifix no longer represented the forces of light.

"Fortunately, the general rules about vampires still held true. They were specific, not symbolic. Sunlight killed Walsh because sunlight vanquishes darkness by definition."

"Does that help you with von Bern?" asked Megan.

"If we apply the same logic to the German, it does," said Jack. "Since cold iron no longer affects von Bern, it logically implies that the metal was merely a specific example of a general category of objects that harmed the Wild Huntsman and his allies. Over the years, people confused the specific with the symbolic. As was the case with vampires and crosses.

"Time passed, and for some reason I don't yet understand, steel lost its effect against the creatures of the night. If anything, I suspect it became too commonplace, and people no longer believed that it possessed the unique property that originally made it an icon. However, the original symbolism never changed. That's what's really important. Obviously, something else replaced cold iron."

"What?" asked Megan.

"I don't know," said Jack. "First, I need to figure out the general case. In other words, what did steel symbolize? If the crucifix represented the power of light over darkness, what meaning did cold iron possess that made it so deadly to von Bern and his cronies? Once I solve that enigma, it shouldn't require much effort to rationalize that principle for the modern world. Which will enable me to find the proper icon. And the German's weakness, I hope."

"I hope so too," said Megan, reaching for him again. "You're starting to fade. Night must be coming to an end. One last kiss before you leave . . ."

Jack could still feel the warm touch of Megan's lips against his when he awoke. With a smile and a sigh of relief, he realized that he had retained full memory of his dream. Then a frown of concern clouded his features. The sun pouring in through the trailer window signaled it was Monday morning. Each hour brought Beltane a step closer. And with it, the end of civilization. Not to mention the untimely death of the girl of his dreams. Hurriedly, he slipped on his new clothing. There wasn't a minute to waste.

27

"Today," said Cassandra, in a tone indicating no compromise, "we buy a car."

"Whatever you say," said Jack, resigned to the inevitable. Not that there was anything else to do in the meantime.

An hour's worth of discussion had brought them no closer to a solution to the mystery of steel. No one in the entire trailer complex had any idea why cold iron had been once deadly dangerous and now was nothing more than inert metal. Even Simon, the wellspring of obscure knowledge, was baffled. The changeling controlled a vast library of facts, but he was worthless when it came to theory. Even Hazel, in Jack's opinion the wisest person in the camp, was stumped. It was his problem, and he was obviously the only one who could solve it.

"Take Sylvester with you," said Hazel. "He can spot a bargain a mile away. Follow his instincts. You won't be sorry."

"I thought witches and their familiars couldn't be separated by any great distances," said Jack.

"A useful folktale," said Hazel, "but not true. Sylvester and I are linked telepathically, but otherwise he's a completely independent entity. He does what he wants and goes where he likes. He's anxious to help. Will you let him?"

"Why not?" said Jack. "If I can have an Amazon for a bodyguard and a changeling for a reference librarian, a magical cat for an advisor makes perfect sense. Before we depart, though, let's finish my beauty treatment."

After the fiasco the day before, they had settled on a much less complicated disguise. Cassandra dyed Jack's hair and eyebrows white. With his eyes pink from the magic contact lenses, he looked like an albino.

"The best disguise," she declared, "focuses attention on one physical trait or abnormality. People seeing you will immediately notice your white hair and not see anything else. Your features won't register with them. No one will ever connect you with the fugitive drug lord. It's a simple but effective trick. I learned it from Ulysses."

"This stain won't permanently alter my appearance?" said Jack, nervously running one hand through his silver locks. "I don't mind staying silver for a few days. But looking like Elric is carrying my interest in fantasy fiction a step too far."

"Don't you worry, dearie," said Hazel. "A good washing with shampoo will restore your true color. The only magic involved comes from a bottle."

An hour later found Cassandra, Jack and Sylvester at "Honest Abe's Used Car Lot" in the far western suburbs. "Honest Abe," they soon discovered, referred not to Abraham Lincoln, but to Abe Ortigara, the owner of the automobile dealership. A big, hearty man in his mid-sixties with a booming voice and the bushiest eyebrows Jack had ever seen on a human being, Abe himself insisted on accompanying them on their survey of his stock of second-hand cars.

"I always try to spend a little time each week on the lot myself," said Abe, walking them down a row of used autos. "It helps me keep my feet on the ground instead of my head in the clouds. You let your salesmen do all the work, and soon, they're running the whole company. That's the quickest path to financial ruin in the car business. I've owned this place for thirty years and I plan to own it another thirty. No retirement in the picture for Abe Ortigara. Selling cars is my life."

The big man patted the hood of an '88 Oldsmobile affectionately. "Any idea what you and the little lady are in the market for?" he asked Jack.

"We're not married," said Jack hurriedly, seeing the dangerous look on Cassandra's face. "Miss Cole and I are merely very good friends."

"My apologies," said Ortigara, wincing as his gaze touched Jack's bleached hair. "It was just that the two of you made such a nice couple, I assumed . . ."

"A natural mistake," said Jack, cutting off the car salesman before Cassandra exploded. "Actually, I thought I would let my cat make the final decision."

"Your cat?" said Ortigara, the words choking in his throat. His face turned bright crimson. "Isn't that sort of unusual?"

"Is it?" asked Cassandra, her voice cold enough to freeze water to ice. "In our religion, we believe in allowing our pets to select our means of transportation. If they're happy, then we're happy. You're not implying that there's something odd about our beliefs, are you?"

"No, no," said Ortigara anxiously. Sylvester, getting into the spirit of things, rubbed up against Abe's leg, meowing loudly.

Reflexively, the car dealer bent down to scratch the black cat's neck. Instantly, Sylvester bounded away, leaving Abe in a half-crouch, staring at a frowning Cassandra.

"I meant no disrespect," he declared nervously as he straightened. "I would never insult anyone's religion. Honest Abe believes totally in the sanctity of a man's—or woman's—personal beliefs. No matter how strange they appear to be to outsiders."

"How comforting," said Jack, trying to hide a smile. "We're Polymaths, by the way, in case you were wondering."

"Polymaths," repeated the car dealer. "How fascinating."

Desperately, Honest Abe glanced in the direction of his office. "Oh, it looks like they're trying to get my attention back at the main building. Must be someone extremely important on the phone. Darn business can't function with me away from my desk very long. Why don't you folks look around in the meantime? I'll return shortly, or send one of my best sales associates to help you. Nice meeting you."

"Honest" Abe bustled off as fast as possible without running. More than once he peered anxiously over his shoulder, as if reassuring himself he was not being followed. He disappeared into his office, leaving Jack and company alone on the lot.

"Polymaths?" said Cassandra, shaking her head in disbelief. "Where do they worship?"

"At the Temple of Universal Knowledge," said Jack, straight-faced. "At least, that's what I would have told Abe if he had asked."

"Well, he's gone," said Sylvester, arching his back. "And I doubt he'll return."

"Just as well," said Jack. "Dealing with used car salesmen makes me nervous."

He stared at the cat. "We drove by three other lots before you made us stop at this one. Obviously, it wasn't due to Honest Abe's reputation. What's special here?"

"I sensed magic," said Sylvester. "It's located somewhere on this lot. Come on, follow me."

Twenty minutes and several bruised knees and shins later, they stood before Sylvester's find. The cat conveniently ignored the fact that it could travel where Jack and Cassandra could not. During the course of its search, it led them on a convoluted search over the entire lot. More than once, it darted beneath a row of cars, leaving it to the humans to climb over or squeeze through. Covered with sweat and grime, Jack was not pleased when he saw their final destination.

"Is this your idea of a joke?" he asked angrily. "A car from the year I was born?"

The cat had come to rest in front of a 1966 Buick Electra. A huge, four-door sedan with light blue interior, it reminded Jack of the massive vehicles driven in old gangster flicks. Considering its age, the car was in remarkably good condition. Not a scratch marred its finish.

Sylvester sat perched on the top of the hood, licking its paws. It appeared undisturbed by Jack's complaint. "Don't judge a book by its cover," it replied.

Cassandra walked around the car, knocking on its side with one fist. "Body is still in good shape. This car's built like a tank."

"We're not looking for a tank," said Jack testily. "You wanted something fast, remember?"

Cassandra popped open the auto's hood, sending Sylvester leaping for the roof. "Mother Athena," she declared, whistling in surprise. "That's a big engine."

Even Jack was impressed. The motor was massive. Curiosity finally overcoming his annoyance, he read the spec sheet glued to the car's rear window.

"It's 425 cubic inches," he said, "complete with heavy-duty manifold, four-barrel carburetor, dual exhausts, the works. Even with the pollution safeguards added, this baby goes from zero to sixty in seven seconds. If we can believe Honest Abe."

Cassandra joined in. She ran a finger down the car's features. "Power steering, power brakes, power windows—name it, this car's equipped with it." She shook her head. "No one dares build gas guzzlers like this dreadnought anymore. Look at that mileage report—eight to ten miles per gallon in the city, fifteen in the country. The damn thing can pass anything on the road . . . except a gas station. No wonder it requires a twenty-five-gallon tank."

"Those figures can't be true," said Jack. "Maybe they were once upon a time, but all those added pollution devices cut down on engine efficiency."

"Not for this car," said Sylvester unexpectedly. "It's been dwarf repaired. That's why it looks so good. And runs so well."

"Really," said Cassandra. "The Little Men? Now that makes a difference."

"Why?" asked Jack. "Care to fill me in on the secret?"

"Dwarfs are the master craftsmen of the supernatural world," said Cassandra. "When they fix an item, it runs better than new. If a dwarf repaired this car, then I'm willing to believe any of Honest Abe's claims about it. Though I doubt he knows the real truth about the vehicle. Sylvester, you're sure?"

"Positive," said the cat. "Dwarfs have a distinct odor you don't forget. Especially if you possess a cat's nose. Call me a dog and spit on me twice if I'm wrong."

"That's good enough for me," said Cassandra. "What about you, Jack?"

"How can I argue with a cat reciting a line like that?" said Jack. "Who cares that this baby has 180,000 miles on it? If you two are convinced, I won't utter another word. Especially since Cassandra does all the driving. From the looks of things, this beauty has been sitting here for a while. Why don't we find Honest Abe and see if he's willing to bargain?"

He was. An hour later, paperwork completed and cash paid, they drove off in their new chariot. Cassandra's wreck, destined for the scrap heap, they left with Ortigara. Jack prayed they weren't on track for the same fate.

28

Roger frowned. He did not like what he was being told. "You want *how* many chickens?"

"Fifty," said the Lord of the Lions, staring at its fingers for an instant as if verifying the number. Mathematics was not one of its skills. "I want them delivered to my chamber in the basement tonight."

"That's a hell of a lot of birds," said Roger. "Buying them alive isn't going to be easy. You're sure you need that many?"

"Great sorcery requires much blood," said the demigod. "Since we are taking no chances, the fowls provide the essential life. If you prefer, five young women, virgins if possible, would serve equally well. Or a dozen head of cattle."

"I think we'll stick with chickens," said Roger. A vision of him escorting a cow through his house and into the basement flashed through his mind, giving him an instant headache. "Virgins are in short supply these days in California. And cattle are equally scarce."

"As you wish," said the Crouching One. It rubbed its small hands together in anticipation. "I have not attempted this spell in thousands of years. It will be illuminating to learn if it still works."

"What if it doesn't?" asked Roger, thinking of his own bad

fortune. If only he hadn't been so greedy. But moderation had never been one of his vices.

"Most likely, you would experience a wonderful opportunity to discover if your religion's faith in an afterlife is justified," said the Lord of the Lions. Blue sparks flickered beneath its ears. "Beyond that, the resultant psychic backlash would level most of the city, giving you plenty of company on your journey."

"Are you positive this sacrifice is necessary?" Roger asked, feeling the noose tightening around his neck. "Wouldn't a phone call to von Bern prove as effective?"

"Afraid?" asked the Crouching One, a slight smile touching its thin lips. "How typical of you mortals. Frightened of the last and greatest adventure. Have no fear. Your life is in no danger. At least, not from this spell."

The demigod's eyes glowed inhumanly bright. "You yourself pointed out to me how terribly inadequate the Huntsman's performance has been. He is an incompetent fool. Our mutual enemy, Mr. Collins, has outwitted von Bern with appalling regularity. I am forced to agree with you that unless I intervene on a more direct level, the great sacrifice will fail. That is the reason for this summoning tonight."

"A summoning?" asked Roger. "Similar to the one I used to raise you? I wasn't aware such spells required blood."

"Great beasts roam the boundaries of the outer darkness," said the Lord of the Lions mysteriously. "Lesser races feared them, often worshiped them as minor deities. They are extremely powerful but extremely stupid. Such monsters cannot be lured to this plane of existence without warm life. They feed on the living, animals as well as men. With such an ally, the Huntsman cannot lose. No ordinary human can defeat one of the Great Beasts of Eternal Chaos."

Roger quickly turned away from the demigod. Drawing in a deep breath, he repressed the reckless laughter that welled up within him. No matter what happened, the Lord of the Lions never learned from its mistakes. Despite its incredible powers, the entity was no smarter than the lowest demon from the pit. The demigod continued to underestimate its opposition. It refused to change its tactics. Roger doubted that it could.

"I better make a few phone calls," he declared, "if you expect that many chickens by nightfall. It shouldn't be too difficult. Explaining the birds to the neighbors is the real trick."

"Perhaps it is time I taught you the spell of forgetfulness," declared the Lion God. "It is a simple magic that even humans can master. Using it, you should have no further problems with the overly cautious."

Inwardly, Roger exulted. One spell would lead to another. And another. And on and on, until he knew enough to reverse this infernal bondage and put the insufferable demigod in its proper place. Whistling, he headed for the phone.

Unfortunately, Roger also habitually underestimated his enemies. If he thought to glance around as he departed, he would have seen that the Lord of the Lions was smiling. It was not a nice smile. It was definitely not a reassuring one. But Roger didn't turn. He never did.

29

Seven o'clock that evening saw Jack and the others ready for their return to the shopping mall. Cassandra slid into the driver's seat with Jack on the passenger side. In the back seat, Simon and an unexpected guest relaxed on the thick cushions.

Shortly after dinner, Sylvester the Cat had announced he wanted to accompany them on their mission. Recognizing that the familiar's special powers might prove useful, Jack raised no objections. He was willing to accept all the help he could get, human or not.

"Be careful," warned Hazel, as they wedged Cassandra's walking stick over the seats. "Von Bern is not without resources. Nor is the Huntsman a fool. It's very possible he knows you plan to return to the mall this night. Until you know his weakness, he cannot be defeated."

"I'm painfully aware of that fact," replied Jack sourly.

He had spent the entire day trying to deduce the symbolism of cold steel without the least hint of success. Everything hinged on his discovering the right answer, which put enough pressure on him to make logical thought nearly impossible. Jack suspected that the truth was obvious, if he could somehow link together the correct facts. Deciding what mattered was the trick.

"Sylvester, you keep an eye on them," continued Hazel. The cat nodded solemnly. "Drive safe."

Cassandra stepped on the gas pedal and steered the big car onto the road. "I love this monster," she declared, patting the dashboard. "It reminds me of my favorite war chariot. Has the same nice solid feel."

"What's the plan?" asked Simon.

Jack shrugged. "Same as before. You and I enter the mall, leaving Cassandra and Sylvester to guard the car. There shouldn't be any trouble with security tonight, considering my new appearance, but to stay on the safe side, Cassandra can double park by the entrance. The two of us head over to the nymphs' garden. April promised to meet us by the water fountain. We talk to January, learn what she heard, and leave. If we have an extra second, we buy Hazel a box of Frango Mints from Fields."

"That doesn't give us much time for socializing," said Simon. "I was hoping to visit a bit with the nymphs."

"Control your base instincts, faerie," declared Cassandra, an edge to her voice. "There's a proper time and place for all things, but tonight is definitely *not* the night for carnal pleasures."

"I can't help being true to my nature," said Simon. "Like my friend Willy once said, 'The fault, dear Cassandra, lies not in the stars, but in ourselves.' It's as true for supernaturals as it is for humans. More so, actually."

"You constantly refer to Shakespeare," said Jack, seeking to stop the two from arguing. "You really knew him? In the flesh?"

"Certainly," said Simon, sounding quite smug. "We Goodfellows were very close with the Bard of Avon."

He raised a fist with his first and second fingers upright and pressed tightly together. "Willy and me," he declared. "Friends forever. I taught him everything he knew about the fey folk."

"Everything?" repeated Sylvester unexpectedly. The cat reared up on all four legs and looked Simon directly in the eyes. "That's not what I heard."

"Well, perhaps I exaggerated a mite," said the changeling hastily. "Puck was on slightly better terms with Mr. Shakespeare than I."

"Oh," said Cassandra, chuckling. "How quickly the tune changes. Now, it's Mr. Shakespeare. Did you really meet him, Simon? Truthfully."

"I swear it," said Simon. "My cousin, Robin, provided the

playwright with information for several of his productions. You know the ones. Anyway, Puck took me along several times to the shows. Afterward, Shakespeare always asked us our honest opinion of the work. A true craftsman, he valued a straightforward answer. Which is what we gave him."

"Hazel liked Shakespeare, too," said Sylvester. "The old girl loved *Macbeth*. She quoted the three witches' lines for weeks. 'Double double, toil and trouble,' and so on, endlessly repeated, until I started going crazy." He rolled his green eyes. "And it takes a lot to undermine a cat's patience."

"Wait a minute," said Jack. "In all the fantasy novels I read, the supernatural characters try extremely hard to stay out of the limelight. They shun famous people and never, ever interfere with human affairs. The last thing any of them want to do is attract attention. That's not what I'm hearing from you guys."

"That's because we're real and not made up," said Simon. "Don't make the mistake and think we hobnob with every celebrity who comes along. Or that we reveal our true nature other than to a few trustworthy souls like yourself. That would be stupid. But we enjoy mingling with the best and brightest. Your race created us with those desires. It's in our blood. If we wanted to hide in the woods out of sight, we wouldn't have worked so hard learning how to blend in with mankind."

"Don't forget that over the centuries, we've become experts at masquerading as normal humans," said Cassandra. "I've taught six different movie stars self-defense. Simon's studied with three Pulitzer Prize winners. None of them guessed our secret. Combine our talent with modern man's skepticism of anything he can't taste, touch or feel, and we're home free. The world is filled with magic, Jack. You humans just refuse to admit it."

"Watch the Grammy awards now that you're able to spot auras," said Simon. "You might be surprised."

"Better yet," said Sylvester, "turn on MTV."

"Enough chatter," said Cassandra, a hard edge back in her voice. "There's the mall up ahead. Jack, you and Simon get ready. I'll drop you off at the same door as yesterday. From what you told me, it's the closest one to the nymphs' oasis. When you've finished talking to Jan, return there and I'll pick you up. If there's any sign of trouble, I'll send Sylvester into the mall with a warning. Got it?"

"Got it," said Jack. He peered out the car window. "It looks pretty quiet out there."

"The exact same words King Priam uttered while his people pulled the wooden horse into Troy," said Cassandra.

"How cheering," said Jack, and then they were there.

Doors opened, and he and Simon headed for the entrance to the mall. As the Buick disappeared into the darkness, Jack's hands unconsciously clenched into fists. A premonition of impending danger raced through his mind. He had a feeling that things were not going to proceed as planned tonight. Which, on a moment's reflection, seemed to be the story of his life lately.

30

January's long tangled hair was white as snow, and her deep eyes were an icy blue. Tall and busty, she looked more like a Norse goddess than a Greek nymph. But she was anything but frigid in her greeting, insisting on a very long, lingering kiss with both Simon and Jack.

"Humans express their desires so much better than the fey folk," she explained, reluctantly releasing Jack from her embrace. "Kissing you is a tremendously rewarding experience."

"Glad to oblige," said Jack, trying to catch his breath. "The feeling is mutual."

Fortunately for his presence of mind, all of the mall nymphs were fully dressed tonight, though their skin-tight skirts and stretch knit tops left little to the imagination. Jack wasn't sure if the girls looked sexier with clothes or without them.

"Cassandra's waiting at the car, Jack," declared Simon impatiently, catching Jack completely by surprise. Simon was the last one he expected to be in a hurry. Then he realized the changeling was only being true to his nature. Closing his mind to temptation, Jack concentrated on their reason for seeing the nymphs.

"May thought you heard von Bern drop a hint where his hideout is located," said Jack. "I need to find the place. Fast. Can you help?"

January nodded. "The girls told me the whole story. I'm glad to cooperate. Human sacrifice is so . . . uncivilized."

She paused for a second, drawing in a deep breath and setting Jack's pulse racing. "Dietrich was bragging how powerful he was going to become once the ceremony took place. According to him, the Old One promised that he would have complete control over Chicago and all the Midwest.

"I remember thinking to myself that that would make life here in the mall insufferable when he launched into this long tirade about how incredibly stupid you humans were. Since that's one of his favorite themes, I tuned out most of what he was saying. However, one line stayed with me. The Huntsman was mocking the police. I remember his exact words. He said, 'The fools hunt desperately throughout the city for my captives, while all along the ones they seek are right beneath their feet.' Then, he changed the subject and never mentioned the women again. Does it make any sense to you?"

Jack frowned. "Not instantly. His headquarters can't be located in the subway system. All of the tunnels are in use. None of them have been abandoned. Maybe he's using the basement of an old warehouse?"

A stray thought about tunnels tickled his consciousness. Jack recalled his conversation with the taxi driver a few centuries ago. The cabbie mentioned that all of the women who vanished had disappeared from the buildings in the Loop. Again, the notion touched a strand of memory. Anxiously, he tried to wrestle the notion to the surface.

"Underground tunnels," he muttered, eyes closed tightly shut as he concentrated. "Tunnels. Passageways. Corridors. Beneath the Loop corridors. Old railway tunnels . . ."

A black ball of fur exploded through the secret doorway of the nymphs' lair. Moving with astonishing speed, Sylvester shot across the glade and into Jack's arms. Immediately, all of Jack's mental groping about old abandoned passageways collapsed.

"Cassandra sent me to fetch you two," the cat gasped out, hardly able to speak. "She senses evil approaching. Amazons possess a talent for that. No more time for talking. We gotta run."

"Von Bern and the Gabble Ratchets," said Simon. "It must be them."

The changeling grabbed Jack by the arm, sending Sylvester tumbling to the floor. "Sorry to kiss and run, girls," Simon said, "but we're history. And if the German catches us, we're dead history."

Her face twisted with worry, April escorted them through the magic door and into the mall. "Be careful, Jack," she said, holding him tightly for an instant. "For all our sakes."

"Thanks," said Jack, reminding himself that this stunning young woman attracting the attention of every male in the immediate surroundings was over three thousand years old. "I plan to be back."

Eyes damp with tears, April let him go. Then she grabbed his shoulders before he could move. "I just remembered! Late last night, long after you were gone, we felt an abrupt rip in the outer darkness. Something massive, something ancient, entered our world. Entered nearby.

"May and June are certain it's one of the legendary Great Beasts. Ask Simon about them. He knows their history. My sisters think von Bern, or his master, summoned the Beast to destroy you. It's out there, somewhere, waiting for you."

"Damn," said Jack. "I wish I justified all the attention these fiends are wasting on me. I've yet to prove myself much of a threat to their plans. April, thanks again for everything. Keep your fingers crossed that von Bern and company are right and I'm hell on wheels. See you soon."

He dashed after Simon and Sylvester. As he ran, Jack wondered what horrors hid behind the title "Great Beast." He wasn't sure he wanted to know.

They burst out the doors of the mall together. Cassandra had the car pulled up to the curb, thirty feet away. She waved at them frantically, urging them to greater speed. But, before he could take more than a few steps, Jack heard the howling—the howling of the Gabble Ratchets.

For an instant he froze, his gaze sweeping across the parking lot searching for the Corpse Hounds. It didn't take long to find them. Their fearful baying attracted more attention than a malfunctioning car alarm. There were three of the monsters, heading directly at them from the west. As of yet, there was no sign of their dread master.

Jack tore his attention away from the beasts. Running, he could reach the car long before the hounds arrived. Trying to stay calm, he dashed wildly for the auto. And tripped over the motionless body of Sylvester the cat.

The familiar was frozen stiffer than an icicle. Eyes popped out of its head, fur standing on end, it looked like a prop from an old horror film. Jack swore as he hauled the beast up into his arms. The unearthly howling of the Gabble Ratchets had completely immobilized Sylvester.

The cat was surprisingly heavy. Stumbling, Jack staggered for the car. Never once did he consider leaving Sylvester behind. The supernatural beast was part of his team. Abandoning it to the mercies of the Corpse Hounds was out of the question.

The Gabble Ratchets were less than twenty yards distant and closing fast. Jack knew he would never make it to the auto. Desperately, he dropped the frozen cat at his feet and stood waiting for the monsters, hands clenched into fists. Jaws dripping slaver, eyes burning with unholy light, the three hounds bayed in triumph as they hurtled forward.

"Out of the way, Jack," said Cassandra, seeming to appear out of nowhere. Calmly, she shoved him behind her and raised her staff as the three Gabble Ratchets launched themselves into the air.

The Amazon whipped her walking stick around faster than the eye could follow. One end caught the first of the hounds square in the throat. A quick flick of the wrist sent the beast flying in the air over their heads and into the mall wall.

Meanwhile, the other silver cap pounded the second dog right in the nose, smashing it to ruins. Shrieking in pain, the hound scrambled backwards, blood gushing from its face.

The third Ratchet, its jaws spread wide, almost made it to Cassandra. Just when it appeared impossible that she could avoid the monster's fangs, the Amazon slammed the center of her staff into the beast's mouth. The hound's teeth clenched together, but on wood, not Cassandra. Releasing her grip on the walking stick, the Amazon let the dog fall to the ground. Twirling on the balls of her feet, she kicked it in the throat. Choking, the hound released the staff and collapsed.

"Watch it!" shouted Jack, as the first dog Cassandra faced charged her for a second time. Howling madly, the beast leapt for her throat.

The Amazon dropped like a stone, letting the hound sail right over her head. Before the dog could recover, Cassandra was on her feet again, both hands gripping one end of her staff. She swept it around in a short, vicious arc ending with the Gabble Ratchet's skull. With a crunch of bone, the monster dropped unconscious to the pavement.

"Bravo!" exclaimed a voice that Jack recognized instantly. "Poetry in motion."

Dietrich von Bern stood less than ten feet distant. By his side whimpered the second Gabble Ratchet, blood dripping in bright red droplets from its crushed nose. In one huge hand, the Huntsman held his terrible sword.

Parked behind von Bern, less than a dozen feet away from their Buick, was the Huntsman's black limo. Leaning against the car, arms folded in disinterest, was Charon. The sight of the ancient Greek ferryman reminded Jack of the insurance nestled in his pocket. Tonight he would learn if his hunch concerning the items was correct.

"A magnificent fight," declared von Bern, taking a giant step forward. Effortlessly, he raised his massive sword shoulder high. The blade glowed with a sinister light. "I doubt that anyone else in the world could defeat three of the Gabble Ratchets unaided. Too bad you struggle for a lost cause, Cassandra. As always."

The Amazon twirled her staff in a circle over her head. In seconds, she had it moving so fast that it blurred in the starlight. Her eyes never left the big German. "It's never over till the fat lady sings, von Bern," she declared.

To Jack, she whispered urgently, "Get in the car, fast. There's no way I can beat the Huntsman with a wood stick."

Jack needed no prompting. He flung Sylvester's petrified body into the back seat and scrambled in after it. Huddled behind the steering wheel, hands trembling with fear, was Simon.

"Welcome to the Flying Dutchman," said the changeling, his teeth chattering. "Ready for takeoff."

For each step forward taken by von Bern, Cassandra paced one back. She was only a few feet from the Buick.

"My master wants Collins eliminated," declared the Huntsman. "Move out of my path or be destroyed."

"Over my dead body," said Cassandra.

"Your choice," said von Bern, chuckling. In the blink of an eye, he raised his sword over his head and slashed downward. The air screamed with its passage.

Cassandra's staff barely slowed the weapon's descent. The massive blow sliced through the wood as if it didn't exist. It would have sheared through the Amazon's skull with equal ease if she had remained motionless. But the sword cut only empty space. Moving with superhuman agility, Cassandra was already in the Buick, the door slammed behind her.

"Hit the gas," she commanded, and Simon obeyed.

Cylinders growling, the car tore out of the shopping mall parking lot and into traffic. Behind them, Jack glimpsed von Bern and Charon scrambling into the black limo. The chase was on.

"They won't give up this easy," said Cassandra grimly, echoing Jack's thoughts. "Slide beneath, Simon, and let me take the wheel. Charon drives a lot better than you. Unfortunately, I'm not much competition for him, either. We'll head for the country. Maybe we can outrun them."

Gunning the motor, Cassandra steered the car southwest, onto a seldom traveled country highway. In minutes, they left behind the lights and congestion of the shopping mall. Only the harsh glare of their headlights broke the absolute darkness that threatened to swallow them up.

"Gabblerats," muttered Sylvester, stretching out on the back seat of the car. "Ware gabblerats."

"Sounds like the spell is breaking," declared Simon. "The howling of the Corpse Hounds petrifies any beast that hears it, natural or supernatural. Sylvester will be fine in an hour. Assuming, of course, any of us are alive in an hour."

"Bandits moving up fast on our side," said Cassandra, checking the rear view mirror. "And they don't look friendly."

Jack stared out the back window. There was no mistaking the black limo creeping closer to them. The giant car cut through the night like a shark circling in on its prey. The rear passenger door was wide open. Balancing there, his drawn sword blazing with blue fire, stood Dietrich von Bern. The twin scars on his cheeks glowed blood red in the moonlight.

"The Sword of Chaos," muttered Simon. "It feeds on innocent souls."

"Shades of Michael Moorcock," said Jack. His brow wrinkled with sudden inspiration. "Chaos? Light versus darkness, order versus chaos. That might be it."

"Hang on," advised Cassandra. "I'm putting the pedal to the floor."

The Buick's motor roared. The car surged forward, the acceleration knocking them back into the seats. Cassandra fought with the steering wheel, trying to keep the auto from skidding off the highway. Clinging to an armrest, Jack risked a look at their pursuers. He groaned in frustration.

"No use," he declared. "They're closing the gap. We can't outrun them."

A dozen yards separated the vehicles. Seconds later, it was five. Then, with a burst of power the Buick could not match, the trailing car pulled even. A gap less than six feet wide separated them.

"Now," bellowed Dietrich von Bern, his triumphant face only a few feet from Jack's, "this game comes to a proper end!"

Balanced in the limo's doorway, one foot propped against the window to hold him steady, von Bern swung his huge sword with both hands. Metal shrieked against metal as the Huntsman's blade bit into the reinforced steel roof of the Buick—and through it. Jack cursed in astonishment as the Chaos Sword passed within inches of his nose.

Twisting the steering wheel with all her strength, Cassandra pulled the two cars apart, trying to wrench the sword from von Bern's hands. But, reacting with inhuman speed, the German slid the blade free. It took him only a second to regain his balance. Laughing insanely, he raised the Chaos Sword over his head for a second attack.

"There's no escape," cried Cassandra. "If he can't reach you, he'll change tactics and kill me instead. I can't steer and avoid his sword. We're finished."

"Maybe not," said Jack, reaching into his coat pocket and grabbing his bag of insurance. "Roll down all the windows."

Unquestioning, Cassandra used the master control to do as she was told. Surprised, von Bern hesitated. "It's too late to plead for your miserable life, worm," he snarled.

"Don't hold your breath waiting," answered Jack. He wasn't concerned with the German.

Through the limo's open door, Jack could see the back of the driver's head. "Charon," he called, emptying the contents of the pouch into one hand. Jack held out a handful of silver coins. "*Oboluses.*"

The ancient Greek ferryman's head jerked around sharply, his red eyes flaring. Reacting to his motion, the limo swerved closer to the Buick. Startled, von Bern tumbled back into his car, the door slamming shut after him.

"Oboluses," repeated Jack, and with a laugh, tossed them over his shoulders and out the opposite window. The coins hit the pavement and disappeared into the night.

Tires screamed and rubber burned as the Greek jammed on the huge limo's brakes. Swerving back and forth across the highway, it skidded hundreds of yards before coming to a full stop. In seconds, darkness swallowed the car as if it never existed. The Huntsman's shrieks of rage followed them a moment longer, then they too were gone.

"I think you can slow up," said Jack. "By the time Charon finds those coins, it will be daylight."

"Oboluses?" asked Simon.

"I bought them from the numismatist in the Loop after our first encounter with von Bern. From your description of Charon's personality, I suspected he couldn't resist their lure."

"In my time," said Cassandra, "the dead paid the ferryman a silver obolus for passage across the Styx."

"Four thousand years later," said Jack, "he remained true to his nature. Luckily for us."

He glanced at the speedometer. They were cruising along at nearly seventy miles an hour. In the blackness, it felt like a hundred.

"The danger's past," he said to the Amazon. "There's no reason to drive this fast."

Cassandra shrugged, looking embarrassed. "It's not my doing. The brakes refuse to work, and the car won't slow down."

She raised her hands off the steering wheel. It remained fixed. "I'm no longer in control. The automobile is following someone else's commands. Until we arrive wherever it's taking us, we're stuck inside. Unless you feel like jumping."

"No, thanks," said Jack, watching the scenery fly by. This latest turn of events left him unmoved. He was starting to expect the unexpected. "I'm willing to wait for the car to run out of gas."

Folding his elbows behind his head, he stretched out on the back seat. "Besides, long car rides make me sleepy. I want to confer with Megan Ambrose about an idea that occurred to me during our fight with von Bern."

Yawning, he shut his eyes. "Wake me when we arrive," he declared and drifted off to sleep.

31

Jack peered through heavy eyes at Simon. "How long was I asleep?"

"Two hours," said the changeling. "We drove through half of Illinois before we arrived here. Wherever here is."

Jack squeezed his eyes shut, then opened them, trying to force the grogginess out of his system. Yawning, he turned his head and stared out the window. It was difficult in the moonlight to make out their surroundings. They appeared to be in the parking lot of an old service station. Not far from where they were stopped was a solitary gas pump. A sign over the front door of the office ten yards distant proclaimed that this was "Fritz's Fast Service."

"No idea where we are, huh?" he mumbled.

"Not a clue," said Simon. "The Buick pulled off the road and stopped moving fifteen minutes ago. We thought it best to stay inside the car. Nobody's shown themselves yet. The place appears deserted. You learn anything important from Megan?"

Jack shook his head glumly. "I couldn't contact her. Not a nibble the whole time I was asleep. Hazel's spell enabled me to remember my entire nap, but none of it involved Megan. Instead, I had this terrible nightmare about some gigantic shapeless monster chasing me."

He paused. "The words 'Great Beast' mean anything to you? April thought they might. She said something about sensing one in the neighborhood."

Simon turned brilliant green. His hair stood on end and his eyes burned bright red. Jack groaned and covered his eyes with his hands. "I wish you wouldn't do that. I gather these Great Beasts are bad news?"

"Remember what I told you about the Old Ones—the ancient Gods that disappeared as mankind disbelieved them out of existence." As he spoke, the changeling's features slowly returned to normal. "Well, not all of humanity's early gods looked like men. A goodly number of them were monsters. Primitive man worshiped the dragons that swallowed the sun, the serpent whose body encircled the earth, and many many others. They had frightful names like Tiamat and Fenris and Azreal.

"With the advent of monotheism, most of those Great Beasts disappeared into limbo. But an equal number of them became part of Christian tradition. Revelations had a great red dragon and a seven-headed monster. There were dozens of others scattered throughout the Old and New Testaments. These monsters, incredibly powerful, monstrously evil, haunted the outermost darkness. They were never disbelieved into nothingness.

"Happily, most of them are as stupid as they are strong. No one imagined them being intelligent. Even when summoned to the Earth, they cannot act without direction. That's the good news. The bad news is that if April sensed one of the Great Beasts in the vicinity, Dietrich von Bern must be controlling it. And that's very bad news."

"Another brick in the wall," said Jack stoically.

Leaning forward, he tapped Cassandra on the shoulder. "I'm tired of sitting and waiting for our mysterious host to arrive. I think it's time for us to find him."

"I agree," said Cassandra, opening the car door and stepping outside. "Patience is not one of my virtues."

Jack, Simon and Sylvester joined her. Seen in the moonlight, the dilapidated old service station didn't appear very threatening. By now, Jack knew that appearances could be deceiving. The office building and accompanying garage were completely dark. There were no lights anywhere.

Sylvester, quiet as a mouse since recovering from his paralysis, raised his head into the night air and sniffed deeply. "I should have guessed," said the familiar. "Dwarf."

Cassandra turned to the Buick and ran a hand along the gash in the roof made by the Huntsman's sword. She nodded slightly, as if mentally answering a question.

"The Little Men take great pride in their work," said the Amazon. "When they do a job, they do it right. Perhaps our vehicle carries a lifetime warranty."

"My thoughts exactly," said Sylvester. The cat paused for a second to lick its paws. "After sustaining major damage, the Buick was compelled to return here for repairs."

"Hold on," said Jack. "We're talking about a car, not somebody's pet. This isn't Lassie. It's a hunk of metal."

"In Norse legends didn't Thor's hammer, Mjolnir, return to his hand after he threw it?" asked Cassandra. "And in those swords-and-sorcery novels you enjoy so much, what about Elric's sword, Stormbringer? I recall it flying back to him more than once."

She laughed at Jack's astonished expression. "You're not the only one who reads that stuff, Jack. Lots of supernaturals keep up with the fantasy field. It's quite entertaining."

Cassandra winked. "I've even heard a few of us write it."

Before Jack could ask who in particular, Simon interrupted. "Quiet down. I think I hear someone coming."

By now, Jack's vision had adjusted to the moonlight. His eyes widened when he saw the figure pacing towards them. Walking in slow, measured steps, swaying from side to side, the being was as broad as he was tall. Five feet high and five feet wide, he resembled a gorilla with short stumpy legs, huge arms that dangled almost to the ground, and a thick bullet head perched directly on his immense shoulders without benefit of a neck. But no gorilla in the world wore a bushy black beard and long curled mustache. Nor did any ape hum the tune to the Don McLean song "American Pie" as he walked.

The dwarf, for he could be nothing else, stopped short when he spotted the four of them clustered by the Buick. He was dressed in a loose-fitting brown uniform with the namepatch "Fritz" sewn over one pocket.

"A greasemonkey," Simon whispered to Jack. Seeing his friend's confused expression, the changeling hurried to explain. "When the dwarfs came to this country, most of them drifted into the automotive repair field. They have a strange bond with cars.

Notice the grease stains on his hands and face. That's how they gained the nickname."

"We're closed," the dwarf announced in a surprisingly mild voice. Jack had expected a tone deeper than a coal mine. "There's a 24-hour service station two miles down the road."

"We passed it on the trip here," said Cassandra pleasantly. "Our car refused to stop. It was determined to return to this particular location. A matter of a guarantee, I suspect."

"Hmm," said the dwarf and stepped closer. He stared at each of them for a second. "Three of the fey folk and a mortal?"

He focused on Jack's face, then shook his head as if amazed. "And him wearing rose-colored contact lenses. An odd grouping, I should think. Not that it's any of my business."

Reaching out, he touched the Buick's hood. His grease-stained fingers, the size of small sausages, gently caressed the metal. "My work, of course. Three summers ago, I rebuilt this car from scratch. The owner, an old schoolteacher who lived down the road, wanted a warranty in writing. I gave her a lifetime one covering all major repairs."

His gaze traveled across the auto until it rested on the huge rent in the roof. "That definitely qualifies," he declared, frowning so hard that his bushy black eyebrows almost covered his eyes.

"A college prank with buzzsaws?" he ventured.

"Try the Chaos Sword wielded by Dietrich von Bern," replied Jack. "What happened to the schoolteacher?"

"I heard she died," said the dwarf. "Never gave much thought again to the car. Glad it wasn't junked for scrap. I put a lot of work into the old wreck. You did say Dietrich von Bern?"

"Right," said Jack, catching the note of distaste in the dwarf's voice. "Also called the Master of the Gabble Ratchets, the Lord of the Wild Hunt, and assorted other less honorable titles. You know him?"

The dwarf spat on the ground. "I am Fritz Grondark, of the family Grondark, of the Olden Folk who mankind calls dwarfs. Two hundred years ago, Dietrich von Bern approached my people about a special sword he wanted forged. Strictly neutral in the war between good and evil, we accepted his commission on the condition that the weapon be used only in battle. The Olden Folk wanted, even indirectly, no innocent blood on their hands. Von Bern readily agreed to our terms. We should have known better."

"The Huntsman didn't keep his end of the bargain," said Cassandra, a knowing expression on her face.

"Aye," growled the dwarf. "The German betrayed us. He bathed the steel in the blood of the weak and the poor, the sick and the lame, the young and the defenseless. 'The Sword of Chaos,' men named the blade. And cursed the fools who made it."

Face twisted with anger, the dwarf gnashed together square yellow teeth. "Worse yet, the Huntsman never paid his bill. He was not only a liar, but a cheat!"

"Dwarfs are notoriously sensitive about debts," whispered Simon in Jack's ear. "Grondark could prove a useful addition to our party."

"My thoughts exactly," muttered Jack to the changeling.

The dwarf ran his thick fingers over the cut metal. "I can taste the blade's poison sinking into the steel," he declared, grimacing. "This wound requires immediate attention."

He stroked the Buick on the side, like a man petting a dog. "To the garage with you," he said, his voice gentle and caring. "Fritz Grondark honors his promises."

The Buick's engine coughed to life. Headlights flicked on. Gears shifted into drive. The emergency brake popped. Slowly but steadily, the unmanned auto drove off towards the rear of the old service station.

"Nothing to worry about," said Grondark. "It remembers where to go. My repair bays are in the back of the garage."

The dwarf squinted at Jack. "I gather you're the leader of this party. What's your quarrel with the Huntsman?"

"It's a long story," said Jack. "One that might interest you if you're willing to listen. There's a chance for money to be made. Maybe even offer a bold dwarf the possibility to collect on a long outstanding bill."

Grondark smiled. "When money talks, dwarfs listen. Come with me to my workshop. We can wet our whistles with some cold beer. And discuss these matters further."

32

They spent the rest of the night and most of the next morning at Fritz Grondark's garage. Cassandra, Simon and Sylvester slept, having skipped resting for long hours, while Jack remained awake and watched the dwarf work on the Buick. Much of that time, Jack related his adventures over the past few days.

The greasemonkey listened attentively, interrupting frequently to clarify specific points. The mention of the Universal Charge Card brought a gleam to his eye. He grunted in disgust at the Huntsman's treachery at the mathematics building. Cassandra's battle with the trolls had him grinning. Dwarfs and trolls, Jack discovered, were mortal enemies. But, more than anything else, the dwarf was fascinated by Jack's musings on the symbolism of cold iron.

"Of all the fey folk, only my people mined and forged cold iron," declared the dwarf as he pounded the Buick's roof with an immense hammer. "As neutrals in the eternal war between good and evil, we were not affected by the power of the star metal. Thus, given to us was the task of creating the great swords of power."

The dwarf smiled as if recalling far-off days. "In our great caverns beneath the mountains, my brothers and I wrought the steel and etched the runes, bringing life to those blades. Even their names were magic—Durandel, Joyeuse, Excalibur. Those were exciting times, Jack Collins, exciting times."

"I understand," said Jack, captivated by Grondark's tale. "But what is the real secret of steel, of cold iron? Swords made from it killed dragons," continued Jack, trying to find an answer. "Peasant folk hung iron horseshoes over their doors to keep out demons. In Roman days, iron coffin nails provided protection against evil spirits. Magicians often used circles of magnetized iron to imprison ghosts. Yet, in modern times, Dietrich von Bern wields a steel sword. And the Border Redcaps use guns loaded with steel-jacketed slugs. What happened?"

"Perhaps," offered Grondark, smoothing out the steel, "it became too common? In ancient times, only the mightiest warriors carried weapons of iron. Oftentimes, charms contained bits of iron, not gold."

"Too common," repeated Jack, his mind whirling. His thoughts from earlier in the evening came rushing back. "Good versus evil, order versus chaos. Symbols and specifics."

"What are you muttering?" asked Grondark.

"You mentioned the great swords of power," said Jack, leaping from one idea to another. "Why were all the famous weapons swords? Why not spears? Or axes?"

"There were a few of those," said Grondark, frowning, "but not many. Magic swords were always the weapon of choice. Heroes preferred them two or three to one over other killing devices. They loved their swords. Oftentimes, the damned fools insisted on being buried with them. As if grave robbers wouldn't dig them up a week later for the booty. At least Roland tried to destroy Durandel. Not that it did him much good. We built swords to last."

Like all the supernaturals, Grondark exhibited a tendency to rattle on if given the chance. Ordinarily, Jack would have found his meanderings fascinating, but not at the moment.

"Why swords?" Jack asked again, trying to steer the dwarf back in the right direction.

"They combine fire and iron," declared Grondark dramatically. "Swords are forged. They are fire and iron, united. A strong blade is the marriage between the two greatest forces of order."

Seeing the sudden look of comprehension on Jack's face, he asked, "Is that the secret, Jack Collins?"

"*Yes*," said Jack, the truth bursting within him. "Yes, that is the secret, Grondark."

"Then would you please explain it to me," said the dwarf, "because I have no idea what you are talking about."

"The important word is order," said Jack, slipping into his teaching mode. "Most superstitions are grounded in a fear of the unknown, of chaos. Primitive man was frightened by many things he did not understand, so he personified them—gave them form and substance. Which is how the first supernatural beings came into existence. They were creatures of the fear, the disorder, that surrounded and threatened early mankind.

"Then came the first major step in human progress. The taming of fire. Using it, man was no longer afraid of the dark. The night was still threatening, but it was not overwhelming. Fire was symbolic of the triumph of order over chaos, civilization over anarchy."

"What about cold iron?" asked the dwarf.

"Order over disorder, law over chaos," declared Jack. "That's the symbolism I was searching for. The conquest of fire led to the mastery of metal. Again, mankind used cold iron, used steel to transform society from the chaotic to the orderly. Iron weapons, iron horseshoes, iron nails brought order to the world. It drove out chaos.

"By definition, most supernatural beings, especially those of evil, were creations of chaos. Even the faeries, like Simon and his relatives, were considered mischief makers, trouble bringers. They were symbolic of disorder. That was why iron hurt them as well as the dragons, the monsters, the bogies. Order triumphed over chaos. That's the key."

"The key to what?" asked Cassandra, wandering into the garage, rubbing sleep from her eyes. "What's got you so excited, Jack?"

Swiftly, Jack outlined his theory to the Amazon. She remained silent until he finished.

"Not bad," she said. "But, if that's the case, why doesn't cold iron hurt Dietrich von Bern still? He's definitely a creature of chaos. As are the Border Redcaps."

"Because iron ceased to be symbolic of order a long time ago," said Jack. "The same applies to fire. Once, they both worked as forces of good in the world. Fire destroyed the worst evils; iron weapons killed terrible monsters. But Fritz hit the nail on the head when he said they became too common. Iron and steel were used not only for good, but for evil. Innocents as well as villains were burned to death by fire. Good people as well as bad were put to the sword. Each crime, each outrage, lessened their powers. Humanity no longer thought of cold iron being used only for righteous deeds. Once mankind realized that steel was neither good nor evil, but merely an extension of the user's desires, it lost all power as a symbol."

Jack shrugged his shoulders. "Guns don't kill people, as we've been told again and again. People kill people. Cold iron doesn't defeat evil because it no longer is symbolic of the triumph of order over chaos. In modern times, cold iron serves both law and chaos."

"Then nothing can defeat the Wild Huntsman," said Cassandra, her face ashen. "Nothing in this modern world is symbolic of the supremacy of order over chaos."

Jack smiled. He felt almost lightheaded, as revelation after revelation filled his consciousness. Unexplained mysteries suddenly made perfect sense.

"That's not true," he said cheerfully. "There are lots of things that fill the bill these days. We're surrounded by things that bring order to a chaotic universe. You merely have to change the way you're thinking. Von Bern is powerful and he has powerful allies. But I have a few surprises for our German friend."

Jack laughed out loud. "Everything fits together like a jigsaw puzzle. Order versus chaos. The Wild Huntsman has a Sword of Chaos, a Great Beast, and the Border Redcaps. That's a pretty awesome force. But we have logic on our side."

Jack was glowing with energy. "And, let me tell you, in the entire universe, nothing is more powerful than logic. Nothing at all."

33

"Y ou want to go *where*?" asked Simon, late that afternoon.

"Back to campus," said Jack. "Tonight."

"That's what I thought you said," declared the changeling. "At least, now I know I'm not going crazy. You are."

Jack laughed. He and his friends sat clustered around Witch Hazel's tiny kitchen table. The addition of Fritz Grondark made conditions even more crowded than before. But, somehow they all fit in the front room of the mobile home.

"I'm tired of being chased, Simon," said Jack. "Ever since Merlin and Megan were kidnaped, I've been on the run. Von Bern and the Border Redcaps have kept me off balance so I can't interfere with their devilish scheme. Well, the time has come to stop running and start fighting."

"That's my type of talk," said Cassandra.

Fritz Grondark grunted in agreement. The dwarf, who had followed them back to the trailer camp in a massive tow truck, carried an immense monkey wrench hooked to his belt. Fritz made no secret of the fact he intended to use it on the skulls of any Border Redcaps, distant relatives of trolls, he encountered.

"The other day," Jack continued, "Hazel remarked that perhaps science and sorcery are actually the same but we're just too ignorant to realize it. There's a great deal of truth in what she said. I know how to defeat Von Bern and the Border Redcaps. But the equipment I need is at the college."

"Can't we buy the stuff?" asked Simon. "Or build it?"

"If we had the time," replied Jack. "But we don't. Tomorrow evening is Beltane. Trust me, Simon, raiding the college laboratories is our only chance to obtain the proper tools."

"For what?" asked Hazel. "You still haven't told us what weapons you intend to use against the Huntsman."

"Light defeats darkness," said Jack, smiling. "Order defeats chaos."

"Water washes mud," said Simon. "Which is about as clear as you've been lately. What does it matter, anyway? We still don't know where to find the German and his prisoners."

"Oh," said Jack. "I forgot to tell you. Right before von Bern attacked us on the highway, I figured out where he's holding the women captive."

For a moment, no one said anything. Then, the trailer rocked with the collective shout, "WHAT?!"

"Sorry," said Jack. Actually, he wasn't the least bit ashamed. After all the half-told stories, hints, and unexplained remarks made by the supernaturals, it felt pretty good to catch them completely by surprise.

"Once I combined all the clues, the location was obvious. January told us that the Huntsman bragged that his prisoners were beneath the feet of the police. That implied an underground hideaway. Megan mentioned a huge chamber, so I knew it couldn't be the basement of a warehouse. All of the kidnappings took place in the Loop and nowhere else, so it seemed logical to assume there was a reason for that. It was then that I remembered that when Merlin was kidnaped, no one saw his captors leave the building. Combining the two facts, it was obvious that they hadn't."

"Huh" said Simon. "Where did they go, then? Underneath?"

"Exactly," said Jack. "The Border Redcaps carried Megan and her father to the basement of the tower and then below it. As they did with all the women they captured."

He drew in a deep breath. "I phoned the main library information center an hour ago and had them do a quick search for me. Each and every one of the Loop buildings where a disappearance took place was once connected to the old underground tunnel transportation network beneath the Loop. That's where von Bern's hideout is located."

"The same tunnels that flooded a few years back?" said Hazel. "The ones used in the 1920's to bring goods into the Loop from the railroad yards?"

"That's them," said Jack. "The tunnels are all but forgotten now, but at the turn of the century they were considered an engineering marvel. The dirt excavated in their construction was used as landfill on Lake Michigan and became the site of the Field Museum."

"Excuse me," said Cassandra, "but I'm lost. I've only lived in Chicago for a few years. You're not talking about subway tunnels?"

"Those were constructed years later," said Jack. "These tunnels preceded them by decades. They were narrow passageways, just wide enough for a railway handcar. Barely lit, they were not intended for commuters but for commercial goods."

Jack paused, putting his thoughts in order. "At the end of the 19th century, traffic in the Loop was so bad that merchants were having difficulty getting their goods from the railroad yards on the south side into downtown. The abundance of wagons, carriages and trolley cars on the streets made deliveries nearly impossible. Goods could only be transported late at night, which made most store owners quite unhappy. That all changed when a system of underground tunnels were built, linking the railroad yards with the Loop.

"Goods were unloaded from the incoming freight trains, transferred to handcars, and then sent from the train station to a central receiving depot deep beneath the central commuter railroad station downtown. There, the products were sorted and forwarded to their final destinations, again by handcar, through branch tunnels that snaked all through the Loop. Nearly a hundred different buildings were serviced by this unique underground delivery service. Each stop had its own receiving dock, located in the subbasement of the structure.

"The network even ducked beneath the Chicago River and supplied stores on the near north side as well. It stayed in service until the early 1930's, when shipping by trucks replaced most railroad deliveries."

"The tunnels were closed and abandoned," said Hazel. "The owners shut off the power, but otherwise left the system intact and undisturbed. During World War Two, I recall talk of opening them up and using them for POW camps. What a crazy idea. Later, in the 1960's, an alderman proposed they be converted into giant bomb shelters. Happily, no one took him seriously."

"A few years ago," said Jack, "as a result of a series of bureaucratic blunders centering around bridge repairs, a hole was punched in the top of the tunnel passing beneath the river. Water rushed into the system and flooded the basements of half the buildings in the Loop. It knocked out electricity throughout the near north side. The accident nearly shut down the entire city, and things didn't return to normal for weeks. Among other problems, the flood forced the closing of the subway."

"That I remember," said Cassandra. "I thought they plugged up the system with cement."

"Not really," said Jack. "The city engineers closed off the section beneath the river, but the rest of the network remains open. And von Bern and his captives are down there."

"Any idea where?"

"Megan mentioned a huge chamber. The only place that fits that description is the old central shipping depot. According to the city librarians, the center resembles a gigantic amphitheater a hundred feet beneath the streets. Doesn't that sound like the perfect arena for conducting a blood sacrifice to an ancient God?"

"I'm convinced," said Cassandra. "How do we stop it?"

"Tonight we raid the campus and get the necessary equipment for my secret weapon," said Jack. "It's all stuff available only in laboratories. Tomorrow, we go shopping. There's a bunch of things I want to buy for additional protection.

"After that, we head underground. The sacrifice is scheduled for May Day Eve. We'll attack during the daytime, when the forces of darkness are at their weakest. Still, I suspect von Bern and his Border Redcaps are expecting us to show up. They'll be ready and waiting no matter when we arrive. But this time, we're going to be the ones with a few surprises."

34

They arrived on campus shortly after midnight. Cassandra drove, with Jack in the other front seat and Simon and Fritz Grondark in the back. Dark clouds hid the moon and stars, shrouding the laboratories in blackness.

"You two know exactly what I want?" Jack asked Simon for the tenth time.

While he trusted his allies, there was no time left for mistakes. After the affair at the math building, he suspected Benny Anderson had tightened campus security. Stealing what they needed might prove to be difficult. There definitely wouldn't be a second chance.

"Nothing to worry about," said the changeling. "We're looking for the battery pack belts used in the film classes run by the photography department. The type that the TV news stations power their minicams with. I never used one, but some of the girls I dated produced their own films for class, so I'm real familiar with the belts.

"It shouldn't take us too long to find them in the photo lab. They keep the expensive equipment locked up but Fritz assures me that he can open anything."

The dwarf flexed his huge fingers. "One way or another, we'll manage the task."

"Try not to cause too much destruction," said Jack. "Dealing drugs on campus is old news. Nobody cares much. Stealing college property gets you in trouble with the Dean's office. That's a black mark on your transcript you can't erase. Someday, I still plan to obtain my degree."

"Stealth is my middle name," proclaimed Simon. "Where are you heading?"

"Cassandra is going to park the car by the chemistry building," answered Jack. "Then the two of us will visit the labs upstairs. I'm pretty sure they have what I need in one of them."

"Which is?" asked Simon.

"Order to fight chaos," said Jack, smiling. "Light to battle the darkness. You'll find out soon enough."

Simon and Fritz, resembling a very odd Mutt and Jeff, departed a few minutes later. Neither of them carried a weapon, though Fritz's monkey wrench dangled from his belt. The dwarf, who had trouble entering doorways unless he turned sideways, didn't need anything else. Though Fritz refused to brag about his fighting prowess, Cassandra respected Grondark's skills, which was testimony enough for Jack. Once Simon and Fritz obtained the battery belt pack, they planned to rendezvous with Jack and Cassandra in the chemistry building parking lot in forty minutes.

Watching the pair amble down the path to the photography department, Jack murmured a silent prayer. Simon meant well, but his mischievous nature played havoc with the best-laid plans. Tonight, they couldn't afford any mistakes. The fate of civilization rested on their shoulders. Jack's back ached from the weight.

A padlock on the front door of the chemistry building made it quite clear that security on campus had been tightened. After checking carefully for wires indicating alarm systems and finding none, Cassandra casually snapped the lock with her new staff. Von Bern had cut one walking stick to kindling, but the Amazon had a half-dozen replacements in reserve.

"There's no way of protecting a building this size," she said to Jack, walking into the main hall, "without using trenches, barbed wire and extensive electronic surveillance equipment. And, even then, a trained, determined professional can, in most cases, infiltrate and compromise any location."

Smiling, Jack nodded his head. It required no guesswork to substitute Cassandra's name for that of a trained, determined professional. Over the course of history, he suspected the Amazon had experienced enough adventures to fill an encyclopedia.

With four chemistry labs on the second floor, they decided to split up to save time. Jack described in great detail to Cassandra the objects they were hunting. After agreeing to meet in the center in twenty minutes, they started searching.

Jack found the device five minutes after he walked into the first lab. He also discovered trouble. Benny Anderson, armed with a police special, was hiding in the shadows of the room, watching and waiting for Jack to make a wrong move. Picking up lab equipment obviously met that requirement. Seconds after Jack pulled the long tube off a storage shelf, the security chief stood up, making his presence known simply and effectively.

"Freeze, drug-scum," he announced, his voice a harsh whisper. Though the lawman's body trembled with emotion, his gun hand never wavered. It remained fixed in a direct line with Jack's crotch. "Make one false move and I'll blow off your balls."

Jack froze, the black rectangular tube clutched close to his chest. "Take it easy, chief," he said loudly, hoping Cassandra was within the sound of his voice. "I'm unarmed. And this isn't as bad as it looks."

"Sure," said Anderson, motioning with the gun for Jack to lower his prize to the shelf. "First it was selling drugs. Now you're stealing school property."

The chief's voice rang with contempt. "Your kind make me sick, Collins. Always whining how unfairly you've been treated. Damned pampered rich kids don't know how tough life really is. Try earning a living the hard way—honestly. Then tell me stealing isn't as bad as it looks."

"I'm neither pampered nor rich," began Jack, then closed his mouth, realizing he was wasting his time. No matter what he said, the chief wouldn't believe him. Anderson had made up his mind and there was no way Jack could convince him otherwise.

"I figured you probably used the chem lab to brew up those artificial narcotics so popular with the rich suburban punks," said Anderson, sneering. Pulling a pair of handcuffs from his pocket, he stepped closer to Jack, the gun steady as a rock in his grip. "So, I personally staked out this building ever since you disappeared. Sooner or later, I knew you would show up again."

"The criminal always returns to the scene of the crime," said Jack. "That's nuts."

"Sure it is," said Anderson. "But look who's here. Put your hands out in front of you, Collins. Real slow, now."

"Don't bother, Jack," said Cassandra from the front door of the lab. The Amazon moved so quietly that she had approached completely undetected. Her staff lashed out like a snake, its silver tip kissing Anderson's hand. Bones cracked like peanut brittle. The security chief yelped in pain and dropped his gun. But he refused to give up.

Lurching forward, Anderson slammed his body into Jack's. Together they tumbled against a lab table. Not bright, but tough, the security man knew exactly what he was doing. A raised knee caught Jack in the groin, bringing tears to his eyes. Shielding his broken hand with his body, Anderson whipped his other arm around Jack's neck. Straightening, he wrenched Jack upright, so that the two of them stood facing Cassandra.

"Do anything stupid, sister," said Anderson, "and I'll break your boyfriend's neck."

Jack gasped for air, feeling lightheaded. He wished the security chief hadn't used the term "boyfriend" with the Amazon.

Cassandra, her walking stick aimed like a spear at the security chief's head, hesitated. "Let him go," she finally declared, "before you make me *really* mad."

Anderson laughed. "I'm shaking." With a snarl of rage, he tightened his grip around Jack's neck. "His windpipe can't stand much more pressure. One more twist and your druggie friend is in the obituary column. Time for you to drop the stick. Now!"

Her eyes burning with anger, Cassandra lowered her staff to the floor. For a second, Jack suspected she planned to launch the stick like a spear at Anderson. Evidently, the same thought occurred to the security chief. Carefully, he shifted his position so that Jack's body completely shielded him from the Amazon. Raising her empty hands to indicate her compliance, Cassandra backed away from the wood staff.

"Smart girl," said Anderson. Grunting with effort, he slowly started to shuffle to the door of the lab, dragging Jack along with him. "Stay right where I can see you. Benny Anderson knows all the tricks in the book, and then some. Twitch funny and Collins's neck goes snap."

They were less than five feet from the exit when an unexpected figure filled the doorway.

"What is the meaning of this disgraceful conduct, Mr. Anderson?" declared Darrell Quiggly, Dean of Students. A tall, thin man, with iron-gray hair and distinguished features, Quiggly filled many roles on campus, including that of Anderson's boss. "Release that young man at once."

"But, Dean . . ." began Anderson, swinging around to confront the official. "This is that drug . . ."

"No excuses, Anderson," interrupted Quiggly, his voice raised in anger. "I said release him. Violence against students is strictly forbidden, no matter what the reason. Immediately, if you value your job at this university."

The Dean's appearance and the confusion he caused was all the diversion Cassandra needed. Jack sensed rather than saw her grab her walking stick, position it correctly, and thunk the security chief across the head in the span of mere seconds. Silently, Anderson released his grip around Jack's throat and collapsed to the floor unconscious.

Swallowing and rubbing his neck, Jack stared at the Dean, waiting for Quiggly's reaction. Surprisingly, a broad grin crossed the school official's face.

"Fooled you too," he chuckled, his features already twisting like Silly Putty. "Damn, I'm good."

"Simon," said Jack, barely able to speak. "You're the best."

"Lucky we found those battery packs as soon as we entered the photo department," said the changeling. "I sent Fritz to the car with them and came to lend a hand here. Anderson's ranting and raving cued me in on what was happening and I reacted accordingly."

Gingerly, Jack touched the unmoving security guard with his foot. "What do we do with Benny?"

"Leave him there," said Cassandra, with a shrug. "The tap I administered should be good for an hour or more. That's plenty of time for us to disappear. Considering your reputation already, a few broken bones and stolen equipment won't change anything."

"It might add a few more years to your sentence," declared Simon. "Assuming your case ever makes it to trial. I figure fifty years to life at the moment."

"Maybe longer," said Jack, grinning. "We better save Merlin, because there's no way in hell I can salvage my reputation on my own anymore."

Stepping over Anderson's body, he walked over to the storage

shelves. Carefully, he lifted the long black rectangular tube from
where he had placed it only minutes before.

"See if you can find another one of these," he said to his
companions. "The one thing I've learned from reading hundreds
of fantasy novels is that it never hurts to have a spare super-
weapon when dealing with the forces of darkness."

∞

35

Roger hated animals. He considered them dirty, stupid, and useless creations, placed on Earth for one purpose and one purpose alone—to serve as food for people like him. Not surprisingly, he had never visited the municipal zoo. If asked to list a hundred places in the city he wanted to visit, the zoo undoubtedly would be number one hundred, following even hospital emergency rooms at midnight, unsupervised kindergarten classes, and hare krishna festivals. Yet, despite his inner revulsion for the surroundings, he found his trip to the zoo on May first strangely fascinating.

His "uncle," as he named The Crouching One for those few mortals who encountered the demigod, had insisted on the excursion. Ever since learning of the existence of the zoo from a newspaper article a week before, the Lord of the Lions had pressed Roger to schedule an afternoon sojourn at the wild-life preserve. It seemed singularly appropriate that they visit the park on what was scheduled to be the day of the ancient god's greatest triumph. Or, as Roger secretly hoped, his greatest failure.

Dressed in a bright yellow shirt adorned with red flowers, loose-fitting slacks, and sandals, the Crouching One appeared a typical senior citizen out for a day of sun and relaxation. Dark sunglasses kept hidden its blazing eyes. It walked slowly and carefully, avoiding human contact as much as possible, and remained surprisingly polite considering its godlike pride. Even Roger, expecting a disaster of near biblical proportions, was impressed by the Lord of the Lions's demeanor.

They spent most of the day at the lion enclosure. A warm spring sun had lured the beasts outside, and they rested on the rocky perches and grassy knolls of their huge compound. The zoo tried to duplicate their animals' original habitats as closely as possible, and the lions appeared quite comfortable in their savannalike surroundings. A high concrete wall and wide trench separated them from the idle and the curious.

The Crouching One stared at the huge beasts with a single-minded concentration that after a few minutes Roger found disturbing. Though he knew the origins of the demigod's title, the Lord of the Lions, for the first time he realized exactly how true was that name. The shape and form of the Crouching One's skull uncannily resembled that of a jungle cat. Even the way the demigod stood unmoving, as if ready to pounce, approximated that of the huge beasts.

"Talking to them?" asked Roger, only half in jest as he noticed the Couching One's lips mouthing words without sounds.

"Of course," replied the ancient God, turning its head for a second to stare at Roger. Even the dark glasses could not hide completely the glow of its eyes. "Though men worshiped me, these here," and it gestured with gnarled fingers at the lions, "are my children."

The Crouching One returned its attention to the beasts. "These few are much different than the great killers of my time. Instead of hunting, they are content to be fed. They are lazy, preferring to spend their time resting in the sunshine instead of searching for prey. Civilization has ruined them, made them weak."

The Lord of the Lions smiled its unpleasant smile, the smile that twisted its face into a shape not the least bit reflecting humanity. "All of that shall change shortly. When my rightful powers return, I will shatter their cages. And the hunting cry of my children will once again echo through the land."

Not wanting to irritate the demigod, Roger decided not to mention that these days, half the citizens in California owned enough legal and illegal firepower to stop a herd of rampaging elephants, much less a pride of old and near toothless lions. There were certain truths about modern civilization that the Crouching One was not yet ready to accept.

Roger looked down at his watch. "Only a few more hours till sunset in Chicago. According to the last call from von Bern, everything is running on schedule."

"As I predicted," said the Crouching One. "Exactly as I predicted."

"Maybe," said Roger, treading on dangerous territory. "Still, the German never caught Jack Collins or his friends. The computer news service from Chicago reported a robbery last night at Collins's college. The security chief's account of the affair was pretty garbled, but it sounded like our enemy. And he took some pretty fancy scientific equipment."

"Bah," said the Crouching One, and it flicked one hand in an angry gesture of dismissal. On the other side of the moat, several of the lions growled loudly. "I refuse to let this mortal worry me any longer. He is a thinker, not a fighter. His allies are few and relatively powerless. They are helpless against the Huntsman and his Border Redcaps. That they have avoided death is a tribute more to their luck than any special skills.

"Tonight, if they dare try to stop the sacrifice, they will have to confront von Bern in his den. The German has recruited nearly a hundred more Redcaps to his banner. What can a handful of do-gooders manage against von Bern and his legions? Science is no match for sorcery. And, do not forget the presence of the Great Beast. Mr. Collins has been a persistent nuisance, but after tonight, he will be a dead nuisance."

"I hope you're right," said Roger, not hoping that at all.

Unlike the Crouching One, he possessed a healthy respect for the miracles of modern technology. After all, it was his own scientific expertise that had gotten him in this mess. From what the wire service reported, Collins only stole a few items from the laboratories. Evidently, the mathematics student had some very specific ideas how to deal with von Bern. Without thinking, he spoke aloud the question that had troubled him for weeks. "Why him? What makes him so special?"

"Nothing," declared the Crouching One, with a sneer. But there was a bare trace of doubt in its voice. "The magician you named

Merlin made a mistake. This pesky student is not the champion I feared."

Behind them, the lions roared in approval of their patron's words. Roger kept silent. He felt sure Merlin had not erred; that Jack Collins was the right choice. But he had no idea why.

36

"What do you mean, I'm not going?" demanded Simon angrily. The changeling's face was a brilliant shade of purple, and he appeared ready to explode. "Why not?"

"I just finished explaining that, Simon," said Jack apologetically.

He had put off this confrontation as long as possible, but now he had run out of time and destinations. It was time for the final confrontation between good and evil, between Jack and his friends and Dietrich von Bern and the forces of darkness. But Simon could not participate.

"Though you're oriented towards the light, you are still partially a creation of chaos," said Jack. "All faeries are. It's the mischievous, trickster part of you. There's no changing that. As you've said many times, it's built into your basic character. You can't alter it. And, like it or not, that's the reason you can't come with us."

"You mean you don't trust me?" asked Simon, the purple changing to blue. "Just because I'm chaos-born."

"Of course not," said Jack, feeling exasperated. Arguing logic with supernaturals was like trying to build sand castles with a thimble. It was possible, but barely so. "Trust has nothing to do with it.

"I selected my weapons very carefully. I dared not use anything that might harm Megan or her father. Everything in the backpacks I've prepared should cause maximum damage against the servants of the dark, the followers of chaos. But, that's the problem. There's no way I can protect you from their effect. If you accompany us into the tunnels, the inventions I use to destroy the Border Redcaps will have the same effect on you."

Jack put a hand on his friend's shoulder. "I value you too much, Simon, to be the one who murders you." He grinned, breaking the solemnity of the moment. "Even if sometimes you deserve it."

"All right," grumbled the changeling, resuming his normal shading. Several people in the Field Museum who had been watching his color changes from a safe distance shook their heads in disappointment and wandered off. Jack suspected the onlookers thought that his party consisted of visiting aliens from space. Which, considering Simon's various facial hues and Fritz Grondark's size, didn't seem far off the mark.

"Besides," said Jack, "if we don't succeed, at least you and Witch Hazel can continue the fight. I left a notebook filled with my deductions back at the trailer camp. If you take it to a major science fiction convention, I'm sure you can recruit a new champion. Several of them, probably, if Hazel performs a bit of real magic as a convincer. Just don't show the papers to any editor there. They're much too practical to believe in faeries and trolls and ancient gods returned to life."

"Enough chattering," said Cassandra impatiently. "It's time we got started. Nighttime isn't that far off. I'll bet von Bern is practicing lighting bonfires with his Zippo while we speak."

"The tunnel entrance is located in that small glade of trees by the bandshell," said Jack, pointing across Lake Shore Drive. "According to the book describing the system that I found at the library, there's a metal grating covering the passage leading down. We'll have to move it before we can descend to the underground railway."

Grunting, Fritz Grondark effortlessly hauled two backpacks filled with supplies onto his massive shoulders. He patted the handle of his monkey wrench with one huge hand. "I'm ready. No more talking. Let's do some serious troll-busting."

"Agreed," said Cassandra. She twirled her wooden staff about in a semicircle. "I'm itching for a nice squabble."

Jack shook his head. He was the only sane one of the bunch.

Though, considering he was about to challenge a hundred or more supernatural villains with a hodgepodge of scientific knick-knacks, he didn't feel particularly stable himself.

Around his waist he wore the battery power pack stolen from the photo lab. It was connected by wires to the black rectangular tube from the chemistry department. Along with the items he had purchased that morning from a local electronics shop and now packed in the bags on Fritz's back, it was all he had to stop the human sacrifice scheduled to take place in a few hours. Hard, cold logic told him that he had made the right choices. Quite illogically, he prayed that he was correct.

For the dozenth time, he wished he had been able to contact Megan in the dream world. But, as had been the case two nights ago, he had been unable to locate her in his sleep. Only Hazel's reassurances had kept him from assuming the worst. The dead obviously didn't dream. The witch swore that the presence of the Great Beast so near made psychic communication impossible, and that Megan was still safe. Jack could only hope Hazel was right. He would find out the truth soon enough.

The light on Lake Shore Drive turned red, halting traffic. "Come on," declared Jack, pushing away all thoughts of despair. "We're off to save the world."

"About time," grumbled Grondark. "Damn humans and faeries talk too much. Dwarfs know better."

"Don't worry, Simon," Jack said to his changeling friend. "We'll be back."

Waving goodbye to the despondent faerie, they ran across the street. The CD boom box Jack insisted they bring with them clattered noisily against Cassandra's walking stick. None of his companions had questioned his odd selection of weapons, though Cassandra had balked a little at his choice in music.

They found the entrance to the tunnel network without much trouble. It resembled a giant raised manhole cover some eight feet across. A massive rusted metal grate covered the opening.

Reaching into a backpack, Jack pulled out three miniature flashlights. After giving one to each of his companions, he shone his into the darkness. After a second, he spotted a ladder leading downward. It started two feet below the grate.

"Out of the way," commanded Fritz Grondark, removing the pack from his shoulders. He pulled the monkey wrench from his belt. "This is dwarf work."

Six bolts fastened the cover to the cement. Six times Fritz raised his wrench and slammed it into the concrete. By the time he finished, it looked like someone had used sticks of dynamite on the opening.

Tucking the tool back into his belt, Grondark bent over and grasped the grate with both hands. His fingers tightened on the rusted metal. Muscles like steel bands rippled in his gigantic shoulders. Groaning, the dwarf slowly straightened up, pulling the immense cap with him. Balancing it like a giant steel waffle, he turned and walked to an open section of the glade. Carefully, he laid the grate to rest on the grass.

"I don't like damaging city property," he explained, brushing flakes of rust off his palms. "I'll put it back where it belongs when we return."

"We'll probably use another exit," said Jack, still not sure he believed his eyes. "The Park District can take care of the grate. Assuming they have a crane handy."

Cassandra leaned over the edge of the pit and shone her flashlight into the depths. "The ladder descends about thirty feet to the floor. There's a big block of wood there. And a tunnel leading towards the city."

"It's the end of one of the rail lines," said Jack. He drew in a deep breath. "According to the maps, this passage should take us on a direct route to von Bern's headquarters. It's several miles away, but we have plenty of time before nightfall. Let's go."

Descending the ladder into the blackness of the pit, Jack gazed up at the bright blue sky. Silently, he prayed it wasn't going to be the last time he saw the sunshine.

"Order over chaos," he whispered softly. "Good over evil."

Smiling faintly, he patted the odd weapon that bounced against his chest. "Logic over superstition." He drew in a deep breath as he recited the final line of his mantra. "Light over darkness."

37

Using his pocket flash, Jack peered into the concrete passage. It was nine feet high, six feet wide, oval-shaped with a flat floor. A railway track stretched out into the darkness. The air, while stale and somewhat musky, was cool and breathable.

"Anyone claustrophobic other than yours truly?" he asked his two companions nervously.

"My folk lived in tunnels like these for hundreds of years," said Grondark. "They don't scare dwarfs."

"Nothing frightens me," said Cassandra unnecessarily.

Jack shook his head in disgust. At least Simon provided a little comic relief. Shrugging his shoulders, he reached into one of the two backpacks.

"Take these," he said to Cassandra, handing her two plastic containers, each filled with ten thin, black plastic, rectangular discs. "Hopefully, you can use these like throwing stars."

"Of course," said Cassandra, balancing one of the rectangles in her hand. "I've used toothpicks as darts when necessary. But these things don't have sharp edges. They won't cause any damage."

"Yes, they will," said Jack. "I'm not sure exactly how they'll affect the Border Redcaps, but I think the results should be spectacular. When we're attacked, use these first before resorting to your staff."

Rummaging through the bag, he pulled out nearly a dozen small plastic boxes. "Stuff these into your pockets," he told Fritz. "Keep them handy. We'll need them if we encounter the Gabble Ratchets."

"These things?" asked the dwarf, doing as he was told. "You can buy them in any electronics store in the country. Even some supermarkets handle them."

"It's not how rare they are that makes them powerful," said Jack, grinning. "It's what they symbolize. Trust me. I know what I'm saying."

"You're acting very mysterious, Jack," said Cassandra.

"My privilege," replied Jack. "I'm the hero. Besides, who knows what powers von Bern controls in these tunnels? He could be eavesdropping on our every conversation. The one thing I've learned the past few days is that anything's possible. The less I tell you, the less he knows. And the more he worries."

"Makes sense to me," said Fritz. "If you're finished handing out surprises, I'll lead. Dwarfs have perfect underground vision. We don't need flashlights to see in the dark. You two keep your lights focused on the ground. That way, we won't warn anyone we're coming."

They started off at a brisk clip. Fritz was first, with Jack second, and Cassandra third. The tunnel sloped gently downward, making walking easy. Within minutes, they had left the dim light of the opening to the surface far behind. While occasional vents dotted the walls and ceiling, providing a steady flow of air, none of them offered a hint of light. Except for their two flashlights, the passage was oppressively and totally dark.

Jack had been joking about claustrophobia, but within a few minutes he was painfully aware of the tons of earth over his head. That the concrete tunnels had lasted nearly a hundred years without collapse seemed relatively unimportant. The one-in-a-million chance that the passage might suddenly buckle beneath the pressure had Jack walking very gingerly.

After twenty minutes, the tunnel leveled out. "We're beneath the city streets," whispered Jack. His voice echoed and re-echoed through the silent passage. "No sign that anyone's used this branch in years. Hopefully, we'll catch von Bern by surprise. So far, so good."

"Maybe," rumbled Fritz Grondark. "Maybe not." He waved a massive hand in the direction they were going. "Something's up ahead blocking our way. I can't make out what it is. Shine your flashlights on it."

Jack and Cassandra both raised their beams. Fifty feet away, a railroad handcar rested on the track. Filling it nearly to the ceiling were a dozen big wooden crates.

"I thought you said they removed the handcarts from the tunnels fifty years ago," said Cassandra as they slowly walked forward.

"They did," said Jack. "Unfortunately, they stored them in the roundhouse station von Bern is using as his base. Much as I hate to say it, I'm willing to bet those boxes are filled with finishing bricks kept there as well. The German probably blocked all the direct routes to his hideout with obstacles like this. Not that we have the time to find out otherwise. Somehow we've got to unload enough of those boxes off that damned thing so that we can pass through, or we're finished."

Fritz leaned on the handcar. "Too heavy to push ahead of us. And whoever left it here probably wedged the wheels on the other side."

Cassandra reached for one of the boxes. As predicted, it was filled to the top with bricks. Even Fritz couldn't move one by himself. It would take hours to clear enough room for them to wiggle over the top of the blockade.

Jack paused. If not over, why not under? Crouching, he checked the bottom of the handcar. There wasn't much room, but it looked like enough. For two of them, at least.

As he expected, the dwarf did not like the idea.

"Crawl under the car? My shoulders are too wide. I'll never fit."

"I know, Fritz. That's why you'll have to stay behind. Cassandra and I are slender enough to wiggle through. We have to go on without you."

Grondark scowled. He reached out and grabbed one of the wood boxes. Angrily, he jerked the container forward. Decaying old wood collapsed beneath his fingers, leaving a pile of finishing bricks in its place. Furious, Fritz kicked the handcar. It didn't budge.

The dwarf's huge hands knotted into fists. "You're right," he said. "I understand. There is no time for delay. Do what you must. It is the only way. But that doesn't mean I like it."

Reaching into his pockets, Fritz pulled out the plastic boxes Jack had given him earlier. "Don't forget these gadgets. Now, go. I'll remove these boxes as quickly as possible and follow. Perhaps, if I'm lucky, there'll still be a few trolls to smash when I arrive."

"We'll save some just for you," promised Jack.

Cassandra, ever cautious, went first. It was a tight squeeze, but after a few curses and kicks, the Amazon made it to the other side. Using her staff, she pulled the two backpacks through. Then it was Jack's turn.

"Goodbye, my friend," said Grondark as Jack knelt on the concrete. "And good luck."

"Thanks," said Jack. "Like I told Simon, we'll be back."

Hurriedly, Jack scrambled through the space beneath the flatcar. If his feelings of claustrophobia had been bad a few minutes ago, now they were overwhelming. Especially when he was beneath an old wooden handcar filled with bricks. He sighed with relief when Cassandra finally grabbed his shoulders and pulled him through.

Before proceeding, Jack carefully checked the wires leading from his power pack to the rectangular box he called his secret weapon. All connections remained intact. If he was going to fail in his quest, it wouldn't be because he was careless.

Once he was convinced everything was functional, he shouldered one of the two backpacks. Cassandra took the other. Walking stick in one hand, CD boom box in the other, she took the lead. Without the dwarf to guide them, they were forced to use their flashlights to point the way.

Behind them, for a long time after they left the handcar, they could hear Fritz Grondark cursing as he heaved brick after brick to the concrete floor.

38

Five hundred feet further, the tunnel curved to the right.

"It's heading towards the Loop," commented Jack.

"Stay alert," said Cassandra, stuffing a handful of black discs into her pockets. "This spot would be a wonderful location for an ambush."

"I don't think . . ." began Jack, only to have the rest of his sentence drowned out by the shouts of a pack of Border Redcaps charging out of the darkness.

There were seven of the fiends, dressed as always in black leather jackets, dirty old jeans, and bright red baseball caps. They were armed with chains, knives and lead pipes. None of them carried guns, worried perhaps by possible ricocheting in the narrow passageway. Except for the sameness of their expression and a certain indefinite inhuman tinge to their features, they could have been members of any of a dozen street gangs roaming the streets of Chicago.

Calmly, Cassandra dropped the CD boom box and her staff and retrieved the discs she had just put in her jeans. The nearest Redcap was less than ten feet away when, with a quick flick of the wrist, she sent one of the hard plastic rectangles flying into his face. Not one to waste an effort, Cassandra aimed it for the fiend's open mouth. The black disc hit the astonished attacker in the teeth.

Even Jack, expecting the unexpected, was surprised by the results. With a flash of light so brilliant that it lit up the entire tunnel, the Border Redcap disappeared. All that remained of the monster was a slightly singed plastic disc and his red cap.

Unable to stop running, two more of the Redcaps met the same fate, as Cassandra flung the black rectangles with incredible speed and accuracy. Both of the fiends vanished in identical explosions of light, leaving only their baseball hats behind as evidence of their passing.

Von Bern's minions were dumb, but they weren't suicidal. Screaming in fear, the other four Redcaps turned and bolted back into the darkness. Cassandra flipped several more discs after them, but without scoring any hits. Seconds after the attack had begun, it was over.

"Pretty neat stuff, Jack," said Cassandra, bending over to collect the three red baseball caps. "I'm extremely impressed. Would you care to explain to me what the hell happened? Or are you still keeping secrets?"

"No reason why not," said Jack, drawing in a deep breath, the first one he had taken since the ambush. Until that moment, he had been working on logic alone. Now, finally, he knew his deductions were correct. "Seeing that our element of surprise is past."

"Those dark discs," began Jack, then glimpsed a blur of motion behind the Amazon. "Cassandra, watch out!"

The Amazon barely had time to straighten up when the Gabble Ratchet slammed into her. Instinctively, she threw up her arms and caught the gigantic Corpse Hound by the throat. But the force of its impact sent both of them tumbling backwards to the concrete.

Growling horribly, the Doberman snapped at Cassandra's face with yellow teeth the size of ten-penny spikes. Saliva dripped in pools on the Amazon's neck as she desperately fought to keep the dog's jaws from ripping her features to shreds. Standing, she was a match for the monster, but trapped against the concrete, she was unable to push the creature back. Its red eyes glowing like hot coals, the beast pressed closer and closer.

With all of his strength, Jack smashed the CD boom box onto the Gabble Ratchet's head. Plastic splintered from the impact, but the hound remained unmoved. Cursing, Jack raised the player and crashed it into the dog's head a second time. The Corpse Hound growled in annoyance, but continued to concentrate all its energies on savaging Cassandra.

Finally, remembering the fight at the shopping mall, Jack rammed a speaker into the Gabble Ratchet's nose. Blood spurted in crimson jets from the hound's face. Howling in pain, the Doberman turned from the Amazon and focused its red eyes on Jack.

Anxiously, Jack scrambled away from the beast. Now that he had the monster's attention, he wasn't sure what to do next. He doubted that the plastic discs that had worked their magic on the Border Redcaps would have any effect on the much more powerful Corpse Hound. But the small plastic boxes in his pockets should.

Grabbing one of the instruments, Jack flung it into the hound's snarling jaws. Jerking its mouth closed, the dog ripped the box to shreds. Bits and pieces of metal and plastic flew across the concrete floor. Nothing else happened. Jack swallowed, feeling his heart rise to his throat. He had just run out of tricks.

Snarling, the monstrous hound tore itself free from Cassandra's grasp. For an instant, it remained motionless, muscles tensing, readying to attack its new enemy. It was during that brief respite that Jack realized his weapon symbolized nothing unless it was fully functional.

He flipped the ON switch to the machine as the Gabble Ratchet launched itself into the air. Desperately, Jack thrust out his hand holding the device. The plastic barely grazed the Doberman's flesh, but that was all the contact needed. A burst of light greater than any of those previous filled the tunnel. The Gabble Ratchet vanished in a streak of white fire.

Wobbly, Jack staggered over to Cassandra. The Amazon was already pushing herself off the floor. She was covered with blood, but none of it was hers. Taking a few deep breaths, she rose shakily to her feet.

"You saved my life, Jack," she said, her voice trembling with emotion. "A few seconds more and that hound would have ripped my face to ribbons."

"Think nothing of it," said Jack, feeling slightly embarrassed. "You saved my neck more times than I can count."

"No matter," replied the Amazon. "That is my nature. I can do no less. For me, choice does not exist. Your rescue demonstrates true courage. It is a debt I will not forget."

"Forget it," said Jack, blushing. Seeking to change the subject, he examined the CD boom box with which he had hammered the Gabble Ratchet. "Other than the plastic casing being smashed, this thing still appears intact."

Cassandra shook her head. "How are you planning to use a CD player against von Bern? Or is that a secret better left unsaid?"

Jack smiled. "The CD players won't hurt the German," he stated. "But the music I brought along might cause him a few problems."

"The music?" repeated the Amazon. "You're going to drive the Huntsman crazy with rock and roll?"

"Something like that," replied Jack. He glanced at his watch and yelped at the time. "We better move along. Those four Border Redcaps who escaped ruined any chance of our surprising their boss. If we don't hurry, the Huntsman will mass all his forces at the entrance to this tunnel. And that could prove to be a challenge even my musical surprise can't handle."

Regaining their possessions, they hurried down the concrete corridor. No longer worried about secrecy, they kept their flashlights on and made no attempt to muffle their footsteps or voices. May Day Eve was drawing closer by the minute.

"What was that thing you threw at the Gabble Ratchet?" Cassandra asked curiously as they jogged over the railroad ties. "And why didn't the first one you tossed at the beast harm it?"

"A pocket calculator," said Jack, pulling yet another one of the machines from his pocket. "The ultimate symbol of order over chaos."

"Huh?" said Cassandra. "You defeated the Corpse Hound with a miniature adding machine?"

"It's not the object," said Jack, "but what it represents. That's why the calculator didn't harm the Doberman originally. Without power, it's merely a collection of circuit boards and batteries encased in a plastic shell. But, when the adding machine is working, it symbolizes the triumph of logic over disorder, of intellect and reason over anarchy."

Cassandra looked at Jack with wide eyes. "All that from a pocket calculator? You realize I have absolutely no idea what you are talking about. Besides, those plastic discs you gave me to throw at the Border Redcaps worked without power."

"As minor menaces, the Redcaps needed lesser remedies," said Jack. "You destroyed them with three-and-a-half-inch computer floppy discs. Again, a modern icon representing the triumph of reason over irrationality."

"Computer discs, adding machines," said Cassandra. "I'm beginning to sense a pattern emerging."

"Of course," said Jack. "It came to me during my conversation with Fritz at his garage. I needed to take the long view of history to understand. A very long view.

"At the dawn of civilization, fire represented the triumph of good over evil, light over darkness. Fire symbolized the rule of order over chaos. It served man, warmed him, helped cook his food, protect him from the beasts that sought his life, held the night at bay.

"But, after an age, fire lost its symbolic power as men used it to destroy as well as protect. Fire became too common, too easily used for both good and evil. Replacing it as a symbol of order was cold iron. Forged into weapons and tools, iron helped civilization develop, society to advance. For more than a thousand years, it represented justice and fairness in a cruel, unjust world. As was the case with fire, it symbolized the rule of order over chaos. But then, iron, too, was corrupted as it became commonplace.

"Tyrants and dictators used steel to ruthlessly subdue their enemies, extend their holdings, trample the rights of the weak and helpless. Civilizations not only rose, but fell due to its use. Cold iron no longer symbolized the triumph of good over evil."

"To be replaced by calculators?" asked Cassandra.

Jack grinned. "In the very broadest sense. Actually, iron lost to logic. To reason. To rational thinking." Almost immediately, his features grew serious. "Men feared the dark and used fire to conquer that enemy. Later, they needed weapons to tame their hostile environment, and cold iron and steel served that purpose. Each battle was in essence a collision between order and chaos. But the menaces were external ones. Finally, mankind itself was faced with a more deadly, more insidious challenge. One that could not be defeated so easily. Itself.

"Instead of battling tangible hazards, men now confront—other men. Civilization has grown too complex. Problems are no longer simple, and thus, neither are the solutions. People are murdered because of their religious beliefs, because of the color of their skin, because of the way they talk—the way they look—the way they think. It's madness. The dark is rising, Cassandra, and this time it can't be defeated by things like fire or iron. Civilization faces dangers unlike those of the past. Physical objects are no longer the answer. Instead, these threats can only be stopped by clear thinking. By logical, rational ideas.

"That's where I come in. Merlin selected me to fight for humanity against this ancient menace because I'm a mathematician, a logical thinker, a believer in an orderly universe. Von Bern and his legions are creatures of chaos and unreason. I refuse to accept the irrationality they represent. And, as a lifelong fantasy and science fiction fan, I realize what's necessary to fight back.

"Computer floppy discs and adding machines are only a small part of the solution. They represent logical, rational thinking applied to modern technology. Each of them brings order to anarchy. In essence, they are the new icons of good over evil. They are symbolic of man's conquest of irrationality and chaos. They are the new weapons of order in a disordered world."

"I'm not sure I follow your thinking very well, Jack," said Cassandra. "But you sound pretty convinced yourself. Which is good enough for me. Especially since the tunnel is widening a bit. There's light ahead. Unless I'm mistaken, we're about to see how well your theories deal with Dietrich von Bern and his Sword of Chaos. Not to mention a horde of Border Redcaps and a pack of Gabble Ratchets. It should prove illuminating."

"Light always triumphs over darkness," said Jack, readying the black tube he held under one arm. It was the one weapon he was saving for their direst emergency. "And this particular light will defeat the blackest night."

39

They emerged from the passageway into a huge underground railway yard easily a hundred yards across and fifty yards wide. Constructed entirely of concrete and steel, nearly a hundred pillars held up the roof thirty feet above their heads. A score of old wood and steel tracks crisscrossed the floor, leading to twenty different tunnels that dotted the walls. But Jack spent little time examining his surroundings.

His attention was completely fixed on the thirteen huge wicker cages that hung from heavy ropes from the ceiling. Each basket held seven women, most of them screaming at the top of their lungs. The sound of their voices, echoing through the immense cavern, was deafening. The reason for their distress was frightfully clear. Below each cage, groups of Border Redcaps were stacking large piles of wood for bonfires. Jack and Cassandra had arrived barely in the nick of time.

"Company, Jack," warned the Amazon, dragging his thoughts away from the prisoners.

He had been searching the baskets, without success, for some sign of Megan or Merlin. Neither the girl nor her father was in any of the cages. Nor was he able to find, scanning his surroundings, Dietrich von Bern. Jack felt positive that when he located Megan, he would discover the Wild Huntsman as well.

A wall of Border Redcaps advanced slowly on their position. Nearly fifty of von Bern's henchmen crowded in a solid line that formed a semicircle around the spot where Jack and Cassandra waited. Many of them carried handguns; a few even held rifles. Mixed among the fiends were the five remaining Gabble Ratchets. Thirty feet away and closing, neither the gang members nor the Corpse Hounds appeared in any hurry to lead the final charge.

"They must have heard what happened to their friends," said Cassandra, filling her hands with floppy discs. "That's the only thing holding them at bay. None of them is willing to make the first move. As soon as one builds up the necessary courage, they'll roll over us like a tidal wave. Or blow us away with automatic weapon fire."

"Maybe a little music will change matters," said Jack, calmly. He pulled out a CD from his backpack, slipped it into the boom box, and pushed Play. Turning the volume control to the max, he placed the machine at his feet, facing the oncoming horde. "Listen."

All motion stopped. Every eye fastened on the boom box, whirring happily to itself. Jack's reputation as humanity's champion had obviously grown by leaps and bounds during the past ten minutes. The Gabble Ratchets snarled, the Border Redcaps raised their knives and chains. And the CD player bellowed rock and roll.

The music hit the waiting crowd with the force of a tornado. Dropping their weapons, the Border Redcaps shrieked in sudden, unexpected agony. Clutching their hands to their ears, they broke formation and scattered through the railway yard. Many of them ran for the tunnels leading into the darkness. Their screams remained long after they disappeared.

The Corpse Hounds fared little better. The Gabble Ratchets collapsed to the ground and rolled back and forth, baying at an unseen moon. Recognizing a perfect opportunity when he saw it, Jack quickly ran over to the monstrous beasts and dropped a functioning pocket calculator on each of them. They vanished in satisfying bursts of white flame.

"What is that song?" yelled Cassandra, catching up to Jack. "And why is it devastating von Bern's allies?"

"Electronic music," said Jack. "Generated by a computer, naturally. My encounter with the banshee gave me the idea of returning the favor. It's not bad stuff, though I prefer Emerson, Lake and Palmer when it comes to synthesizer."

He gestured at the boom box. "Carry it with you. Sooner or later, some of the Redcaps will plug up their ears. But until then, the music should provide us some protection. Let's cut down those wicker baskets. Until those women are safe, the Huntsman is still a menace."

As if replying to Jack's concerns, Dietrich von Bern's voice, magnified by a portable amplifier, boomed through the immense cavern. "Cover your ears, you fools. The music can't hurt you if you can't hear it. Remember, there are only two of them. Surround them. Use your guns. Stop them. Prepare the fires. And release the Great Beast!"

"Release the Great Beast?" repeated Jack. "I don't like the sound of that. Come on."

A half-dozen Border Redcaps, wads of cloth dangling from their ears, their baseball hats holding the material in place, waited for them beneath the nearest cage. Grabbing a handful of floppy discs from his pockets, Jack sent them sailing at the fiends. Years of goofing off in computer lab finally paid off, as he flipped disc after disc with uncanny accuracy.

Aware of their peril, three of the Redcaps managed to duck out of the way of the plastic rectangles. The others shifted position, but not enough. One touch of the hard plastic was enough to send them to limbo. By the time Cassandra arrived, the number of their enemies had been cut in half.

Faced with a trio of foes, Cassandra completely forgot the discs she was carrying. Instead, releasing the CD player, she lunged at the first Redcap with her staff, catching the killer hard in the chest. Bones cracked, and the fiend tumbled to the concrete floor. He showed no further interest in the fight.

Twirling her walking stick like a baton, the Amazon slammed the second Redcap sideways across the face. Like the first, he crumpled to the ground, unmoving.

The third gang member pulled an automatic from inside his shirt. He never had time to aim and fire. Cassandra's staff smacked the gun from his hand, then sent him joining his companions on the floor with a smash to the forehead.

Hurriedly, Jack deposited a floppy disc on the chest of each of the fallen Redcaps. With satisfying bursts of light, all three vanished.

"Sorry," said Cassandra, tearing at the pile of wood located beneath the cage dangling high over their heads. "I got carried away."

"No problem," said Jack. He pointed upward. Seven anxious faces peered down at him. Seven terrified women, hoping for rescue, screamed words of encouragement. "How do we get them down?"

"Von Bern must have a block and tackle somewhere," said Cassandra. "That cage is tied to a girder in the roof. Releasing them will take hours. And we don't have the time."

She gestured with her stick at an object at the center of the pile of timbers. Jack cursed in dismay. Von Bern's henchmen had placed a can of gasoline and a timer between the logs. Set for six o'clock, the mechanism was already counting down the minutes. Jack checked his watch. They had less than an hour to disarm thirteen bombs scattered throughout the huge cavern.

"Smash it," he said to Cassandra, pointing at the timer. "We'll free the women after we deal with von Bern."

A roar so loud that it set the wicker basket above them swaying cut off the Amazon's reply. Guessing why her eyes had widened in shock wasn't difficult, though. Turning about, Jack Collins faced the Great Beast.

40

It waddled towards them from the other end of the railway yard, its intense bellowing shaking the walls. Seventy feet long, the Great Beast stood twelve feet high at the shoulder, balanced on four short, stumpy legs, and was ten feet wide. Fifteen feet of its length consisted of a gigantic mouth filled with teeth the size of bar stools. Its milky white eyes were the size of pizza tins. Assorted spikes decorated its back and sides. Dark brown, with splotchy spots of green, the monster bore an uncanny resemblance to a gigantic alligator.

It wasn't hard to guess its true identity. At least, not for Jack. After reading hundreds of fantasy novels from Adams to Zelazny, he was an expert on mythical creations. The monster could only be Leviathan, the monstrous sea creature mentioned in the Book of Job. Though the Bible described the creature as a serpent, according to earlier Babylonian and Canaanite myths, the creature was actually a giant sea dragon. Or, in more prosaic terms, an alligator the size of a steam locomotive.

Watching the Great Beast approach, Jack experienced a curious sort of déjà vu. His mind flashed back to dozens of 1950's science fiction B-movies, filled with giant ants, flies, wasps, and grass-hoppers. But now the menace was a monstrous alligator demon, and instead of watching the film, he was living it. He only hoped that his plan was the equal of those dreamt up by Kenneth Tobey, Steve McQueen, or Peter Graves.

For all its immense size, Leviathan moved surprisingly fast. The beast ignored minor obstacles in its path like Border Redcaps, stomping over any of von Bern's henchmen too slow or too stupid to get out of its way. Though it kept its gaze fixed on Jack and Cassandra, the monster allowed itself a few quick snacks as it approached, swallowing several gang members foolish enough to dart in front of its huge mouth. Chewing and swallow its prey didn't slow it down a step.

Jack estimated the Great Beast would reach them in only a few minutes. While he had a general concept of how he planned to stop the monster, he was still short on specifics. He would have to improvise on the run.

"What should we do?" yelled Cassandra. Even though she was screaming at the top of her lungs, it was hard to hear what she was saying, between Leviathan's bellowing and the horrified cries of the imprisoned women. The Border Redcaps, for all their faults, perished quietly.

"Split up," shouted Jack. "Leviathan's after me. Keep out of its way and knock over the rest of the bonfires. Von Bern's troops are pretty well scattered and they shouldn't prove much opposition. In the meantime, I'll handle the Great Beast."

"On your own?" cried Cassandra, looking concerned. "That thing's awfully big, Jack. And it looks pretty hungry. Floppy discs and pocket calculators won't stop a Great Beast. I hope you brought something special to handle it."

Jack pulled off his backpack and emptied the contents onto the concrete floor. "You take all the discs and calculators," he shouted to the Amazon. His hands latched onto a thin box the size of a small attache case. "This baby is going to give Leviathan indigestion."

Then there was no more time for talk. Grabbing the hard plastic case, Jack sprinted for the tunnel from which they had first emerged into the underground railway yard. As he predicted, Leviathan ignored Cassandra and pounded after him. The Great Beast evidenced no signs of great intelligence, but obviously it possessed more brains than the dinosaurs it resembled. Jack was its quarry, and wherever he went, the monster followed.

Running full speed from the creature, Jack vowed to take up

jogging if he survived this latest round of supernatural battles. Being a hero, at least in his case, seemed to involve a tremendous amount of running from various menaces. That thought annoyed him, though he had no plans to stop moving in this instance in protest. In most of the novels he read, the hero rarely ran. Usually, the protagonist walked towards his enemies, not ran in terror from them. That was the dividing line, he decided, between fact and fiction.

As he ran, Jack fumbled with the lock holding his briefcase closed. Unfortunately, the clasps required more attention than he could spare. Risking a quick glance over his shoulder, he noted that Leviathan was less than fifty feet away and closing fast. The tunnel entrance was about half that distance ahead. Performing some quick estimates and algebraic calculations in his head, Jack concluded he would reach the passage mouth two seconds ahead of the Great Beast. Considering a margin of error of plus or minus three seconds, Jack redoubled his efforts, forcing his aching muscles to try harder.

He hurtled into the opening with two-tenths of a second to spare. The Great Beast's head crashed into the concrete passage with rock-shattering force. The entire corridor shook from the impact, and thin spiderwebs of cracks darted hundreds of feet into the darkness. But, try as it might, the creature's head was too large to fit into the tunnel. Jack collapsed in a heap ten yards into the passage, praising an orderly universe that dictated underground tunnels in Chicago were no more than six feet wide by nine feet high.

The corridor's measurements provided the Great Beast with no pleasure, as it tried again and again to widen the passage by pounding the cement opening with its head. Fortunately, the founders of the underground railway system had built it to last. Except for the hairline cracks in the walls, the tunnel was otherwise unaffected by Leviathan's attention. Jack wondered, however, if high above on the streets of Chicago, residents were experiencing a mild earthquake.

Steadying himself on the concrete, he managed to pop open the lock on his case. Opening the top, he examined the insides of the portable laptop computer with extreme pleasure.

If floppy discs and miniature calculators served as minor modern icons in the eternal battle between order and chaos, then a 486DX, 33 megahertz computer, albeit a portable one with backlit screen, had to be the equivalent of St. George's lance or St. Patrick's staff. And, knowing the type of monster he was going to face, Jack had loaded the computer memory with something special.

Ignoring the beast huffing and puffing only a few steps distant, Jack powered up the laptop. Getting a C prompt in DOS, he pulled up the Bible search program he had installed on the hard drive earlier in the day. After entering "Exodus" for the book name, he specified Chapter 20, Verse 3.

"Thou Shalt Have No Other Gods Before Me," Jack read aloud. According to Simon's explanation, that was the commandment that had doomed the ancient gods to the outer darkness. What worked once, Jack reasoned, applying the most basic tenet of logical thought, should work a second time.

Rising to his feet, he waited patiently for Leviathan to open its mouth and bellow in rage. The monster obliged less than a minute later.

"For I am a jealous God," declared Jack, and he flung the portable computer as far as he could into the Great Beast's throat. When the machine finally made contact, Leviathan screamed. It continued to scream for an eternity.

Picking himself off the tunnel floor some minutes later, Jack decided that there were certain sounds so painful that mere words could not adequately describe them. He had always felt that human fingernails drawn slowly across a blackboard led that list. Not any more. Leviathan's shriek of fury/agony/pain/distress dropped that noise to twentieth position. The beast's cry of dissolution filled all the other spots.

Both Great Beast and laptop computer were gone. Jack regretted losing the machine. It was a lot nicer model than any he had ever owned. In retrospect, he decided, it was a small price for vanquishing one of mankind's oldest foes.

Emerging from the tunnel, Jack spotted Cassandra a hundred feet away, ripping to pieces another of von Bern's bonfire devices. There were no Border Redcaps in sight. Jack suspected the death cry of the Great Beast had taken the fight out of the remaining gang members. For all of their nastiness, the villains remained true to their basic character and were, at heart, cowards.

Not so Dietrich von Bern. The Wild Huntsman's proud voice rang through the underground rail station.

"You've defeated my underlings, Collins. And triumphed over

the Great Beast as well. But not me! I still hold your woman and her father captive. They are my prisoners. Come, release them if you dare. Fight me for them. I, Dietrich von Bern, Lord of the Wild Hunt, am waiting for you!"

Sighing heavily, Jack shook his head in despair. A hero's job was never done. He was tired and sore and weary of combating the forces of darkness. But Megan and Merlin needed rescuing. And he was the only one capable of defeating the Huntsman.

Lifting his secret weapon, Jack checked the wiring for the fiftieth time. Everything was in order. Feet throbbing, back aching, he set out on his final quest. Softly, he began humming "You Light Up My Life."

∞

41

He found them at the middle of the underground railway yard. Years ago, it must have been the center of operations for the entire complex, but now it was merely a raised cement platform, fifteen feet on a side, six feet off the floor. Von Bern stood there, gripping the Sword of Chaos with both hands. Off to one side, trussed up with ropes like a prime roast, was Merlin the Magician. A few paces behind the Huntsman stood Charon. Trapped between his unmoving arms, struggling without the least sign of success, was Megan.

"I salute you, Collins," said von Bern, raising his sword as Jack approached. "You accomplished the impossible. Neither I nor my dread master treated you with the respect you deserved. We vastly underestimated your talents. I assure you, we will not make the same mistake twice."

"You won't have the chance, von Bern," said Jack, continuing to walk towards the German. "Release Megan and her father, and maybe I'll consider letting you escape. Maybe. Otherwise, you're due to follow Leviathan to limbo."

The Huntsman chuckled. "Not very likely, young man. Charon has his orders. If anything happens to me, he will crush the pretty Miss Ambrose to a pulp. After disposing of her, he will do the same to her illustrious father. Recall, please, that the ferryman is neither good nor evil, but neutral. Your unusual armament cannot harm him."

Von Bern's voice hardened. "I am the one who is in charge, Mr. Collins. Put down that strange weapon you carry and perhaps I'll consider letting *you* escape. You have my word on it."

Jack snorted, remembering from their encounter at the math complex how much the Huntsman's promise was worth. Casually, he flipped the button turning on the power to his secret weapon. He was less than twenty yards from the German and closing quickly.

"Stop," cried von Bern, his voice rising a note. "Take another step forward and the girl is dead."

"Then what?" asked Jack. "With her gone, you have no one to hide behind."

"Still," said the German, raising his Chaos Sword high in the air and turning to Megan, "I'll vanish knowing that I made your life miserable. Make your decision now, Collins. Does the girl live or die?"

"Leave her out of it," said Jack. "Fight me. I'm your enemy, not Megan. There's no honor killing defenseless women."

"Honor?" laughed the Huntsman. "Only fools believe in such concepts. I led the Wild Hunt for centuries because it kept me alive, eternally young. Justice and fairness mean nothing to me. I refuse to fight you because I know I cannot win against your magical devices. And I only engage in battles that I am assured of winning."

"Just as I suspected," said Jack, raising the black rectangular box chest-high. Perched on its top was a sighting device much like that of a high-powered rifle. "You're so afraid of dying that you'll stoop to any level to stay alive."

"Perhaps," said the Huntsman, pausing dramatically. "But better . . ."

Not waiting for the German to finish his sentence, Jack fired. The one fact he had learned from his dealings the past few days with the supernaturals was that given the slightest chance, the fantastical entities loved to talk. They had a flair for the dramatic, and none of them could resist having the last word. One and all, they were hams. Which gave Jack the necessary few seconds he needed to aim and fire his weapon.

A slender beam of red-orange light like that of a neon tube leapt from the end of the box. Slender as a pencil, the ray caught von Bern in the chest. The look of absolute shock that crossed the Huntsman's face lasted less than a heartbeat. Then, he was gone, the Sword of Chaos dropping like a stone to the concrete.

"Helium-neon laser beam," said Jack unnecessarily, but quite satisfied with the correctness of his deductions. He swung the beam so that it touched the cement at Charon's feet. "Coherent, *ordered light*. The ultimate icon of order versus chaos. It's definitely the final word in the battle between light and darkness."

"It doesn't scare me," said Charon. Megan, her eyes wide with fear, pushed hopelessly at his encompassing arms. His voice cold and deep, rumbled like thunder. "I am a creature of neither."

"But you are a stupid old fool, honoring bargains with darklings," declared Cassandra, directly behind the ferryman. She had silently mounted the concrete platform from the rear during Jack's confrontation with von Bern. Feet spread wide for optimum effect, the Amazon swung her walking stick in a short, brutal arc at Charon's head.

With a crack audible throughout the entire underground complex, the staff connected with the ferryman's skull directly above his left ear. Charon staggered a few inches, then righted himself, as the pole exploded into shards the size of toothpicks. The Amazon's jaw dropped in amazement.

Looking puzzled, Charon turned and stared unhappily at Cassandra. "Why did you do that? I wasn't planning to hurt the girl. After thousands of years of comradeship, you should know, Cassandra, that I would never obey an order like the one given to me by von Bern. The Huntsman believed only in himself. I served him because he paid me well, but I retained my own ideals. And killing the helpless was never among them."

As if confirming his words, the ferryman opened his arms and let Megan free. By the time Jack reached Megan, she had nearly finished untying her father.

"Good to see you again, Jack," said Merlin, stretching and turning his long fingers. "Sorry I never provided you with the information you needed in your quest. Though you seem to have managed quite well on your own."

The magician surveyed the underground train yard, with the thirteen wicker cages filled with women dangling from the ceiling. "Cleaning up this mess and explaining it to the media is not going to be easy. But it shall be done."

Merlin's gaze touched the gas laser hooked onto Jack's belt. "Coherent light to battle the forces of darkness. Nice touch. We'll have to discuss the notion when there's more time."

Basking in the magician's praise, Jack swiveled to Megan— only to have her catch him square in the face with a slap that nearly jarred his eyeballs loose.

"That's for acting silly with those outrageous mall nymphs," said Megan. Then, before he could recover, she wrapped her arms around him and kissed him with all the intensity of their dream embraces. This time, however, it was real, and left them both, several minutes later, breathless.

"And that," she stated once she regained her voice, "was for rescuing me."

Arms around his neck, she looked deep into his eyes, waiting for another kiss. After a few seconds, she grew impatient for his response. "Kiss me, you fool," she declared. "I won't bite."

"Uh, Megan," said Jack, feeling very ill at ease, "it's not that I don't enjoy kissing you. I do. Very much so. Too much so, I think, for a casual romance. That's the trouble. What with the difference in our ages . . ."

"Casual romance?" repeated Megan, frowning. "Difference in our ages? What are you mumbling about, Jack? You're not *that much* older than me. I turned twenty-three last month."

"Twenty-three?" Now it was Jack's turn to be confused. "But, you're Merlin's daughter. He's hundreds of years old."

"So what?" asked Megan. "I'm a halfling—half-supernatural, half-human. My mother is a perfectly normal middle-aged woman. She married Merlin knowing full well that someday age would part them. So far, she's been remarkably happy. Mom's been visiting relatives in Florida the past few weeks. She probably never knew we were gone."

Megan glanced at her father proudly. "The old boy is pretty lively, considering his age. From what I gather, he's fathered more than a few children over the centuries. Being supernatural doesn't mean you're sterile, Jack. I thought you knew all about this."

"How?" said Jack. "How was I supposed to know?"

"Your friend Simon, the changeling," said Megan. "Didn't he tell you when we had our first dream talk? He must have realized then that I wasn't a supernatural. The fey folk don't dream. Only humans or halflings can. That's why Father never made contact while you slept. He couldn't."

Storm clouds gathered in Jack's face, as he remembered an abbreviated conversation. "Simon was about to tell me once. Then he changed his mind. Instead, he remained true to his nature and never said a word."

Megan grinned, an impish smile that lit up her entire face. "If that's the case, I bet he never mentioned anything about your ancestry, either?"

Jack's eyes bulged. "My ancestry? What are you talking about?"

"Dream communication, my darling," said Megan, her fingers twirling through his hair, making concentration difficult. "It's a rare talent. Only halfings can do it. On both ends."

Jack shook his head, trying to make sense of what Merlin's daughter was implying. "But, what you're saying is that one of my parents . . ."

". . . is a supernatural," said Megan. "That's why I was so surprised when you first walked into our office. Father cast a spell on the newspaper ad insuring that it would only attract halflings with the talents we felt necessary to defeat the forces of darkness. Never once during the semester I audited your class last year did I suspect you might be the one."

"You audited my class last year," said Jack, feeling he was fast losing track of the conversation. "Real Variables?"

"Right. Remember, I sat in the fifth row, in the back?"

Jack's eyes narrowed. "No wonder you looked familiar. But your hair was a lot darker and not so long."

Megan laughed. "Some magic comes from bottles, Jack."

"A halfling," he said. "Which means one of my parents isn't human but a supernatural entity. It can't be my father. He has a family tree longer than your arm. That leaves Mom."

He closed his eyes as if recalling old memories. "Very interesting. How very, very interesting. I can't wait to phone home. This puts a whole new twist on the old family business."

Together, they rose to their feet. Merlin, who had studiously ignored them for the past few minutes, was busily talking with Cassandra. There was no sign of Charon.

"I let him go," the Amazon replied to Jack's question about the ferryman. "What else was there to do? He harmed no one. And, despite his immense age, he could probably whip the bunch of us with one hand tied behind his back. I thought it best to allow him to depart in peace. We won't see him again."

"One less loose end to tie up," said Jack. "Fine with me. Leaving us with ninety-one women and one battered reputation to save."

"Reputation?" asked Merlin. He squinted at the wicker cages, rubbing his beard in concentration. "Whose?"

"Mine," said Jack. "Let's rescue these prisoners first. They're the real problem. I can tell you the whole story over dinner. After sleeping for days, I bet you're rather hungry."

"Starved, actually," said Megan. She patted Jack on the arm. "Don't worry, Jack. Father's terrific at repairing reputations."

"So I've heard," said Jack. "The nymphs—uh, I mean, Witch Hazel mentioned the King Arthur mess. Hopefully, my problems won't prove to be so much trouble."

"Oh, I don't know," said Megan, smiling a smile that set Jack's heart racing at an unhealthy speed. "Sometimes a little trouble can be fun."

42

The phone rang. Its inhuman face twisted with unspeakable rage, the Lord of Lions beckoned to Roger. "Answer it," hissed the Crouching One.

The demigod wore a plain white cotton robe, decorated on each shoulder with a golden lion's head. On its feet were simple leather sandals. In one hand, it held a slender polished wood scepter. On its hairless head, the Crouching One wore a gold circlet. It sat on a throne specially constructed of white marble, in the center of Roger's library. It had been waiting there for lightning to strike for the past five hours.

Roger, dressed casually in blue jeans and a sweat shirt, hurried to pick up the receiver. He caught the phone on the third ring. After listening to a few words, he turned to the Lord of the Lions. "It's for you," he declared solemnly. "From Chicago. I don't recognize the voice. It's definitely not the German."

Snarling in rage, the Lord of the Lions grabbed the telephone from Roger. "Speak," it commanded. "I am listening."

Silently, the Crouching One stood there, one ear glued to the receiver. The scowl on its face changed first to a look of absolute astonishment, then swiftly switched to anger, then finally ended in a mask of grim resignation.

"Thank you," it said into the mouthpiece, catching Roger completely off guard. "Your information is greatly appreciated. When my day comes, you will be richly rewarded."

Hanging up the phone, the demigod shrugged its shoulders in a very humanlike expression of disgust. "Collins defeated von Bern and all his minions."

"The Great Beast?" asked Roger.

"Sent back to the outermost dark," said the Crouching One. "Obviously, you were correct. I underestimated our foe's ability and ignored the Huntsman's glaring faults. Those were mistakes I will not make again."

Roger sincerely doubted that, but he knew better than to say anything.

"If von Bern and his troops were destroyed, who was that on the phone?" he asked instead.

"A contemporary of mine," said the Crouching One, sounding almost nostalgic. "His people, the Etruscans, called him Charun. Like me, he was originally a death god. However, when his followers died out, the ancient Greeks adopted him into their religion, but no longer as a God. They renamed him Charon and made him a ferryman, a mere servant of their own gods. A reversal of fortunes, to be sure, but ultimately it worked in his favor. He escaped the exile the rest of us suffered centuries later, with the rise of the One God."

"Why did he call? Old friend or not, he never phoned before."

"Charon is interested in the welfare of only one being," said the Lord of the Lions. "Himself. He loses nothing in informing me of Collins's victory, and puts me in his debt. If I triumph, he claims a reward. If I do not, he is out nothing. He is an opportunist."

"What now?" asked Roger. The Crouching One was accepting this setback with amazing equanimity.

"We wait. We watch. We plan." The Lord of the Lions's eyes glowed yellow as blue sparks creased his fingertips. "We devise a scheme avoiding the errors of this first attempt. We find new allies, stronger and more dependable allies.

"In the meantime, we leave Mr. Collins and his friends strictly alone. Let them wait and wonder until the moment is right. Then we strike, seizing power and crushing them with the same stroke."

"You sound pretty positive," said Roger, "for having lost the first round of the fight."

"I am a God," said the Crouching One, "and Gods are very patient. A battle was lost," and blue sparks flashed across its features as it spoke, "but the war is far from over."

∞

Epilogue

Chicago's newspapers reported several unusual stories the next morning.

The most dramatic, making both the local and national TV news, was the discovery of the ninety-one kidnapped women in an abandoned underground railway yard beneath the city streets. What kept the report in the public eye for more than a week was not the details of the story but the lack of them. For despite the vast diversity in age, nationality, and intelligence of the victims, not one of them remembered a single detail of their capture or imprisonment. It was as if someone or something had gone through each of their minds and erased all memories of their experiences involving the crime.

A few tantalizing details of odd and unusual discoveries in the underground tunnel network raised more questions than they answered. Who had blocked certain passageways with handcarts filled with bricks? And, more importantly, why?

A thorough examination of all the entrances to the system revealed the crooks' method of stealing away their victims without being discovered. But, again, no one could explain why an entrance to the network located by the Field Museum, far away from the scene of the criminal activity, showed definite signs of having been recently disturbed. Nor could investigators explain the smashed concrete at the mouth of that same tunnel, as if it had been hit repeatedly by a gigantic battering ram.

There were whispers, too, of giant wicker baskets found on the floor of the railway yard and ropes dangling from the ceiling. No one, other than the most outrageous tabloids, seemed willing to connect the two, and even those papers dared not suggest anything as incredible as ancient sacrificial rites involving human beings. Though there were those stacks of timber directly beneath each of those ropes, and the remains of timing devices filled with gasoline. It was all quite mysterious.

The police and FBI tried to maintain an aloof attitude towards the press's questions, but neither department was able to hide its frustration dealing with the kidnap victims. If it could happen once, the Federals argued, it could happen again. So they had to know the truth, the whole truth, to prepare for any future disappearances. But they soon discovered that wanting and learning were two entirely different matters.

It wasn't that the women weren't cooperative. By and large, they wanted to know as much as the investigators what took place in that vast underground railyard. But try as they might, they couldn't remember. Not a glimpse, not a hint, not a word of what took place remained. Their minds had been swept clean of every detail.

It was incredible. Even supposed flying saucer victims were troubled by partial memories or weird dreams. Not so with the "Chicago 91" as they were dubbed by the media. Drugs and hypnosis proved equally ineffective. They just could not remember. It was uncanny. It almost seemed . . . supernatural.

In any case, none of the women suffered for their ordeal. They were given a standing ovation by the Chicago City Council, received special letters of thanks from the mayor, and even got a call from the President of the United States. Several of their group, chosen by a random lottery, appeared on Oprah. And several enterprising local firms produced a full line of novelty T-shirts, caps and buttons featuring witty sayings about the women or their ordeal.

Despite the lack of facts, all three major TV networks announced immediate plans to film a made-for-TV movie about the disappearance. Hollywood insiders confirmed that each production featured a different explanation—ranging from visitors from another planet, to a top-secret Army experiment with nerve gas, to a fiendish scheme by a well-known Arab potentate whose dream of revenge against America was foiled by a secret government task force. Needless to say, none of the explanations came close to matching the truth behind the kidnappings.

A second story, pushed back to the center of the newspapers and the second half of the local evening newscasts, concerned a major scandal breaking at Chicago's largest engineering college. A British exchange student, Simon Fellows, had uncovered shocking evidence that the school security director was also the mastermind behind a campus illicit drug ring.

Using his position to monitor and threaten any potential rivals to his gang, Benny Anderson had been selling dope on campus for nearly four years. When a local street gang recently made a move on the security chief's turf, Anderson had diverted blame by accusing an innocent mathematics graduate teaching assistant of his crime.

Refusing to believe his professor guilty as charged, Fellows spent his free time trying to learn who benefited the most from the allegations. Surprisingly, the trail led right to Anderson, an outspoken foe of illegal drugs. Investigating further, the exchange student discovered the security chief needed the money to support his extremely expensive sexual escapades.

Evidently sensing something amiss, Benny Anderson fled campus a step ahead of the police officers coming to arrest him. Though the security chief was still at large and described as "armed and extremely dangerous," his capture was expected at any moment.

Jack Collins, absolved of all guilt, returned to campus from hiding to collect his possessions from storage. Leaving school to begin work for a consulting firm, he was especially concerned over the whereabouts of his collection of science fiction and fantasy paperbacks. Assisting Collins was a stunning young woman, Megan Ambrose, one of the principals of his new employer. Various descriptions of her invariably relied on the terms "elfin" or "pixieish." Though the young couple refused to comment on anything but Collins's recent ordeal, the frequent glances they exchanged left no doubts to their feelings for each other.

In a third story, totally unrelated to the other two, buried in the back of the papers and not even reported on the TV news, Russian

President Boris Yeltsin announced that, in keeping with the new spirit of openness that had swept his nation, he was releasing the secret KGB files dealing with secret biological warfare experiments carried out in the late 1980's. Most experts on Soviet affairs agreed that Yeltsin was merely reacting to documents leaked to the press a few days earlier and which could no longer be suppressed.

According to the secret papers, early in 1989, in St. Petersburg, more than sixty people died when an experimental airborne anthrax plague germ was released into the atmosphere. Authorities had succeeded in stopping the spread of the killer disease only through massive efforts of the army and secret police. Briefly noted at the end of the story was that the developer of the plague, Dr. Sergei Karsnov, had vanished shortly afterward. Presumably, he had been executed by the KGB, though no report of his death could be found in the agency's records.

Reading different stories in Illinois and California, a master magician and ancient demigod both nodded in satisfaction.